Fangs for Nothing

Shannon Ryan

Broken Typewriter Press
5001 1st Ave SE
Ste 105 #243
Cedar Rapids, IA 52402

Broken Typewriter Press
http://brokentypewriterpress.com

First Printing, August 2012
Second Printing, August 2015

Version 1.2.0

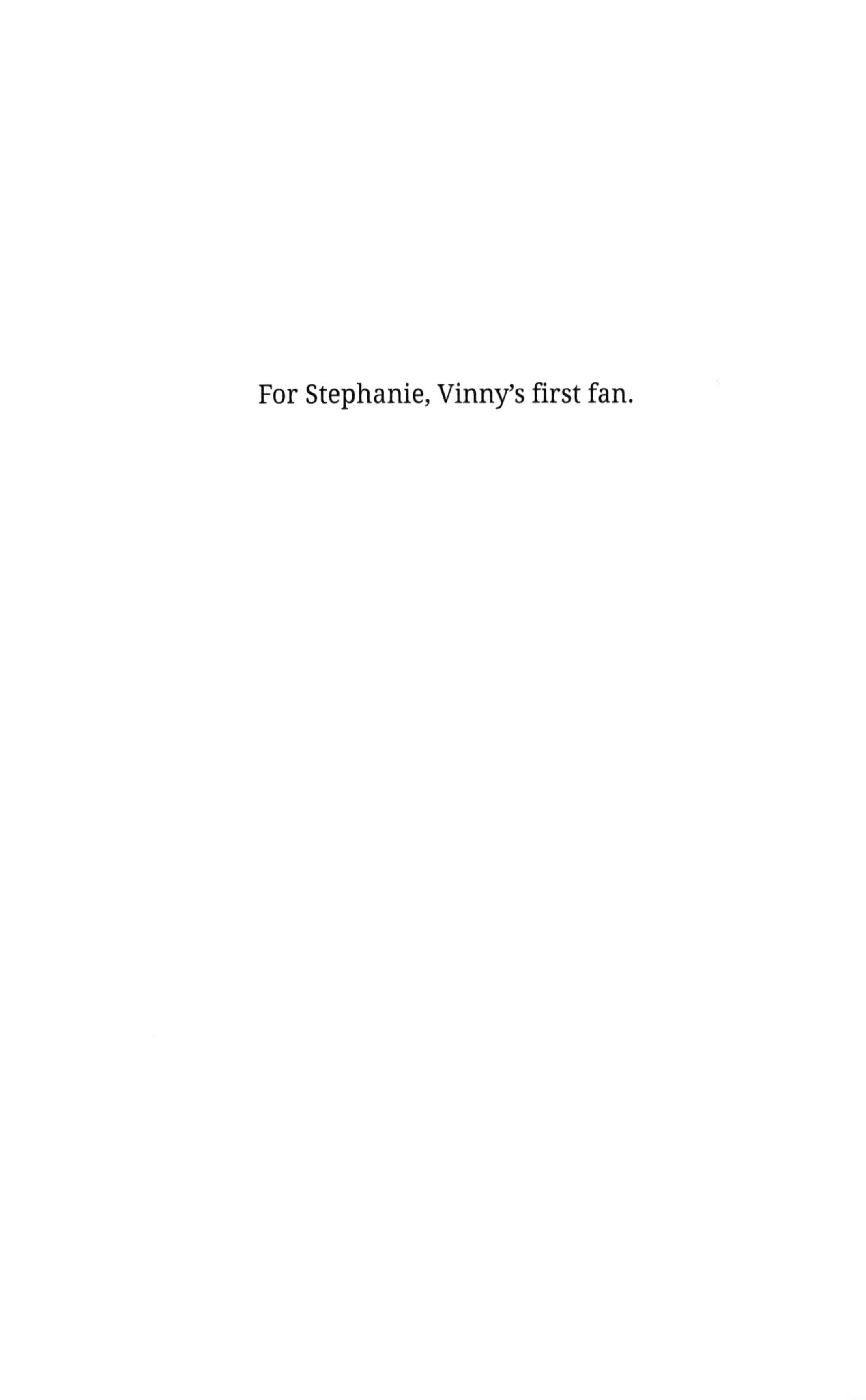

For Stephanie, Vinny's first fan.

Contents

1   Where Vinny goes to Karaoke Night   1

2   Where Vinny attacks a woman in an alleyway   19

3   Where Vinny gets a job   37

4   Where Vinny gets an extreme makeover   49

5   Where Vinny discusses the facts of life with his father and then puts on a dress   65

6   Where Vinny leaves home   79

7   Where Kyle and Margot return   93

8   Where church goes to Vinny   107

9   Where Vinny tries to meet his maker   119

10   Where Vinny goes to the cleaners   133

11   Where Vinny joins Brad's organization   147

12   Where Vinny does a bad thing   161

13   Where Vinny runs errands for Brad   173

14   Where Vinny goes on another outing   187

15   Where Vinny's investigation of the ranch yields a surprising result   203

16   Where Vinny goes to the hardware store with murderous intent   217

Where Vinny goes to Karaoke Night

Blood. I thought about blood all the time. I would lay in my bed, staring at the ceiling, thinking about how I wanted to sink my fangs into somebody. Blood. Blood. Blood. I needed blood.

However, the whole predatorily-attacking-people thing bothered me. I've never been much of an athlete. I just couldn't see myself chasing girls down alleyways, and if they could outrun me, that would be so embarrassing.

To satisfy the urge, I would sneak upstairs in the middle of the night, when I knew my mother was thawing hamburger for the next day, and drink the puddle of blood that had collected in the tray. This tactic for survival was less than successful. I spent my first decade as a vampire sickly and weak.

Things would turn around though. Eventually, I did get to taste the nectar of human life. The first time I tasted human blood was a Wednesday, Karaoke Night.

It started like many other nights of my unlife. While I was sleeping peacefully, my mother came down the stairs and yanked open the curtain of my tiny basement window. My skin blackened like a steak after a week on the grill and let out a puff of smoke. I scurried under the covers to avoid bursting into flames.

"You've been smoking down here," my mother accused.

I held the covers over my head, hoping I had completely covered my exposed skin in time to avoid becoming an unholy fireball. "Mom, what have I said about coming into my room?" I really shouldn't have whined like that. I was twenty-seven years old and dead. By the time he was my age, Vlad Dracula had crossed the Danube and was busy devastating Serbia. I bet he didn't whine at his mother. "Besides, I don't smoke."

"I don't care what you've been doing. It stinks down here. You really need to clean up this room, get up, and get out of the house. Did you even look for a job today?"

Since my ungodly transformation, my parents had been in denial about my "condition." Sure, they might admit I had a nasty sun allergy, but anything beyond that got conveniently edited out of their reality. Plus, they were really getting sick of having me around the house, especially now my sister was heading to college in the fall. At least they couldn't complain about the food bills. I didn't have much luck with human food.

"Mom, you know I have a sun allergy."

"You have a disability. You have to learn to overcome it. Now, how are things on the job front?"

"I guess I can look for work tomorrow." I just said it to make her leave. There was no use in arguing. We'd had the same conversation on and off for the last ten years—after my high school had let me graduate on accumulated credits due to my "illness."

"You know I just nag because I love you." If she really loved me so much, why did she try to douse me in sunlight? I'm sure Vlad Dracula's mother never tried to do anything like that, or if she did, she never got a chance to do it twice.

"Yeah, Mom. I love you too."

The weird thing about my mother is I actually did believe she loved me. Sure, her attempts at immolation seemed contrary to that opinion, but they were half-hearted at best. Attempted murder was just the way she dealt with her subconscious resentment of my basement-dwelling, or at least, that's what my friend Ernie said, and he knows things—he's a bartender.

She left without another word—and without closing the curtain. This left me with two equally sucky choices: I could remain in bed, hiding under the covers for two hours until the sun went down, or I could try to close the curtain while staying out of direct sunlight. If I tried to close the curtain, there was a chance of exposing myself to too much sunlight and dying, but if I stayed under the covers, there was a serious risk my mother would come down the stairs and harass me until I came to supper.

I decided to risk it. I leapt up, holding my blanket in front of me like a shield, and ran for the window. Halfway there, I stepped on my acoustic guitar, putting my foot through the shell—if only my parents had bought the solid body Stratocaster I had asked for, this wouldn't have happened. When I lifted my foot, the guitar came with it. The neck of the guitar hooked in my blanket and pulled it from my hands. Sunlight hit me straight in the face. I struggled to close the curtain as my skin blistered and smoked. Off balance and desperate, I frantically lunged and jerked the curtain closed. Overbalanced, I fell into a heap of my dirty underwear. I might have passed out from the pain, but the undead funk rising from my dirty underwear acted like smelling salts, jolting me awake.

I really hate the summertime. In the winter, it was dark by the time my mom got home from work, and she couldn't try to kill me with sunlight.

After I removed my foot from the guitar, I stood up. My burnt skin crackled like aluminum foil. I walked to my bed, knelt down, and felt around until I found a one-gallon baggie filled with moist soil. I pulled it out and smiled. Just what I needed to take my pain away. I reached into the bag, pulled out a big handful of dirt, and sprinkled it all over my bed.

I got the idea from Bram Stoker's Dracula, not the book, the 1992 movie starring Gary Oldman. In the movie, Dracula has to travel with soil from his native Transylvania. Since I was born and raised in suburban Omaha, and there are plenty of gardens here, it wasn't hard to get a few handfuls of soil. And in this rare case, it turned out the legends were right. The soil did have a restorative property, which I needed to use quite often given my general sickliness and my mother throwing open curtains with wild abandon. Mom always got annoyed my sheets were so dirty—in the last ten years, our family had gone through three washing machines.

Once I had an even covering of soil on my sheets, I slipped off my jammies and climbed naked into the dirty bed. The moist soil felt like cool tendrils soothing my burned skin, like a cool shower on a hundred degree day. My anxiety level dropped. The pain left me. I flipped over, covering my back in the cool soil. I took a breath, and my nostrils filled with the earthy perfume of topsoil: dirt, moss, roots, and worms. Covered in dirt, I glowed with calm wellbeing. I luxuriated in the soil of my birthplace for almost a half hour.

Then I went to the bathroom and washed all that crap

off my body. As I was showering, I noticed the water wasn't running down the drain very fast. Dad would have to call Roto-Rooter soon. The soil didn't do much for the drainage in the basement shower either.

I brushed my teeth. As a vampire, I'm pretty sure I don't have to worry about tooth decay. I haven't had a cavity in the last ten years. After my ungodly transformation, all my fillings fell out and my enamel re-grew, which freaked out my dentist. But trust me on this, being undead gave me wicked bad breath, or maybe it was drinking from raw hamburger trays.

My mother had placed a basket of clean underwear in my room, along with a note to put them away. Ten years out of high school, and she still treated me like a teenager. I located a pair of jeans and a t-shirt that weren't too smelly. I slipped on my watch; it was about an hour until sundown, an hour until I could escape the house.

"Vinny, honey," my mother's voice came down the stairs. "Are you going to come to dinner tonight?"

"I don't really want to," I yelled back. I could eat human food. I mean, it wasn't poison or anything. But it provided me with no sustenance and often made me sick to my stomach, especially cooked meat.

"You should come up and join your family."

Why did she always want me at dinner? She knew I couldn't really eat. But now she'd started, she wasn't going to give up. She would badger me until I came up to dinner, and if I didn't come up to dinner, she would come down and badger me more. "Okay, Mom. I'll be right up."

I climbed up the basement stairs with little enthusiasm, stopping at the top. The stairs opened into our kitchen, and already the smell of cooking meat was making my stomach jump. I held my breath. Yes, vampires breathe, but it's not because we need huge amounts of oxygen, it's because we have a keen sense of smell, which doesn't work without taking in air. Also, see how long you can talk without breathing. I'm good at holding my breath though—my record is two hours, after that I get bored.

From this side of the kitchen I could see the dining room curtains were closed, but most of the kitchen gleamed with the burning white sunlight. My mother had left the blinds open above the kitchen sink. I edged around the outside of the room, pressed against the wall commando-style, aware any misstep could be my last. When I reached the kitchen blinds, I yanked them shut, blocking-out the deadly beam of sunlight.

Our dining room was a typical suburban model complete with china hutch and oversized oak table. It seemed small with the curtains drawn, but I wasn't about to complain. Mom, Dad, and Jennifer were already seated. They spoke excitedly about something, but when I appeared at the doorway, they abruptly stopped. They all looked up at me. "What?" I asked.

"Hello, Vinny, my boy." My dad always talks like that, calling me "son" or "my boy." I'm told it sounds creepy if you aren't used to it. "We were just discussing your sister going to college in the fall. She got her acceptance letter to Yale today."

"Not that we love you any less," my mother chirped in. "You just have a different path for your life, of course. Still, we feel like it's an appropriate time to celebrate your sister's accomplishments. She received some important news today."

"Yeah, whatever," I said magnanimously. "Yale, huh? Must be tough to get in there."

Jennifer smiled up at me. "Yes, and I owe it all to you, big brother. One of the most important parts of the application is your personal statement essay. I wrote about how I needed to go to a good school, like Yale, because I would have to, one day, take care of my deadbeat older brother."

"Hey—"

"I may have implied you were mildly retarded."

"You little brat—"

"Vincent Price Lester!" my mother snapped. "Don't talk to your sister like that."

Silence prevailed for a moment as Jennifer and I stared across the table, daring each other to make the next move. In the kitchen, the timer started to beep.

Mom and Jennifer went to the kitchen to get the food. My mom and dad are socially conservative; they believe in traditional gender roles. They hated I lived in the basement, and I am still surprised they wanted Jennifer to go to college. I don't think Dad would have even let Mom work, except he likes the money.

Left alone with me, Dad felt it necessary to make conversation. "Vinny, my boy, what have you been doing today?"

"Oh, a little of this and that," I said.

Jennifer chose that moment to walk in with a bowl of peas. "Mom said Vinny slept all day."

Dad shook his head. "It's that stupid bar you're always going to..." He paused while he thought of the name. "...Ernie's. I don't want you going there anymore."

"But Dad, I'm twenty-seven. I'm an adult."

"I don't care how old you are. You're living under this roof, and until you can go out and get a job like your mother and I, until you act like an adult, you can't expect to be treated like one."

Mom and Jennifer finished setting food out. The pork chops were burned. I could smell them across the table. I used to love pork chops, but now they smelled like rot and corruption. My stomach heaved, just a little.

I stood up. "I think I'm going to skip dinner after all."

My father stood. He already had a napkin tucked into his pants. "Sit down. You are not excused from this table. You'll at least stay while I say grace." He thumped the table for emphasis, and the napkin fluttered to the floor.

I sat.

My father returned to his seat. "Oh, Heavenly Father, bless this food and the people who sit around this table. Deliver us from evil..."

I started to squirm. I'm not sure if there really is a God, but if he does exist, there is a precedent that he's not really on my side. Jesus might love the little children, but he was silent on the subject of bloodsucking fiends. Not that I had ever sucked any blood, unless you include licking the hamburger tray, but I was looking forward to doing it someday.

"What do you think, Vinny?" While my mind had turned to theological matters, my father had finished blessing our meal. He was asking me a question.

"What?"

He shoved a fork full of burned pork chop in my face. "Do you want to try a chop?"

My stomach crawled up into my throat as the piece of burned meat hovered next to my face. My father should have known better. He knew I couldn't stand cooked meat. He might as well have shoved a lump of Kryptonite at Superman.

My body reacted without thinking. My arm went up at impossible speed, knocking fork and chop out of my father's hand. The pork chop bounced off two walls before skidding to a greasy, charcoally stop on the dining room carpet. The fork embedded itself two inches into the plaster of the dining room wall.

My father stood. "What the hockey sticks did you do that for? Your mother worked hard to prepare this food for us."

"I'm sorry. You were waving it in my face. It was reflex."

"She works all day and comes home to fix your dinner, and this is how you show your appreciation?"

"I said I was sorry."

"That's not good enough. Go to your room."

"Fine," I said, standing from the table. "I didn't want to eat your stupid supper anyway."

Mom looked ready to cry. She didn't like it when Dad and I fought.

"Nice going, butthead," my sister said as I left the room.

On the way through the kitchen, I stole a twenty from my mom's purse. I know, I'm a low-life. Whatever. I was broke, and my parents had enough money to fly to Florida last year just to see the Huskers play.

The weirdest thing about being made into a creature of darkness—okay, the second weirdest thing after the whole lusting after blood and bursting into flame in the daylight thing—is being able to feel the sun set. The feeling is hard to describe. It's disorienting. It doesn't hurt or anything. It's a jolt I never quite expect, like walking into a screen door when you think it's open. I think that's where the whole vampires waking up at sunset thing comes from. If my mother didn't wake me up every day, the feeling of sunset would. I also get a bit of a rush when the sun goes down. For a few minutes, I actually feel a little like a superhero with fangs.

I opened the basement window, and pulled myself up through the opening. I took to the street and jogged twelve blocks to the bar. While becoming a vampire hadn't given me super speed—I doubt I could make a high-school track team—running wasn't so bad if you couldn't get winded. It's a small conciliation for not having a car, but at least I could get around. I wanted to get to the bar early. It was Karaoke Night at Ernie's.

The best part about Karaoke Night was getting to see my best friend Kyle. Kyle and I had gone to school together, and he had supported me during my nosferotic transformation. Kyle was making a life for himself, and we didn't see each other as much any more. He had gone to work for my dad, doing the job Dad had intended for me, selling plumbing fixtures, and he was making real money. He still came to Karaoke Night though.

From across the street, I could see Ernie had a new bouncer. This was going to be fun—that was sarcasm, by the way.

I walked up to the bouncer and showed him my driver's license, trying to remain positive. I smiled at him, showing off my perfect teeth, most of them anyway. My fangs don't show unless I'm... aroused.

The bouncer was a beefy guy with bulging biceps and a crew cut. He looked like he tanned. He looked like he probably spent lots of time working on his lats, and really wanted to discuss his lat journey. He looked the driver's license over carefully. "Sorry kid. Nice try. The ID's perfect, but there's no way you're twenty-seven."

"I am twenty-seven. I just look really young for my age. Hold up the license to the light. The hologram is completely intact. Where's Glen? Glen lets me in all the time."

"I'm not Glen. I'm Tony. And I don't care if you can pass the Glen test. All I care is you can't pass the Tony test."

"But I'm twenty-seven. Ask anybody. Ask Ernie."

"I don't care how good it is. It's still fake. I'm not going to bother the boss with this."

"Fine, whatever. Just give me back my license, and I'll be on my way."

Tony held the plastic card away from me. "Sorry kid. I'm going to have to keep this to teach you a lesson. It's a civic duty thing."

I waved my finger at him. "Look, jerk. That's my driver's license, and you have no idea how hard it was for me to get that." Convincing a DMV tester I needed to wear a big hat, ski mask, and dark glasses for the test had been a bitch.

I jumped, snatching the license out of his hand. I ran a dozen steps and glanced over my shoulder. Tony was following me. The idiot wasn't going to give up. What did he think he was going to do when he caught me? Beat me up for my driver's license? I had to think up something fast. I held up my hand. "Stop!"

Tony stopped. Don't think it was some kind of fancy vampire mind control. He was just that dumb.

Still, Tony's pause gave me the moment I needed to come up with a reason not to be chased. I pointed back to the front door of the bar. "You can't leave your post."

Tony looked at my driver's license, still clutched in my hand. Then he looked back at the front door of Ernie's. I swear I could hear the squeak of the rusty hamster wheel in his head. He looked back and forth between the door and me. I was about to turn and run for it when a group of people walked up to the door.

Tony ran back to the bar. "Hey! Stop! Let me check your ID."

I strolled around the back of the building and went in through the kitchen. Okay, I'm acting all nonchalant about it, but for a minute there, I thought Tony was really going to kick my ass.

In the kitchen, the fryers were shut down—Ernie didn't offer food after eight. Under the bright lights, stainless steel surfaces shone and composite flooring gleamed. The kitchen was the cleanest part of Ernie's, the only clean part of Ernie's, and unlike the rest of the establishment, Ernie was determined to keep up on the cleaning.

Ernie himself was sitting on a milk crate drinking a beer. He raised his beer in a salute. "Vinny! How's my favorite customer?"

"That depends. How about the line of credit I asked for?"

"If I ran you a tab, you wouldn't be my favorite customer."

"Maybe you have a point."

He took a swig from the beer. "It's Karaoke Night. Are you going to sing? They've got a whole new song collection tonight, Super Sweet Seventies Sounds."

"I'll take a look at that." I stood for a moment wondering if I should squeal on Tony.

"What? What's bothering you?"

"Well, you know that new bouncer, Tony? Could you tell him I'm not seventeen?"

Ernie looked embarrassed; he knew all about my condition. "I'm sorry, Vinny. Did he give you a tough time? I should have thought about that."

"Oh, don't worry about it." I didn't want Ernie to feel bad. He felt guilty enough about what had happened to me in his bar. I really should flash back to it right now, but I'm going to make you wait because I want to get to Karaoke Night.

"Don't worry, I'll get him off your ass."

"I know you will." I patted him on the shoulder. "See you in there." I pushed through the kitchen door.

In the bar, Karaoke Night was already in full swing. A guy who looked like a used car salesman in his cheap suit was belting out "Friends in Low Places," looking out of place with a comb-over instead of a cowboy hat. Most of the tables were already taken, and beautiful women displayed themselves at the bar, looking for losers to buy them drinks.

Ernie's barroom was the exact opposite of his kitchen. It smelled of stale beer and, if you had a sensitive vampire's nose, a decade of vomit—heightened senses can soooo be a pain in the ass. Even with my superhuman ability to see in the dark, I had to pause after heading into the bar. After dark, when the kitchen shut down, Ernie's turned into the neighborhood dive, where the local drunks went to puke and pass out after more reputable bars had tossed them into the street. Usually if you were a regular of Ernie's, you were self-medicating some deep-seated emotional issue, like vampirism.

On Karaoke Night, things changed. It was still dark. It was still smelly. I still had to be careful not to rest my hand on a table, lest it stick badly enough to warrant field amputation. But on Karaoke Night, the usual clientele of people slowly killing themselves with alcohol poisoning was absent, or at least shoved into an especially dark corner. For one night a week, Ernie's was ruled by young professionals, looking for an opportunity to embarrass themselves publicly via the works of Kenny Chesney and go home with anonymous sex partners. The lights were kept somewhat higher, as was the water content of the drinks. All the beautiful young women came to sing, and I came to drink their blood. Or at least I came to fanaticize about drinking their blood. So far, all blood-drinking attempts had proved unsuccessful.

I grabbed a beer from the bar, and then, I checked out the three-ring binder containing the Karaoke song list, slowly scanning the newly printed and laminated section titled "Super Sweet Seventies Sounds." I sipped my beer to stretch my dollars. I didn't have a great deal of money, and I was hoping to buy some lucky victim a drink.

After signing up for a song, I made my way over to a recently vacated booth. I have a feeling it was recently vacated because a petite blonde woman in the next booth was puking her guts out. I marveled at how such a tiny woman could contain so much vomit. Sure, it was gross, but also fascinating. Where was she keeping it all?

I didn't mind sitting next to her anyway. It could have been much worse. I mean, it wasn't chunky or anything. She pretty much was just puking up a bunch of mixed drinks. In fact if she threw it all up into a bucket... No, sorry, I'm going too far, just forget I said that. I settled back and listened to her pleasant retching, which I found preferable to the atonal rendition of country music. Ah, Karaoke Night at Ernie's.

After about an hour, Kyle finally showed up. He was wearing a sport coat and a purple tie. He looked successful yet accessible, the epitome of everything the modern plumbing fixture salesman should be, according to my father at least. He set a beer, dripping condensation, down on the table, and shook my hand in a bone-crushing grip. "Hey, Vinny. How's the talent tonight?" He always called young women "the talent" like he was casting a porn movie.

"Not too bad, I guess. There are some cute girls by the bar."

He looked over at the bar. "Well, yeah, if you like old barfly skanks." He nodded at the young professionally-dressed women in the booth next to me, sitting uncomfortably around a table covered in vomit-covered napkins. "What's their story?"

"They were here when I got here. The little blonde one lost her cookies big time."

"That all came from her? Where did she keep it?" Kyle yanked his beer from the sticky table and took a big gulp.

"I was thinking the same thing."

I set down my empty beer bottle. "I'm going to get a fresh beer and check out the song list."

As I walked up to the bar, I saw an attractive woman sitting alone. I sauntered up to her. "Hi, can I buy you a drink?" I had asked this question hundreds of times on Karaoke Night, but I could count on my hands the number of times I had gotten a yes. The last time had been three years ago, and the woman who had accepted the drink had talked briefly to me before finding out I lived at home.

She smiled at me. "Sure, you can buy me a drink." She spun on the stool to face me, uncrossing and re-crossing her muscled legs. I had heard this was a good signal. She caught the eye of Tina, Ernie's night bartender, and ordered a twelve-dollar drink. I gave up the money, wishing I could put down a couple dollars to tip Tina, but now I only had enough left for two more beers.

She took a sip of the drink and made a shooing motion with her hand. "Thanks for the drink, kid. You can go away now." She turned back to the bar.

I stood dumbfounded for a moment. "You know, when I buy you a drink, we're entering into kind of a social contract. You're agreeing to at least talk to me for a couple minutes."

She shook her head. "What's the point? It's not like it will get you anywhere."

"What's so wrong with me?"

"Well, you have no physique to speak of. Your oily, nasty face is covered in zits. You look like you're maybe fifteen. You didn't tip the bartender, so you're either poor or cheap. Your shirt is stained. And you smell funny. Have you heard enough, or should I go on?"

"I guess you have a point." I snatched her drink off the bar. "I'm taking this back though."

"Asshole." She kicked out at me with her pointy shoe, nearly nailing me in my soft undercarriage and causing me to jump out of the way, spilling part of the drink.

I swept by the Karaoke list on my way back to the table. I was up in two more songs. Currently, Vomit Girl's party was making their way up to the stage, sans Vomit Girl. I looked across the room to the booth. The girl was still there.

By the time I returned to the table, Kyle was leaning across the back of our booth and chatting up Vomit Girl. Their conversation was one-sided, however, as complete sentences seemed beyond her current scope of abilities.

I set my expensive drink on the table. "Kyle, what are you doing?"

Kyle leaned over and whispered in my ear, "Dude, I'm closing."

I whispered back, "She was closed an hour ago. You know she was up-chucking earlier."

"That's not such a big deal though. You throw up every time your mom makes a pot roast."

"No, I managed not to puke tonight, but it was a close thing—pork chops."

"You and your sensitive stomach." He turned back to the girl. "Shit. Where did she go?"

"She slid under the table." I realized the music had stopped playing and looked up at the stage. "Her group is done singing. You better turn around and pretend you weren't hitting on their friend who is too drunk to sit up."

"Do they even care? I mean, what kind of people leave their drunken friend to get date raped while they sing 'We are Family?' There should be a fucking law."

The voice of the DJ boomed from the sound system, "Vinny. It's time for Vinny to sing 'Sweet Child of Mine.'"

I started to stand, but Kyle pushed on my shoulder. "Let me take your spot. I've got to leave early, big meeting to-morrow."

I shrugged. So much for hanging out. "Okay, go for it."

Kyle walked to the stage, taking the microphone as the music started. He raised the mic to his mouth just in time to sing the first line. The opening words ground out of his mouth with the intensity of a dozen Axel Roses. As one, the entire room turned to watch him. His golden voice resonated with Axel's nasally twang, filling the hearts of every woman in the room with lust. When he finished singing, there was a moment of silence, followed by a standing ovation.

He stepped down from the stage, and a woman from the bar, the woman who had tried to steal a drink from me, walked up to him and whispered something in his ear. She tugged his arm, and he whispered something in her ear. She nodded and walked out the front door.

He dodged back through the crowd to me. "Hey, I gotta go."

"I thought all the women at the bar were old skanks?"

"Dude, she's not that young, but she's no skank."

I nodded. "All right. See you next week."

"If I'm still alive."

Sure, rub it in.

He made his way back towards the front door, where the beautiful drink stealer was supposedly waiting.

I settled back and watched Karaoke Night unfold. People bought drinks. My high-school chemistry teacher was singing "Don't Stand So Close To Me." Creepy. The women in the booth next to me came back to grab their purses and say their goodbyes.

I wondered if I should call it a night. It wasn't like I was going to score.

"Hey, bro," someone said.

I looked up. Four thick-necked guys were standing by my booth holding beer bottles. "Yes?"

"You mind giving up that booth, bro? This place is packed, and you're all alone."

I nodded to the booth behind me, recently vacated by the We-are-Family singers. "What about that one?"

"Somebody puked all over it."

"Okay." I didn't want an argument. I slid out of the booth and unstuck my mixed drink from the table. Just to prove the booth behind me wasn't that bad, even though it was, I sat in it myself.

I sighed. I might as well go home as well. Kyle obviously didn't feel like hanging out with me tonight, and I didn't have much money left, so it wasn't like I was going to buy anyone else a drink.

Something grabbed my ankles. I jumped, frightened for a moment, and then looked down. Vomit Girl grabbed my legs and rested her head on top of my smelly, old sneakers. Her friends must have left her behind.

I reached down and pulled her up to sit beside me in the booth. Her body felt good, athletic, under her thin, summer business suit.

"Thanks," she muttered. "It's disgusting down there. Somebody puked all over." She looked at me. "Who are you?"

"I'm Vinny."

She shook my hand. "Vicky." She looked around the empty booth. "Are we on a date, Vinny?"
"Yes. Yes, we are."
Score!

Where Vinny attacks a woman in an alleyway

For once, my fortune seemed to have changed. I was sitting in a booth with a cute blonde. The kind of professional woman I had lusted over for a decade of karaoke nights, and she was so drunk she hadn't noticed what a loser I was, yet. I desperately tried to think of something to say.

She squinted at me. "So, what do you do?" she asked.

Hard question, I didn't really do anything. "Well, you know, the normal kind of things... What do you do?"

"I'm a telecommunications specialist." She was still slurring her words quite badly, but as an Ernie's regular, I was an expert at understanding drunk speak. "I work for a collections agency. I call people on the phone and say, 'Pay up you bitches. I know you got money.' Kind of like a loan shark or a pimp." She laughed at her joke, snorting with such gusto that she threw her head back and then slammed it down into the table. Great, now she was drunk and concussed. At least she had managed to face-plant on a section of the table that wasn't covered in vomit. Even still, it hadn't been that clean.

Without raising her head from the table, she said. "Now, tell me what you do, Vernon. Don't be so mysterious." I didn't bother to correct her about the name; between the alcohol poisoning and the head trauma, I took what I could get.

"I have a weird blood condition which prevents me from going out during the day." I decided to go for broke. She was too drunk to care anyway. "Actually, that's just what I tell people. I'm a vampire."

Vicky nodded by rubbing her face against the filthy table. "I was a vampire in college for a while. But it didn't work out. No matter how dark I dyed my hair and wore my makeup, people kept calling me perky. I look like crap with all that eye shadow, and I was shit at dying my hair."

If I had blood pressure, I would have felt it rise. "You weren't a vampire. You were a goth. Vampirism is a serious condition that makes you put your life on the line every time you step out your door. Goths are just pathetic wannabes in black makeup."

Vicky did not seem concerned at my outburst. She turned her head so her cheek rested on the table. It made a sticky sound like Velcro ripping. Strands of her hair landed dangerously close to the vomit-covered napkins from her earlier hurling. "This table is nice," she said.

"That table," I said, "will give you a nasty infection if you have any open cuts."

Vicky laughed. "You're funny."

"Not really. We had this old carpenter who used to come here, Ted. One day, he was tearing out some old cabinets at a job site, and he caught his hand on a jagged piece of metal. He came here with his hand freshly cleaned and bandaged by the emergency room. Three days later he was dead."

"You're too much, Vernon," she said, still resting her face on the table. "Funny."

"His wife didn't think it was very funny."

"Oh, stop it. You're so bad." She attempted to punch me in the shoulder and missed.

We shared a long awkward pause while two drunk women on stage sang "Cat Scratch Fever."

Vicky gave me a considering look from the tabletop. "Let's get out of here."

"I don't think you're safe to drive home. I'll have Ernie call you a cab."

"No, let's you and me get out of here."

"You want me to drive you home? I'd like to, but I walked..." I was never very good at picking up on hints, so what she said next came as a complete surprise.

"Vernon, I want you to take me home." For emphasis, she reached for my crotch and squeezed. This time, she didn't miss.

"Let's go." The answer was autonomic. My mouth moved and the words came out, but I swear, my brain was not involved in any way.

"You don't seem too excited about it."

"Yes. Yes I am. That sounds great. Your mind has produced a jewel. Let's go to your place."

"Good boy." She peeled her face off the table, leaving a good portion of her makeup and a few blonde curls behind.

I helped Vicky out of the booth, trying to keep her on her feet, but I was having trouble. Vicky was small, but a hundred pound woman still weighed a hundred pounds, and did I mention my sickliness? She flopped around like she had no bones in her body. Ernie wasn't going to be happy. He tends to be very hands-off in his bar keeping, but he does have one firm rule: women cannot go home with strangers if they are too drunk to walk. I was desperate for her blood, but I didn't want to be banned from Ernie's.

I looked to the bar, Ernie was selling drinks, and he wasn't looking our way, so I put my arm around Vicky's waist and started guiding her towards the kitchen, the only exit not covered by a bar employee, as it offered no public ingress. I hoped that, from the bar, Vicky just looked friendly and not immobile. Up close, I was fooling no one, and as I pushed through the crowd, people gave me looks of disgust, suspecting I planned to take sexual advantage of Vicky, which was silly—I just wanted to eat her. Fortunately, none of them had the nuts to do anything about it.

Despite my attempt to steer her, Vicky managed to run into a dozen people in the fifteen feet to the kitchen, muttering, "excuse me," periodically. Propping Vicky against the wall beside the swinging door into the kitchen, I scanned the bar to see if Ernie could see us. He was still busy mixing drinks.

"Are we going to your place?" Vicky asked.

"Let's just get through this door first." I grunted, pulling Vicky away from the wall to guide her through the kitchen door. She grabbed the end of my belt and fell into the kitchen, pulling me off balance. I flipped over her like she had done some kind of judo move and slammed headfirst into the hard, ceramic floor. I saw a bright light and then darkness.

When I awoke, Vicky was dry-humping me on Ernie's kitchen floor. Her pelvis rhythmically ground my zipper into my wang like a cheese grater. It was absolute agony. I pushed her off me.

"What?" she asked. "Didn't you like it?"

"It was great. But let's wait at least until we get outside. Somebody might find us here."

Despite being incapable of standing a moment earlier, she grabbed my wrist and pulled me to my feet. I guess the dry humping woke her up a bit. "Come on, then."

I ignored the pain in my aching junk as she let me out into the alley. I felt the weight of ten years as a failure dissipating. I was finally going to get some. Blood! This was going to happen. I was going to do it. I wondered how it would taste.

I walked her through the steel security door, out of the kitchen into the back alley. Here, I felt more exposed in the cold floodlights protecting Ernie's garbage than I had in the kitchen, but I was committed. I pulled her back between the dumpsters and the used grease tanks. It pretty much smelled like death, so I stopped breathing.

Vicky grabbed me and kissed me. "Push me up against the wall. Let's do it right here."

"Sure. Actually, that was kind of the plan. I don't really—"

She grabbed my shirt. "Don't talk, just do it."

I pushed her up against the wall with as much roughness as I could manage. My entire body tingled with anticipation. Again, she grabbed for my belt. She had to lean over to do it, and she stretched her long neck out of the collar of her jacket. My fangs grew, and for the first time ever, I entered the zone, the point of no return, where the human brain checks out and the animal takes over, nothing exists except for the moment, the strike, the feed.

Grabbing the collar of her jacket, I pulled hard, exposing her neck even more. I could see the twitch of her heartbeat in her throat. I could smell the blood coursing through her arteries. Slowly, like winding a spring, I drew my head back to strike.

I struck, bringing my teeth down hard at her exposed jugular–just as she suddenly moved. My canine sunk into her collarbone.

For a woman so drunk just a moment ago, Vicky moved very fast. "You dick!" she yelled. She slammed a fist right into my ear. Then, she kneed me in my crotch, and I fell to the ground. She kicked me a few more times, screaming at me the whole time. "You bit me you piece of shit. What's wrong with you? The first man since my divorce and you fucking bite me?" She kicked me in the balls one more time before leaving.

I breathed deep, rewarding myself with the rich smell of Ernie's dumpsters and a sharp pain, probably indicating a cracked rib. My junk was grievously injured—I think she popped one of my grapes with her last kick — I hoped a handful of garden dirt could fix it. Even with all the damage she had done, I smiled. When my fangs had pierced her skin, a trickle of blood had squirted into my mouth, just enough to taste. It was the most magical thing I had ever experienced. Before, my body had tingled with anticipation, now it burned with pleasure.

I wanted more.

I walked home with a spring in my step and dirt in my underpants. I slid through my basement window, closed it, and carefully arranged the curtains for my day's sleep. My clock read 5:30 AM, the time my parents got up. I lay down and stared up at the pipes and joists of the unfinished ceiling.

I felt the sun rise. Usually, this put me out like a light, but today, I felt awake. Maybe I was drawing power from the drop of blood I had sucked from Vicky, or maybe I was just too excited to sleep. Either way, there was no reason to lay around in bed all day.

I walked up the basement stairs, stopping at the top. While I could just sneak into the room in afternoon light, morning light hit directly in front of the basement door. I could smell breakfast cooking, and for once, it didn't seem disgusting. My mouth wasn't watering at the prospects of egg and sausage, but I felt like I might be able to stand being around them. I could hear Jennifer yakking away about some committee she worked on at school. My sister was always talking about some committee or other. She had joined every committee possible, hoping to get into an Ivy League school.

"Hello?" I called out.

"Vinny?" my mother said with surprise in her voice.

"Do you think you could close the blinds over the kitchen sink? I'd like to come upstairs, please."

After a moment, she said, "Alright, they're closed, you can come up." I ignored the tone in her voice that indicated she didn't think I needed them closed.

I walked into the kitchen. I had not attended a family breakfast in several years, but it was just as I remembered. Mom had eggs and sausage cooking on the stove, and toast and pancakes were piled on serving plates in our breakfast nook. There would also be cold cereals in the cupboard. I wondered if they had Count Chocula.

My mother set a plate and a fork down for me at the breakfast nook. "What do you want, Vinny?"

"I think I'll stick to pancakes for now." I sat down and served myself two pancakes from the stack, buttering them and pouring syrup over the top. I usually just ate to appease my mother—human food had almost no nutritional value for me, and it tasted bad, but today the pancakes actually smelled okay. Even the meats didn't seem that bad. I took a first, tentative bite, and found the pancakes to my liking.

I was three bites in before I noticed the room was quiet. I looked at Jennifer and then my mother. They both seemed frozen. "What?"

"You're up and eating, before noon," my mother said, amazed.

"Yeah, I didn't feel all that sleepy."

"And you're eating," my sister said, a puzzled look on her face. Then again, she'd been in third grade the last time she'd seen me eat breakfast.

I looked at my forkful of pancake. "Yeah. The pancakes are good. Thanks, Mom."

"It's amazing. You have an appetite." My mother clasped her hands to her chest.

Quickly getting over her surprise, my sister rolled her eyes. "Oh, amazing. He can keep down two pancakes."

"Jennifer, be quiet. If you could barely tolerate solid food, I'd be excited about you eating too."

My sister stood up. "I have to get ready for school. Some of us have to deal with mundane accomplishments, like finishing valedictorian." She exited the room quite huffily.

I continued to shovel pancake into my mouth, but after I finished half my stack, I slowed. My stomach started feeling a little tender again. The pancakes started to lose their flavor. I looked up at my mother. She watched me intently. I took another bite. I didn't want to let her down.

"Delicious pancakes, Mom."

"You certainly seem to be doing well today. Do you think maybe you could harness some of this energy and visit your Uncle Ted at the bank? He really likes you, you know, and I think he might offer you a job."

I didn't really want to, but things were going so well, I agreed without argument. "Sure, Mom. I'll go see what he has to say."

"Great." She stroked my hair like she used to. "Do you want to drive me to work so you can take the car to your interview?"

"No thanks, it's not that far, I can walk." With my condition, it was difficult to get a driver's license, and I'm still not a great driver.

"Okay then. Enjoy your breakfast. I'd love to stay and talk, but I need to get your sister out of the bathroom so I can get ready for work."

I thanked her for the breakfast as she left. I even picked up the kitchen a little bit. Breakfast after my first taste of blood was the most perfect experience my mother and I had had for years. I sat back and relaxed for a moment. I still had to get dressed for my interview and walk to the bank, but there was plenty of time, and I played PlayStation most of the morning, so I guess I have time for that flashback now.

———————

When I was in high school, a human with a future, I used to really kick ass at PlayStation fighting games. This always pissed off Kyle. About a month before graduation, we got our hands on a Japanese import, something with a robot pig that fought scorpion creatures. After about three solid hours of getting his ass kicked, Kyle was getting pouty.

"Can we do something else? I'm tired of PlayStation. We need some real action."

"What are you talking about? We're in the suburbs, in Nebraska. There's no action here." This had often been a subject of conversation.

"I heard that new bar, Ernie's, isn't carding."

"Heard it from who?"

"Lots of people."

"So even if this Ernie doesn't card us, we need money for drinks. We just blew our last cash on Mecha Porko."

Kyle held up a crisp fifty-dollar bill. "My mom and dad left on vacation yesterday. They left me money."

"Sweet. Now we can buy another game." I reached for the fifty.

Kyle snatched the bill back and stuffed it in his pocket. "No! We're going to go to the bar like normal teenagers."

I sighed. "Okay. I guess we could give it a try, just once."

We walked to Ernie's and stood outside the freshly renovated building. We were dressed as college students. Kyle wore a flannel shirt—the height of "grunge" fashion. I wore a Notre Dame sweatshirt my Uncle Ted had gotten me—come to think of it, that was the last time I went outside without needing protection from the sun. I wished I could see inside, but the building had security windows, small and high up. My stomach crawled with nerves, but I didn't want to admit I was afraid to go in. If we went in, they would find us out, and then they would call the cops or our parents.

"Are you sure you want to do this?" I said. "We could take that money and buy the new Final Fantasy." There, that should do it. I'd given him an out. We were geeks. There was no way we were going into that bar.

"We'll be alright. It's just method acting. Act like a scared kid, and they'll treat you like one. Believe you belong there, and they won't question you." To my amazement, Kyle strode forward, pushed open the door, and walked in.

I followed behind as he went right up to the bar and sat down on the stool. I waited there, standing by the bar as the bartender, who I would later know as Ernie, turned and took a long look at us. "What?" he said in a voice reminiscent of a choking blender. I jumped just a little.

"We'd like a couple of drinks," Kyle said.

"Well, what do you want?"

"Beer, I guess," Kyle answered

"Beer, you guess. Beer is a pansy drink. Are you a pansy?"

"N... No," Kyle stammered. "What would you suggest, sir?"

Ernie leaned forward. "If I were you, I'd get a Coke and grenadine."

I realized I was standing by the bar. Kyle was sitting and I was standing. The bartender was going to see I was standing and then realize I was a scared kid, too afraid to sit down. I tried to step up to the bar and sit down, but my feet wouldn't move. I just sort of swooned forward and caught myself on the bar.

"Sure," Kyle said, "Coke and grenadine sounds great."

Ernie gave him a nod. "You got it, kid." He snatched the fifty out of Kyle's hand, punched at the register, and put down forty-seven dollars in change. He took a fancy bottle down from the bar and filled two glasses with about an inch of red liquid, and then he used a soda gun to fill the glasses the rest of the way. He picked up the glasses and set them on the bar in front of Kyle. He turned and looked at me. "Are you going to sit down or what?"

I tried to play it cool. "Oh, yeah. I didn't realize I was still standing." I jumped up on the stool.

"So, you boys go to school?"

"No," Kyle said.

"Yes," I said.

Kyle kicked me in the shin.

"We don't go to high school," I said. "We're college seniors." I realized in terror my mouth wasn't going to stop running. "We've almost graduated, so that's why if you asked if we go to school, we could say no, because it's just really a formality at this point."

"Uh huh." Ernie nodded and went to the other end of the bar to serve a customer.

"Let's go sit at a table," I whispered.

Kyle took a drink of his Coke and grenadine. "Why?"

"If we sit at a table, maybe he won't come over and ask us questions?"

Kyle shrugged. "Okay. Have it your way."

We grabbed our drinks and headed towards a table. We were about halfway there when Ernie's gruff voice yelled, "Hey!"

I froze and, to be brutally honest, I also peed just a little.

Kyle turned. "Yeah?"

"You left your change on the bar. Unless you boys are leaving me a big tip."

Kyle walked back to the bar to get his change, and reached a trembling hand across the bar under the watchful eye of the bartender. I expected him to grab Kyle at any moment and demand he show some ID, but Kyle grabbed back his money without incident, leaving a couple dollars for tip.

"Thank you, young sir." the bartender smiled.

Somehow, I managed to turn and walk the rest of the way to the table. When Kyle returned, we sat there sipping our Coke and grenadine, thinking we were men of the world who had put one over on the simple bartender. Months later, I found out grenadine was just corn syrup and cherry flavoring.

After two Cokes with grenadine and two trips to the bathroom, I had convinced myself I was pretty buzzed, as I probably was with the amount of caffeine and sugar I'd had to drink. Kyle and I chatted away happily about the latest Japanese games and the PlayStation 2, which I expected to be released any day, bringing about universal harmony and world peace. I was feeling good, but Kyle didn't seem as happy.

He shook his head. "Let's go."

"What do you mean? Don't you like getting drunk?"

"I thought going to a bar was going to be this great life-changing experience. Instead we're just sitting here talking about video games. That's all we ever do. I thought if we made the effort to get out of our rut, something good would happen."

"Things aren't that simple Kyle. Sometimes, life is just life, boring..."

My mouth stopped working, and even if it hadn't, I had forgotten what I was going to say, because that was when she came in. She was, without exaggeration, the most beautiful woman I had ever seen. She had long brunette hair with wild curls, a little upturned nose, and unnaturally long thighs, mostly visible between a short leather skirt and knee-high boots. I couldn't tell you what specifically was so fabulous about her—a sexy aura just surrounded her. All the men in the bar examined her, and not a casual, she-would-be-ok-to-take-home look. Their looks said, "I would lay down my life to touch this woman's feet." She had that timeless quality some women have, making it hard to tell whether she was twenty or forty. Her eyes looked old though, like she had seen a lot. She carried herself through the leers of the men at the bar with secure dignity, like the stare of every man in the room was natural.

She walked to the bar. "Beer." She spoke the word as a command, but there was something soft and yielding about the command, a command for beer holding the promise of illicit rendezvous and naked moonlight trysts.

Ernie sat a beer on the bar. He didn't ask her for money. She didn't offer. I think if she'd asked him to empty the cash register he would have done it without question.

I lowered my gaze to my drink. This woman was so out of my league that just looking at her caused me pain. The idea I could never be with this woman made me think my life could not possibly be worth living. I felt a tear run down my face. I wanted to look up so badly. I wanted to watch her wrap her lips around the neck of her beer bottle.

She sat down at our table.

I lifted my head, trying to think of something to say. I opened my mouth and no words came out, just a bunch of "ums" and "ahs."

"You do not watch me like the others," she said. She had one of those accents that said, "I have been living in the US for a long time, but I have lived places where borsht is a staple food." I looked up, surprised. She was talking to me. She was looking at me. This was even worse than being ignored. If I messed up now, I would always have to live with the knowledge I had a chance and blew it. I wanted to hide. I wanted to run out the front door of the bar. I wanted to tell her to fuck off and leave me alone, so I didn't get any further before I failed.

I looked at Kyle for moral support, but it was obvious his brain had seized up.

The woman ran her index finger down my cheek and under my chin. Then she pushed up slightly on my jaw, raising my gaze to meet hers. "What is so different about you? Why do you think you are immune to my charms?"

"I wouldn't say immune. I just don't think I have much of a chance. I'm a short, pimply, video-game-playing loser." Ouch. Way to be honest.

She nodded. "True. But so is your friend, and he seems..." She snapped her finger. "Catatonic."

"Well, yeah, but, uh..." I was talking, but all the words were just space fillers. I had no idea what to say.

She leaned over and sniffed me, like a person sniffs the milk carton to see if it's gone off. "What is your name?"

I knew that. "Vinny." I said. My mouth was really dry.

"Are you gay, Vinny?"

"No." I had never questioned my sexuality. I was always too busy thinking about girls.

"Do you like my body? Would you like to make love to me?"

Of course, this is where the stereotypical, red-blooded, American boy is supposed to go apeshit, falling over himself, but honestly, I was scared out of my skin. Everyone in the bar was watching us, and if I answered yes, I was sure she would laugh at me. Even worse, she might take me home with her, and then there would be a whole other load of anxieties to deal with. Then again, saying no was not an option.

Kyle, suddenly awakened, punched me in the arm.

"Yes, please. I would very much like that." The words had been caught in my throat, and Kyle's punch had set them free.

"So polite." She stood and walked toward the front door. "Follow me." I watched her go, swaying her hips all the way.

Kyle punched me in the arm again. "Well, go!"

I stood up and walked towards the door as if in a spell. As I passed by them, I could feel waves of jealousy coming off the other men in the bar. If only they knew what was about to happen to me, they would not have been so jealous.

She stood in front of a bright blue Corvette, parked in the light of a streetlamp. The sun had gone down while Kyle and I had been "drinking" and as I walked to her, I got a good look at her under the harsh lighting. She looked just as sexy as before, but she stood unnaturally still, in a way reminding me of a cat about to pounce. A primitive part of my brain wanted to turn and run home to the safety of my parents. I shook my head. I was being stupid. Still, I wanted to say something, so she would move, or at least do something.

"Nice car," I said, nodding at the Vette. "I think you can really tell something about a person by the vehicle they drive. You obviously like to go fast, and you're into American things."

"It's a rental. I could choose this or a mini-van." She stumbled over the word minivan like she had never put those particular syllables together before.

"Ah." I hesitated, trying to think of something else to say. "So, do you mind if I ask your name?"

"No, I don't mind. I'm Veronica. Are you going to get in the car?"

"Sure." I opened the passenger door and sat down in the seat. Veronica got in and started the engine.

"Your place or mine?"

"Definitely yours." I didn't think my parents would appreciate Veronica's charms, at the very least Mom wouldn't.

Veronica drove in silence for a few minutes. I really got the feeling she would have preferred it if I not talk, but I was too nervous.

"So, of all the guys there, why did you pick me?"

"You wouldn't believe me if I told you."

"I don't believe it anyway."

"I read about you in a book. Your coming was foretold." I had no clue what that meant, but I didn't say anything because I didn't want to screw up when I was this close.

She stopped the car by a hotel, just off I-480 and led me to a room. At this point, I was so nervous and excited I didn't even see the name of the place. She pulled me inside and started pulling off my clothes. I would have felt embarrassed by my nudity, but she undressed me so quickly, I didn't really have a chance.

Then she took off her clothes, and I pushed my embarrassment aside, trying to dedicate all my mental power to recording every detail for posterity. I figured, for me, this was the best it was ever going to get. In fact, if things continued as the had through my high-school years, this would be my only opportunity to have sex with a real woman.

She stood before me, naked and prefect. I felt like I should say something. "Nice room."

"Not really, but it's near the Interstate, and they take cash. Now, shut up." She grabbed my hair, pulling my head back, and licked my neck. She let out a low giggle, and threw me onto the bed. Then she was on me.

First time stories are supposed to be really awkward and embarrassing things are supposed to happen, but Veronica handled me with such skill I really didn't have a chance. She took the lead and I followed, letting myself go to pleasure. Between my sense of awe at being with such a beautiful woman and the wonders of discovering physical love for the first time, I didn't even notice when she tore out my throat—endorphins, I guess.

She drank blood from the wound at my neck. Despite my concentration on what was happening lower down, I knew something was wrong, but I felt disconnected. While I was dimly aware I was about to die, I took comfort in the fact I would not die a virgin.

"Thank you."

She stopped drinking my blood. "What?"

"Thank you, Veronica. Thank you for the most wonderful night of my life. Now I don't have to finish high school a virgin."

She sat up straight. She didn't look happy. "You're in high school." She stared at me in stunned horror for a moment, and then she was across the room, my wallet in her hand. "You're only 17? You're in high school. We have rules, you know. When kids don't come home from school their parents fucking notice." She grabbed my t-shirt off the floor. "Here, hold this to the wound. Press hard."

I took the t-shirt from her and pressed it against my neck. Suddenly, I was wearing clothes, and so was she. She was really quick at dressing and undressing people. She grabbed me, I felt a rush of air, and then I was sitting in the passenger seat of her car. The tires squealed and the Corvette's engine wailed. It smelled like something was burning. I looked out the window to see the guardrails on the interstate flickering by incredibly fast.

"If you're in high school, why were you in a bar?"

"Bartender didn't card me," I said. My voice sounded far away. I closed my eyes for just a second.

"Vinny! Wake up!" Veronica slapped me.

There was warm liquid in my mouth. I swallowed it and opened my eyes. Rough gravel dug into my back. I looked over to see the idling Corvette. "I'm lying on the side of the road."

She shook me, grinding the gravel further into my shoulders. "Look, I gave you some of my blood, enough to keep you alive, but not enough to turn you." She paused to think for a moment. "Well, probably not enough to turn you. It's different for everyone, but I'm sure you'll be fine." I supposed she was trying to convince herself, but at that moment, I couldn't really tell much.

"Why are we on the side of the road?"

She didn't answer. She just threw me back into the Corvette. A few minutes later, she stopped the car.

"Where are we?" I asked.

"Hospital. This is where you get out."

"I..."

She reached across me, threw the door open and pushed me out. I landed on a cement ramp, and rolled over on my back to see two big glass doors with "EMER-GENCY" painted on them. The Corvette sounded two long honks and drove away.

"I had a lovely evening, Veronica," I said to the retreating taillights. "Let's do it again sometime."

Where Vinny gets a job

After some morning PlayStation, I got out my day clothes: ski mask, broad-brimmed hat, wrap-around sunglasses, long underwear, two pairs of socks, pants, two shirts, gloves, and a long coat. I had learned the hard way that this amount of clothing was necessary for my continued survival. And even if it hadn't been deadly, having your foot catch fire because there's a tiny hole in your sock is just annoying.

Before pulling on the ski mask and gloves, I meticulously checked them for small tears. I liked only wearing a single layer over my hands and face, but I understood there were dangers. When I finished dressing, I walked upstairs and waited hesitantly by the front door. If I had made any mistakes in dressing, I would start to smolder.

Then, I'd have to go back inside, cover myself in dirt, and do it all over again.

I opened the door, stepped outside, and waited for the smell of smoke. Nothing happened. I silently counted to thirty just in case. Finally, I knew it was safe to continue. I started walking and noticed a bit of spring in my step. Usually, I felt fatigue when the sun was up, but today, I felt... I wouldn't say I felt alive, but I felt good.

Uncle Ted's bank was ten blocks from my house, a nice walk on a summer's day. I loved the smell of the air; morning air is warm and alive, fresh, the smell of warm grass and flowers. The blood I had taken from Vicky cranked my sense of smell up just a bit further, making me especially aware of all the beautiful smells around me. Still, I felt like an idiot in my daytime clothing. Walking around in all that crap is surreal when everyone else is wearing t-shirts and shorts to beat the summer heat. At least heat doesn't bother me. I don't even sweat, unless I get nervous.

I arrived at the bank just before noon. Despite its proximity, I had not visited Uncle Ted at his office for several years. The building that housed his branch was a one-story brick monument to bad architecture. The south-facing wall of the building was made up of giant brick arches, filled with twelve-foot-high windows. The bank looked like it had not so much been built as thrown together from leftover pieces of other buildings.

I walked into the lobby, which stank of carpet cleaner and old money. All the tellers had short lines in front of them, so I joined a queue and watched the television in the lobby, tuned to a 24-hour news station. How stupid. Just another way in which our society was thriving on sensationalism of...

"I got him!" yelled a voice behind me, and someone big slammed into me, forcing me to the floor. My arms were wrestled behind me, my face was pushed into the floor, and my ski mask turned sideways, blinding me to what was going on outside of my cocoon of clothing. My sunglasses crunched underneath my face. In the distance, I could hear a woman, maybe one of the tellers, screaming.

"Everyone remain calm. I have the perpetrator," said the same voice. It was a male voice, loud and commanding. A cop? A security guard?

I was so panicked that the eyeholes in my ski mask would start my head on fire I couldn't think. I struck out wildly behind me, but my arms were pinned. Cuffs slapped across my wrists, and I was lifted from the floor. "Walk." Someone pushed me, and I started walking forward blindly. Someone yanked up on my handcuffs, and I felt an alien pain like my arm was being pulled from the socket. I felt a wet pop, and heard a sound like wet celery being ripped apart.

I was pushed through the building by my injured arm. When I reached my destination, a chair was pushed into the back of my knees. "Sit." I still couldn't see, but the room smelled like stale coffee and BO. I stopped breathing for the moment.

I sat. "Look, guys, I don't know what you think—"

"Shut up."

I shut up.

"You picked the wrong place to target, you scum. We've called the police. They're on their way," said the voice of the man who had attacked me in the lobby. He pulled off my ski mask, and for a moment, I thought I was done for. Frantically, I tried wrapping my arms around my head to block the sun, but that was impossible with the handcuffs. When I failed to burst into flames, I realized with relief I was in a windowless room.

A heavyset man stood in front of me, wearing, as I guessed, a security uniform. The room had a concrete wall with no windows and a steel security door. An old desk seemed devoted to holding loose papers and dirty coffee mugs. One wall held a row of lockers, labeled with marker and masking tape.

Behind the security guard stood my uncle, Ted. Ted is a big man, a former running back for Notre Dame. He has blue eyes and sandy blonde hair, and every time I see him, I can't help but think of sixties surf movies.

"Uncle Ted? What's going on?" Yuck. I had to breathe in to speak, which meant I had to smell the dank little room.

Ted shook his head and sighed. "Great job, Rusty. You've captured my nephew Vinny. He's here for an interview."

Rusty wasn't smart enough to give up. "Then why the hell is he dressed up like a terrorist?"

"Because he suffers from a skin condition and can't be out in the sunlight. Rusty, just unlock him and go back to the lobby. I'll take it from here."

"I'm sorry, I just saw him dressed like that, and... It's going to be ninety degrees today and I just finished an intensive class on how to spot domestic terrorists. You can't let any suspicious—"

"The handcuffs, Rusty. Oh, and call the police. For your sake, I think you should see if you can save them a trip."

Rusty walked behind me, and unlocked the cuffs. "Sorry about the misunderstanding."

"Don't mention it." I tried to make my voice sound cold, pissed off.

Rusty left quickly, presumably to call off the police, leaving me alone with my uncle.

"Sorry about that," said Ted. "He's an okay guy, just a little jumpy. He really wanted to go to Iraq, but the army found him to be a little..." He looped his finger around his ear in the "crazy" gesture and whistled coo-coo.

"And so you gave him a gun?"

"Well, he really wanted one, and he didn't shoot you, did he?" He smiled. "Speaking of which, how you doing? He didn't hurt you?"

"I'm fine." I could have told him about the dislocated shoulder, but it would be fine once I popped it back into place. He didn't really care anyway. He was just asking to be polite. Well, okay, maybe he did care a little, he did ask me here for an interview after all.

"Want to go to my office?"

I asked the question I always have to ask, "A lot of windows between here and there?"

"Oh, shit, yeah. I forgot. Sorry, Vinny."

"De nada."

"Why don't we just meet here? Can I get you a drink? I've got some nicely aged Scotch."

"Yeah, sure." At least it would get him out of the room for a minute. I needed to knock my shoulder back into place.

I waited for Ted to leave the room and walked over to a bare section of concrete wall. I rammed my shoulder into the wall. It hurt like hell, but it didn't pop back into socket. I took a breath to steady my nerves and rammed the wall harder. It stung bad enough to cross my eyes. I took a half-dozen steps back—this was going to hurt—and ran at the wall, shoulder first. I felt the force of the impact, and then I was flopping on the floor like a dying fish. After a moment, I was able to stand up. I worked my arm a little bit. It seemed to be aligned properly.

Thankfully, I was done flopping in pain and back in the chair by the time Ted returned—I didn't want him to think I was humping the floor. He cleared off a spot on the old desk, pushing dirty coffee cups and papers out of the way, and set down two highball glasses. He pulled a bottle out of his jacket pocket and poured an inch of golden liquid.

After sliding into the wooden chair behind the desk, he raised his glass, "Skoal,"and sipped at the Scotch. "So, Vinny, you're interested in a job at the bank?"

"That's the theory." I took a sip from my glass. It burned. "Mom wanted me to come talk to you at least. I don't know if I can work here, though." Like I would really want to. I just needed to blow the interview bad enough to get Mom and Dad off my back for another few months.

"Good. I like that kind of honesty. So, let's see? Are you good with numbers?"

"Horrible."

"Hmmm." He nodded. "That does rule out quite a bit of what I could offer you. You are a high school graduate though."

"Yes." Probably because teachers took pity on me after my attack, but I did graduate. "Hey, once in high school, I spent an afternoon rolling quarters into rolls. I was really good at that."

"We have a machine that does that. I suppose you could work a security job." He glanced at my outfit. "Probably night security. However..." He gave me a pleading look. "...Rusty would be your boss."

"That guy who just attacked me? The psychopath?" I tried to sound panicked, violated.

"Say no more. I understand. Tell you what. Let me think about this for a couple days. I'll tell your mother you had a great interview and I'll call a few people and see what I can come up with. You might not end up in the bank, but I must know someone who needs a bright, young man like you."

"Yeah, sure." Good luck with that.

He took another drink of his Scotch. "So, nice of you to stop by."

"Yeah."

After a moment of awkward silence, he downed the last of his Scotch. "See you in a couple days. By then, I should have something more suited to your... skills." He stood up and shook my hand. "I hope you don't mind showing yourself out."

"No problem. See you around." I stood and donned my ski mask, broken glasses, and floppy hat.

I walked slowly home. Whatever advantage I had gotten from the trickle of blood from Vicky seemed to have finally petered out. I ended up crawling straight into bed, covered myself up, and went to sleep exhausted. I don't often dream, but that day, I dreamed of Veronica and the night she turned me. Come to think about it, this would have been a much better place to do the flashback, but I already did that bit, so as my friend L'Isle would say, "C'est la vie."

––––––––

A couple unremarkable days later, I awoke to my father shaking me. "Wake up, my boy." This was such a nice change of pace from my mother's attempts at homicide—then again, is it homicide if the victim is already dead?

"I'm awake. What's up, Pop?"

He opened up a newspaper. "According to this, a woman was attacked in an alley behind Ernie's the other night. A guy tried to stab her in the neck. Do you know anything about it?"

I sat up to look at the paper. Why was he reading me this? Had he come out of denial about my condition and guessed I was involved? "Did it say anything else? Do they have a description? One of those artist sketches?"

"No, it was just a little blurb in the crime section. Still, I think you should stay away from that place. Apparently, it's getting pretty rough. I want you to be careful. There are a lot of loonies running around."

I nodded, relieved. My father hadn't figured out I was the mysterious attacker. "Sure thing, Dad. But I don't think it's really all that dangerous. I mean, Kyle goes there all the time."

"Well, I suppose if Kyle's going there, it would be alright for you to go with him, but don't go there alone. I don't want to worry about you dead in some alley." Typical, my opinion was unimportant, but Dad respected Kyle.

"You have nothing to worry about." I waited for him to leave, and he didn't. "Did you want something else?"

"I just wanted to remind you Ted and Loni are coming over tonight. I think Ted's going to offer you a job, so make sure you have some nice clothes. Do a load of laundry if you have to."

"Sure." That wasn't going to happen.

Dad must have detected the sarcasm in my voice. "Now look, son. I know you'd like to sit in the basement all day and play your video game, but you need to get out there and take control of your life. If Ted finds you a job, mister, I expect you to take it. Your mother and I aren't going to let you freeload here forever."

"Okay Dad." He had been making this threat for a decade, but so far, I had been able to talk my way out of any job offers. I already had a reason to stay away from the security guards at Ted's banks, and with the big windows, I couldn't imagine him having a real job for me.

I would be expected upstairs at six o'clock. My father likes things orderly, which meant dinner at six thirty, invitations for six. The meal always lasted at least one hour. The only food that made it to our dinner table was meat, potatoes, and a vegetable. We did not eat pizza. We did not eat tacos. Chinese food was not an option.

After a hunt, I had found a shirt with a collar and not too many holes and matched it with a pair of pants not made out of denim—after my parents came to the realization I was not going to do anything with my life, they stopped buying me nice clothes. I walked upstairs and after determining the blinds were closed, stepped into the kitchen. My mom and sister were working on the dinner, while Ted's fiancé Loni stood to the side. As always, Loni looked unnaturally beautiful, but for some reason, tonight she looked uncomfortable. The air was permeated with the smell of cooking meat, making me nauseous.

"The guys are in the study," Mom said.

My dad's study was right out of the 1970s, paneled with cheap wood, lacking the shelves of unread but leather-bound books so popular in today's home office. He even had an old-fashioned wire TV stand, sagging under the weight of his new 42" flatscreen. Besides the television, the only concession to the modern world was a laptop computer, which my dad grudgingly purchased upon discovering he could no longer buy five-inch floppy disks. As I walked into the room, Ted and my dad were discussing football. "You have to drill your nickel and dime defense, get your fundamentals down first," Dad was saying.

"Well, you could say that," Uncle Ted said with the look of a man who was trying not to embarrass his brother-in-law, "but special teams are just as relevant in the modern game..." My dad had wanted me to play football, but he quit when he realized I would never be big enough for the varsity team, which suited me fine, as I was never really that interested. I sat pretending to listen until Mom came in and announced dinner was served.

In accordance with the ancient rites and traditions, we sat waiting at the table while Mom unveiled a pot roast—which I was expected to praise despite the fact it smelled like death to me. After saying a blessing, my dad served out portions to everyone, while saying things like, "Honey, you've outdone yourself," and "What a feast." Sometimes when I am with my parents, I think the latter half of the twentieth century only happened to other people. All throughout this little show, Loni kept looking at me funny, like I was something nasty stuck to her shoe. I wondered if there was a stain on my shirt or something.

"So, Mom," I asked, "how did you find time to cook all this?"

"Well, if you were ever awake for dinner, Vinny, you would know we often have pot-roast."

"You go to bed that early?" Loni asked.

"No, not at all," Dad said. "Vinny's a night owl, out all hours spreading his wild oats, just like his old man."

"Oh, you," Mom said, "by the time you were Vinny's age, you were already the company's youngest regional manager."

I should explain that my father is a district manager for a chain of plumbing supply warehouses. I always found this completely embarrassing because he drove around in a big truck with a bumper sticker reading, "We do our business in the crapper!" Dad disliked the sticker also, but only because all the interesting things were happening in kitchens.

Lost in thought about my dad's crappy business, I had lost track of the conversation. All of a sudden, I realized Ted was watching me expectantly. A moment later, Jennifer exploded into the maniacal laughter only accessible to the most twisted of siblings.

"What was that?" I asked.

"Vinny! Pay attention," Dad snapped. "You are being offered a job. Jennifer, stop laughing." Jennifer shut her mouth, but her face turned red, and she gripped the table, shaking hard enough to jiggle the water glasses.

"There wouldn't be much money at first," said Ted. "You will be strictly working on commission." Oh, great. He had found a bank job for me after all. Oh well, there were worse places than the bank. "Of course, Loni will train you."

"Loni?" Loni didn't work at the bank. I didn't even know she worked.

Loni smiled forcibly. "Of course you will need more training than the other girls, but if anyone can teach you how to sell Lyle B cosmetics, it's me."

I got a sinking feeling. Something horrible was about to happen. "You mean I won't be working at the bank?"

Ted's broad shoulders shrugged. "I just don't have anything for you. I mean if you could just work during the day, you'd be all right, but banking is a 9 to 5 business, there's just not much to do after dark, and with you being at odds with my security chief..."

"He attacked me."

"Lyle B makeover parties, on the other hand," said Loni "can be scheduled for any time of day. It might be awkward finding a hostess who will have a party after eight, but once the fall comes and the days get shorter, you should be able to find lots of work. Until then, you can learn the business with me. I could use a model. It's hard to show off the best concealer in the business with my perfect skin."

"But only women can sell Lyle B."

Loni shook her head. "Of course not, Vinny. That would be discrimination. Lyle B is about empowering individuals, not telling people what they can't do."

Everyone looked at me expectantly. I couldn't believe this was happening. The room had started spinning around me. I took a deep breath, and the smell of the roast slammed into my throat and mouth, choking me. I stood up. "I'm not feeling so—"

"Here we go again," muttered Jennifer.

I whipped my head round to tell off Jennifer, and my dizziness came back with a vengeance. I grabbed a serving bowl off the table, cupped it in my arms, and started retching into it.

"Oh, Vinny," Mom said. "Not the potato salad."

Loni was looking a little green. "Does he throw up often?" She put one hand over her nose and mouth. She involuntarily rocked forward. "Oh, I think I'm going to be sick."

"Only at dinnertime," Jennifer said.

"I'm going to my room," I announced, not waiting to see if Loni followed my example. My stomach was still jumping, and my arms shook so badly I could barely hold the befouled side dish. Without waiting for permission to leave the table, I walked back to my room, pausing only briefly in the kitchen to throw the potato salad in the garbage, bowl and all.

Where Vinny gets an extreme makeover

Following the ill-fated dinner of pot roast, I had a few days to settle back into my old routine. I went to Ernie's. I hit on babes. I got shot down. I slept during the day. Whatever benefits I had received from my taste of blood were gone, but now that I knew what was missing in my life, I felt a new motivation. I tried to enjoy myself as best I could, knowing I would soon be walking the path of the Lyle B associate. At least now that I had a job, my mother was leaving me alone, which meant no morning barbeques. And humiliation in front of groups of women seemed marginally preferable to waking up as a small pile of dust.

All good things come to an end, though, and on Saturday, my mother woke me up in the usual manner, pulling open the curtain, and frying my butt like a pound of bacon. This time she wasn't lecturing me about finding a job, but preparing me for the crappy one I had. "Wake up, Vinny. You need to get dressed. Loni will be here in an hour to pick you up." She sat down on the bed and patted my head under the covers, where I cowered from the sun. "And don't worry. If this thing with Loni doesn't work out, you can always join the Marine Corps."

I know she was trying to motivate me, but talk about an empty threat. The Marines didn't want vampires. They were more into sunny, outdoor activities, like shooting people in the desert. Then again, I envisioned a squad of vampire marines popping out of the desert sand and eating a group of insurgents in the middle of the night. Maybe they did want vampires after all. Could I be immune to chemical weapons?

After Mom left, I got up and dressed in my daytime clothes. I glanced in the mirror—damn, I looked creepy. Loni was waiting upstairs. When she saw me, she took a step back. "Vinny?"

"I'm in here," I said through my layers of clothes.

"Oh, of course. I'd been told, but I wasn't ready for... Well, honestly, I thought you might be a burglar."

"I get that a lot."

I got into Loni's car and rode in silence for a few minutes. I felt like I should say something, "So, do you and Ted watch a lot of football?"

She didn't even turn to look at me. "You are here for one reason and one reason only. My very wealthy fiancé likes you. I, however, do not. So you're going to shut up, pay attention, and not talk to me unless you absolutely have to. And if you do anything to mess up my relationship with Ted, I'm going to cut your nuts off. Got it?"

"I got it. I got it." Jesus. I could tell she was going to fit in with the rest of my insane family just fine.

"Good. Now, shut the fuck up."

We rode the rest of the way to Loni's apartment in silence.

The most stunning feature of Loni's living area was the large dressing table that dominated the room. It was one of those things with the big mirror surrounded by light bulbs, like what they use in movies when they wanted to show people were about to go onstage. All the seating focused on the makeup table. She didn't even have a TV.

"Do you have a lot of parties here?" I asked.

"Yes. You would be amazed at how many women will use their husbands as an excuse not to host parties. When a customer says she'd like to host a party, but her husband won't let her, I offer my apartment, which I have set up to be the perfect showroom for the product. I also host special events here, which means I get all the hostess bonus items, and I can re-stock my inventory for free. If you want to make it in this business, you have to build up a good collection of cosmetics, both for demonstrations and for free gifts."

"Okay. Whatever."

She shot me a nasty look. "Look, turd. I get the idea you don't think this is a real business. Do you want to know how much money I made last year?"

"Yeah, sure."

She told me. I'm pretty sure Loni was making more than my dad. If I made a go of this, it would buy me a lot of video games.

"Shit. That's a lot."

"Yes it is. So are you about done with all the attitude?"

"I suppose so."

"Good, now let me take your coat, and I'll be right back."

She took my hat, ski mask, and coat into the bedroom and

returned a few moments later with a digital camera and a pile of clothing. "I think these will fit you."

I looked through the clothing— a pair of black panties with a matching bra, a spaghetti-strap top, a black jacket, and a black skirt. "Um... you want me to dress up in women's clothing so you can take pictures?" Loni was slightly more insane than I had estimated.

She rolled her eyes. "I'll turn my back if you insist, but trust me, I can control myself." She turned around and waited.

I picked up the panties. They looked rather small compared to my boxer shorts. I stood looking at them like a deer in headlights.

After a moment, Loni said, "Are you dressed yet?"

"I don't think I can do this."

She turned around and stuck her long, red fingernail out at me. "Look, Idiot, if you want to sell, you're going to listen to me. No woman is going to buy her makeup from a pimply boy. If you can do this, you can make some real money. However, if you don't think you can put on those clothes, I can just open my blinds and see how allergic you really are to sunlight. Personally, I think you're a lazy faker, but I guess we'll find out. My apartment gets wonderful afternoon sun." She reached over to the blinds and wrapped her hand around a cord. She had presented me the carrot of money and the stick of spontaneous combustion.

I held out my hand. "Listen, Loni, you don't want to do that."

She shook her head, and her eyes went all crazy. "Oh, I do want to do it. I'm so sick of hearing Ted say, 'Poor Vinny... Poor, poor, Vinny.' You have no idea how much I want to see if you're just a little faker."

I turned my back to her, quickly slid off my pants and boxers. I stood there naked, holding the panties and really looked at them for the first time. They were tiny and lacy. They seemed designed more for looks than comfort. "Look, are you sure—"

"Do it now, or I swear I'll open these blinds."

At this point, I considered draining Loni's blood and leaving her for dead, but as Uncle Ted and my parents knew I was "training" with her, I didn't really want to explain how I just happened to be the last person seen with someone who ended up a bloodless corpse.

I took a deep breath and slid on the panties. I was surprised to find they weren't wholly uncomfortable. They gripped me a little more tightly than I would have liked, but I didn't find the sensation wholly unpleasant. I started struggling into the bra.

"Put it on backwards," Loni advised. "Hook it in the front and then twist it around back."

I did so, and found it much easier. I put my arms through the straps. I poked at the small cup of the bra. Despite the tiny size, it was filled with air.

"You'll need these," Loni said. Her hand dipped into my bra and slid something in. "Silicone inserts. I use these when I wear party dresses. This is my old pair. You can have them. You'll still be an A cup, but at least you'll have something."

"Great." I slipped on the strappy top, skirt, and jacket, making the transformation complete. Through the entire humiliating experience, I kept thinking about how much I hated those goth wannabe vampires. Being a vampire had taken away my chances at a normal relationship, it had taken away the respect of my family, it had taken away my ability to live in the daytime, and finally, now, it had taken away my manhood.

"That wasn't that bad, was it?" Loni said. "I'll let you wear flats today, but you're going to have to learn to walk in heels. Now, let's put your face on. And Vinny, stop adjusting your crotch."

"Sorry, it's a little snug."

"Well, get used to it."

After taking pictures of my face from multiple angles, Loni spent the next hour "putting on my face." It wouldn't have taken so long, but she would try one product, shake her head, and clean it all off so she could move to the next product. She wasn't gentle as she scraped off each successive layer, and even with my hardened vampire skin, all those chemicals were starting to sting a bit.

Loni sighed. "I'm having trouble matching your skin type. I've never seen anything like this. It's like the product is rejecting you." She picked up a plastic tub and blew the dust off the top. "Let's give this a try." She took a cotton ball and started quickly spreading it across my face. "This is Lyle B Type V Magic Concealer and foundation. It's supposed to be the bestseller, but I've never had any luck..." She stopped talking and gasped, raising her hand to her mouth. Before I could ask her if the nasty stuff was eating through my skin, she scooped up a big plop of the stuff and smeared it all over my face. "I can't believe it."

"What?" I said, a little freaked out.

Before she answered me, she took out a tube of lipstick and applied it to my upper lip. "Go like this." She pushed her lips together.

I did as she commanded.

She shook her head as if not believing what she was seeing. "You're gorgeous." She said it with such conviction that I believed her. I looked into the mirror expecting to see a man in drag. Instead, I saw a beautiful woman. "Now, let me just finish up your eyes and put a little blush on."

"Is all this really necessary?"

"Shut up. I'm a professional." She started messing with my hair, eventually settling on holding it back with a flowered clip. "I'll do better next time. I'm going to teach you how to apply everything Lyle B sells. When I am done with you, you will know more about applying makeup than most women. Lyle B has a limited presence in Omaha and I have more business than I can handle. After I have you trained, you will start doing your own parties. I will be above you and get a cut of everything you sell. Understand?" She looked at me like I might not understand.

"Yeah, I get how it works."

When she was done, she banished me to the kitchen, giving me detailed instructions on how to prepare hors d'oeuvres. Fortunately, everything was sitting out and ready to go, it just needed to be put into dishes and platters. As I worked, I listed to the doorbell and high, excited voices of female greeting. When I emerged from the kitchen fifteen minutes later with a tray of drinks, there was already a small group of women in the living room.

"Everyone," Loni announced, "this is my new recruit, Sally."

I looked around. "Sally?"

Loni gave me one of her nasty looks. "Don't kid around, Sally." I suddenly realized she meant me, which made sense. She couldn't go around calling me Vinny. She passed around the photos she had taken earlier. "These are the before pictures, fresh off the printer."

I had no idea she was going to show off my picture without makeup. I knew as soon as those women saw those pictures, they would know I was a man, but as each woman saw my "before" picture, she looked up in stunned amazement. Sally smiled at their reaction. "This is an excellent illustration of what finding the right product can do for you."

As I stood there with the women examining me, I reflected that after a decade, I had finally found a way to impress women, an unfathomably horrific way to impress women.

We waited for the rest of the women to arrive, and each one took their turn examining my transformation. When everyone was there, we played games, discussed products, and did makeovers. Finally, with Loni's guidance, I learned to fill out order forms.

When the evening was over, Loni added up her receipts. "Well done, Vinny. With you here, I sold almost twice as much as I usually do. You're a good luck charm."

"But why did they see my before pictures and still believe I was a woman?"

"They believed you were Sally because they want desperately to believe Lyle B cosmetics can improve their appearance as much as it can improve yours."

"And does it?"

She shook her head. "As far as I know, you're unique. Still, with these before pictures, you should be able to sell even more than me."

"And then I'll be making as much money as you?"

"No. You're going to be on a tier below me, so you'll make a smaller percentage until you recruit enough girls. Still, there are other benefits to selling Lyle B. For instance, you can buy Lyle B for thirty percent off the retail price, and given the reaction it has with your skin, I think you should wear it all the time."

"I'm not going to live my life as Sally."

She smiled at me. "Of course not, but let me show you how you can disguise your acne and oily skin and still look masculine."

In exchange for my help, Loni offered me a line of credit, and I ended up buying $150 worth of product against the commission on my first show.

Over the next week, I posed as Loni's ugly duckling almost every night, and Loni taught me more and more about how to apply and sell cosmetics. When I was dressed as Sally, she was even a little nice to me. I tried several different products on myself, trying to come up with the best combination. From what I could see in the mirror, I was ready to go outside.

After applying my Vinny face, I put on a black t-shirt and my least faded black jeans. In the mirror, I looked more confident. My skin was perfect. I had one hundred dollars in my pocket—a gift from Loni for helping her sell so much. And it was Karaoke Night. Tonight, I would return to Ernie's a better man. I would seduce a beautiful woman brimming with sticky, delicious blood.

I arrived early to find Ernie working the door. "Hey Ernie, what's up?"

"I've been having trouble with Tony, the new guy. He is a real pain in the ass. You gonna sing tonight?"

"You know it."

He looked at me inquisitively, "You do something different to your hair?"

"Not really. I combed it."

"Whatever it is, you're looking good, Vinny."

I smiled. "Thanks."

Two cars pulled up and a large group of people began to assemble on the sidewalk. "You better get inside while there's still somewhere to sit."

"Okay. See you later."

Inside, Karaoke Night was in full swing. A guy onstage sang Van Halen's "Hot for Teacher." The line to the bar was already three deep, most of the stools were taken, and the noise levels were significant as people strained to be heard over the sound system. Kyle sat in a booth with two beer bottles in front of him.

I walked over and slid into the booth. "You started without me."

"I got a beer. The other bottle was stuck to the table." He poked the bottle with his finger—it didn't move. He looked at me funny. "You get a haircut?"

"No. I haven't changed my hair since high-school."

"Yeah, you don't need to tell me," he said in his sarcastic tone.

"At least it's not a mullet."

"Thank God." He picked up the bottle not stuck to the table and finished his beer. "Sit tight. I'll go get us another round."

He returned a few minutes later, setting a beer in front of me. "So, your dad tells me you have a new job, but he's been kind of cryptic about what you're doing."

"Sales," I answered, hoping without much hope that he would not ask any follow-up questions.

"Who for?"

"It's a direct sales company."

"Well, that's not a big deal. Most of my money comes from commission. I mean there are less honorable professions."

"Like what?"

After a moment, Kyle said, "So, what are you selling?"

"Lyle B Cosmetics."

"Oh dude, you are so lucky."

"I am?"

"You are going to get such crazy amounts of tail. Just thinking about all those excited women is making my dick hard."

"Kyle, it's not like that—"

"Yes, it is, seriously, take a look, I've got wood."

"Kyle, I'm not looking at your junk, especially if you're pitching a tent."

"Have it your way, but trust me, it's there." He took a drink of his beer. "So, how'd you break through the pink ceiling? I thought they only allowed women to sell that stuff."

"I have to wear a dress," I said, trying to make it sound like a joke, which in a way, my entire life was.

Kyle chuckled. "Good one, dude." He lifted his bottle and made a face. "I'm out. Want another?"

"I got this round."

I returned with two bottles of Budweiser and found Kyle with a shit-eating grin on his face. I set down the beers. "What?"

"Dude, I just realized, when you went up to the bar just now, you're wearing makeup."

If there were blood in my body, I would have blushed. "No. I'm not."

"Well, I was kind of guessing, but the look on your face says it all." I must have looked uncomfortable. "Don't worry, dude. It looks good." He smiled evilly. "Queer."

"Hey!"

"Settle down. I'm just screwing with you, but next time, seriously, a little lighter on the eyeliner. It's a dead give-away."

"Thanks for the advice." I paused for a moment to reflect on how weird it was to discuss makeup tips with Kyle while a young professional sang Wang Chung.

The night continued. We drank lots of beer. My song was announced, and I sang "Live and Let Die," the Guns 'N Roses version. Not only did people seem to pay attention, but when I was done, they applauded. Some of the women even gave me looks. Score!

I returned to the booth and Kyle gave me a high-five. "You are on fire tonight. That was spectacular." We drank more. I was proud, having my own money to spend, and I bought several more rounds than I usually did. Buying those drinks made me feel good, like I was giving back for all those years Kyle carried me.

Kyle sang "One Bourbon, One Scotch, and One Beer." He didn't seem to attract as many women as usual. In fact, he seemed sloppy drunk. He kept making eyes at one of the women in the bar, but instead of being sexy and seductive, he was coming off as creepy and stalkerish. I realized there were a great number of empty bottles sitting on the table in front of us. Alcohol doesn't have the same effect on me as it does on mere mortals. I must have bought a few too many rounds.

He returned to the table. "How was I? I think I really connected with that hottie over there. I'm going to go see if she wants some action."

I pulled Kyle into the booth. "I think she went to the bathroom. Why don't you sit down and relax for a minute?"

"Okay, that's cool." Kyle sat back down. He closed his eyes, and a moment later, his head lolled back, and he started to snore. I watched Kyle sleep for a few minutes as I finished my last beer.

Ernie walked up and nodded to the forest of beer bottles adorning our table. "Looks like you guys have been having a good night, but maybe it's time you got Kyle home."

"Yeah, I guess so. Here, help me get his keys out of his pocket, and I'll drive him."

"I don't think you should be driving anyone anywhere. How many of those empty bottles are yours?"

"Well, yeah, I've had a few, but I'm okay." I closed my eyes and touched my nose.

Ernie shook his head. "Forget about it. You're either walking him home or calling a cab."

"I guess I'm walking then." I'd started the night with one hundred dollars in my pocket, but that had almost all gone for beer and tips. I didn't have enough to tip a cabbie.

"Vinny, don't worry about it. I can give you some money for the cab."

"You don't worry about it. I'll get him home in one piece." All night, I hadn't leeched off my friends once. I was not going to start again.

"Have it your way." He patted Kyle down and pulled the keys from his pocket. "Either way, these are staying with me. You can pick them up tomorrow." He worked the car keys off the ring and handed me back the rest.

Kyle's condo was twenty blocks away. He was somewhat capable walking, but he needed steering, which took some serious effort. After five blocks, I seriously regretted not taking up Ernie on his offer of cab money. At ten, I dropped Kyle on somebody's lawn and lay down next to him. I didn't have to catch my breath, but trying to figure out which way Kyle would lurch next was mentally exhausting.

"You're my best friend, dude."

"I know Kyle. You're mine too."

"I really love you, dude. I'm glad you have a job."

"That's great."

"We should find some girls. I like girls."

"Yeah, that would be nice. But let's get you home instead." I pulled him back to his feet and started steering him again. At fifteen blocks, I waited while he threw up. At eighteen blocks, he had to pee. Finally, I walked him up to the front door of his swank condo. He froze, and I nearly knocked him over.

"Wait." He nodded at the glass front door. Through it, I could see an old lady giving us the stink eye. "That's Mrs. Manilow," he whispered, "that evil crone hates young people who have fun. If I walk in drunk, she's going to complain to the condo association. We better go in through the freight entrance."

"Where's the freight entrance?"

"All the way round back, in the alley."

"Of course it is. Come on, Kyle." I steered him round to the other side of the building and through a set of double doors labeled "Service Entrance" to find a big hallway, just a piece of undecorated dead space, with concrete floor and walls. A set of interior doors led further into the building and a large freight elevator dominated one wall. I leaned Kyle up against the wall. "Wait here while I figure out the elevator."

"Okay," Kyle said, and slid to the floor. I tried to pull him up again, but he just slid back down, so I left him there.

With Kyle's keys, I managed to unlock the gate on the freight elevator and opened the doors to reveal a diamond-plate steel interior, big enough to hold a bedroom set. Helping Kyle from the floor, I led him toward the large, metal box. As I guided him inside, he swerved, cracking his head on the gate. I pulled him back—a trickle of blood ran down his forehead.

"Careful, big guy. Just a little bit farther and you'll be home and dry." I shut down my respiration, afraid of what I might do if I caught the scent of his blood. I wrapped my arms around him so he wouldn't fall over while I closed the doors and started the elevator up to his floor, trying to lean him back against the elevator wall when he grabbed me in a tight hug.

"I love you, dude. You are the most awesomest friend ever."

I struggled to push him away, but he held on tight, and without blood for the past weeks, I had become weak again, especially after half-carrying him for twenty blocks. My head rested on his shoulder. I steeled myself to push back once again, and without thinking, I took a breath. I drowned in the smell of his blood. It was only a trickle, but it was enough. The smell crept down my nostrils, down my throat. He had loosened his tie earlier, and I could see his exposed neck. Before I knew what was happening, I was shaking with desire. The man with his arms around me was no longer my oldest best friend. He was my food. And I was hungry.

My teeth closed on his throat, puncturing the artery, and blood leapt into my mouth, hot and sweet, sating my desire, turning my need to pleasure. This time it was no small trickle. I drank mouthful after mouthful. I experienced a feeling of calm and ecstasy I had never felt before, ecstasy I would die for and, if necessary, an ecstasy I would kill for.

With the thought of dying, I realized I was killing my friend. I pulled back from the wound and watched as the blood flow slowed to just a trickle. I licked his neck and watched as his wound sealed shut.

Kyle pushed me away. "Dude, did you just kiss me?"

"No," I said immediately, but then again, it might be a good cover-up for biting him. "Well, maybe by accident."

"Oh, crap. You have a hard on. Dude, I know I'm hard to resist, but it's not going to happen."

I glanced down and saw there was indeed a tent in my pants, probably just a reaction to suddenly having so much more blood in my body. I tried to think of some kind of reason or excuse for my erection, but nothing came to mind. The elevator stopped.

"Just let me explain. You know I'm a vampire—"

Kyle pushed the "open doors" button. He held up a hand between us. "Dude, I'm leaving. You go home. I need some time to think." He gave me a look I couldn't describe. Was it fear?

Without another word, he turned and staggered to his apartment door. I waited, but he keyed into the apartment without looking back at me. I heard him close and lock the door. I stood there for a few minutes watching the empty hallway. My senses were working overtime. All around me, I could hear the people of Kyle's floor, snoring, watching TV, making love, arguing. I could smell their stink and hear their heartbeats. Standing there, filled with the raw power of Kyle's blood coursing through my veins, I realized I was no longer human. I was something different, an immortal who drew his energy from the blood of others. I could never go back to what I used to be, and unless I could find others like me, I would always be alone.

Where Vinny discusses the facts of life with his father and then puts on a dress

"Wake up, my boy."

Dad was sitting on the edge of my bed, shaking me. I glanced at my clock. Another hour until my alarm would go off.

"I'm awake. What do you need?"

"Kyle tells me you made some unwanted advances towards him in a service elevator."

"That's not really what happened," I said, trying to stall for time so I could come up with a story about what really happened. A week had already passed since my attack on Kyle, and I had done my best to avoid him. This mainly meant staying out of Ernie's, but to me, that sacrifice was dear.

"Would you like to tell me your side of the story?"

I searched my mind for an excuse. Empty. "Not really."

"You don't have anything to be ashamed of. It's only natural for two young men, spending time in each other's company, without girlfriends, to feel urges, and through natural curiosity... Well, for instance, when I was in college, my roommate and I were on the wrestling team, and we used to spend long hours in the weight room, sweating and straining our young, toned bodies, and then later, in the showers—" Suddenly, I realized where this speech was going.

"Dad! No! Don't say it."

"I was single at the time and he had broken up with his girlfriend—"

"Dad! Shut up!" There were some things I just didn't want to know.

"There's no reason to be like that. I'm just pointing out it's perfectly natural, and I understand if you have feelings for Kyle."

"Listen, it was all just a big misunderstanding. I don't have feelings for Kyle. I'm not curious. And I don't want to hear about you and your college roommate."

Dad stood up. "Well, if you're going to be that way about it. I was just trying to be supportive." I listened, relieved, to him walking up the basement steps.

I couldn't believe my father would say something so deviant, I thought as I put on a new skirt and a summery blouse. Jenny had bought me the outfit. My little sis had a great eye for what would look good on me, and I felt sure this outfit would be perfect for tonight's party. Then again, I also had my new dress...

A half hour later, I traipsed up the steps in a short, cotton dress. I was still riding the high on Kyle's blood, and

I felt extraordinarily light on my feet. Of course, I would have to wear my horrible daytime clothes on the way to the party, but by the time I was supposed to be there, the sun would be down. I wondered if there was somewhere I could buy a burka.

On my way through the kitchen, I waved to Mom, who was making some final preparations for supper. Dad and Jenny were waiting for me in the dining room.

"Hey, Vinny," Jenny said as I slid into my seat. "Looking good."

"Yeah, thanks for picking out clothes for me. It's hard to go shopping in the day, and all the mall stores are closed by nine. That hardly gives me time to try things on."

"Oh, I like it. It reminds me of dressing up my Barbies. You're really going to have to shave your legs though if you want to pull off that dress."

Mom brought in a large plate of ham. "Oh, Vinny. Do you have to dress like that for dinner?" While she had wholeheartedly supported me working for Loni, she had not realized the job would involve... costuming.

"Sorry, Mom, but I have to leave for a party right after dinner. Loni's going to let me do both makeovers tonight. I'm getting really good."

"I'm not sure you should be selling cosmetics," she said, as if it hadn't been her idea to begin with.

"Oh come on, Mom. This is the twenty-first century. If I want to put on a dress and sell cosmetics, there's nothing wrong with it." While my first night as a woman had horrified me, I found I liked the pageantry of dressing up to go out, and I enjoyed the silky textures of the clothing.

"Well, maybe in places like New York City, that's fine, but this is Nebraska. People talk."

"And they don't already talk about how I sit in the basement all day and don't have a job?"

"Well, at least they used to know you weren't wearing a miniskirt and pumps."

I rolled my eyes. "Mom, I don't even own a miniskirt."

"You really should," Jennifer said. "With your legs, you could totally pull it off."

My mother sat down heavily and buried her head in her hands. "I just want my little boy back."

Dad stood up. "Vinny, I think you should go to your room. You're upsetting your mother."

I sighed. "I didn't do anything. Why doesn't anyone ever worry about upsetting me? I mean earlier you wouldn't shut up about hooking up with your college roommate."

I heard a gasp from my mother and turned to see a look of shock on her face. Tears began to leak from her eyes. "You said you were just wrestling. You said there was nothing between you two. You lied to me. Am I just your fag hag?"

"No, honey. You can't be my fag hag. We're married. You would be my beard."

Mom stood up from the table. "I'm going to my room." She marched out of the room with Dad following at her heels. As they left, I heard Dad say, "I meant that if I was gay, you'd be my beard. Honey, don't be like that."

I crossed my legs and turned to Jennifer. "So, about miniskirts..."

That night we sold a ton of makeup, and I ended up doing three makeovers instead of the regular two. After learning every trick Loni knew, I felt very confident with the tools, and she seemed quite pleased with the job I was doing, allowing me to do makeovers and fill out the paperwork with little or no supervision. We even rolled out a new line of lipsticks, taking the total number of shades to thirty.

After the party, we returned to Loni's house, where we traded our heels for fuzzy slippers and Loni poured me a glass of white wine. "You did really well tonight, Sally."

She still refused to call me Vinny when I was wearing my working clothes.

"Thanks, Loni. I really think I'm getting good with the product. Though I still haven't found anyone else who takes to the Type V Magic Concealer like I do."

"You seem to be unique." She took a sip of her wine. "I can't believe how quickly you've taken to all of this. Pretty soon, you'll be selling on your own. Of course, that will mean having your own product, coming up with promotions, and getting bookings, but I think you can handle it."

"I owe it all to you. You were tough at first, but I've learned a lot."

"I wasn't a tough teacher. I was a royal bitch. Ted begged me to take you on, and honestly, I thought he was crazy. I thought if I was nasty enough, you might go away."

"Little did you know I was too stupid to get the hint."

She took a sip of her wine. "I wouldn't call you stupid. You learned our products so quickly."

"The one gift I was born with. I have near-perfect recall when it comes to things written down on paper. A book, a billboard, or a catalog, I can remember word for word. Without that and the help of my friend Kyle, I would have never made it through high school." Thinking of Kyle reminded me of the precarious position our relationship was currently in. I couldn't avoid him forever—he was my best friend, and even if I didn't see him, I'd want to go back to Ernie's. I realized Loni was saying something. "What was that?"

"I have a surprise for you. I accidentally double booked tomorrow, so I'm giving you one of my shows. Do you think you can handle it?"

"Sure." This was the perfect opportunity for building my customer list.

When we were done discussing the details of the show, Loni drove me home. I got out of the car and stood in front of my house, but instead of going inside, I walked to

Ernie's, still dressed as Sally, with the intention of checking in on Kyle without showing my face, just in case he was still mad at me.

Tony, the new guy, was checking IDs at the door, but he didn't even look at mine, he just waved me through. I sat down at the bar, and Ernie walked up to me. Even though I knew I looked completely different, part of me was still afraid he would recognize me. I ordered a light beer. He sat it down in front of me and examined my face for a minute. "Do I know you from somewhere?"

"Is that a line?"

"No, just natural curiosity."

"I come in for karaoke once in a while."

He looked at my face again, changing position to see it from another angle. "Yeah, that must be it." He opened a bottle of Bud Lite and set it in front of me. "Enjoy."

I sipped the beer and watched a few people sing, waiting to see if Kyle showed up. I was just about to get up and leave when Ernie set another beer in front of me. "That's from Tony, over there."

I looked over to see the bouncer. He swaggered over. "Hi, baby, what's happening?"

"I'm not your baby."

"Then what should I call you?"

"How about you don't call me at all?" I'd been shot down enough times to know how this worked.

"So, you're going to take my drink and not talk to me."

"That's about the size of it."

He tried to snatch the beer away, but I was too fast. "You're a bitch!" He pounded his immense fist on the bar.

I stared into his eyes. "Honey, you don't want to know what I am." I felt a low growl coming from deep in my throat.

He took a step back, but he didn't turn away. It was like I had mesmerized him.

"Tony!" Ernie shouted from across the bar.

The shout brought Tony out of his trance. He blinked a couple of times. "Enjoy your beer," he said sarcastically. I gave the attempt a three out of ten.

After determining Kyle wasn't going to show up, I signed up to sing. Since I had the cover of my Sally persona, I did something I'd always wanted to do. I sang Wilson Philips' "Hold On" to the obvious excitement of the male contingent in the crowd.

Eventually, the evening drew to an end, and Ernie announced last call. I finished my drink and had just started to the door when Ernie stepped up to me. "Can I offer you a ride?"

"Um, no thanks. I'm fine." I didn't know whether Ernie was offering me a ride, which meant dropping me off at the house of his friend Vinny, or he was offering me a "ride," which was just too horrible to contemplate.

"Okay, lady. Just trying to save you some cab fare."

I was anxious to get started with my first solo event, but I needed to borrow the car, and Dad would only give me the keys if I agreed to come to our family dinner. If all went well tonight, I would get bookings off this party, and I wouldn't have to rely on Loni anymore.

My father was waiting to be served, per usual. When he saw me, his face fell. "Vinny, why are you dressed like that?"

I had put on a black skirt and nylons with a white blouse embroidered with a black pattern. "I think I look good."

About halfway through dinner, Jennifer turned to me and said, "You're never going to believe what happened at school today. Mark broke up with Rebecca, and he told Stephen her nose was too big, so now she wants to have surgery."

"You should let me meet Rebecca."

She gave me a mischievous look. "Why, are you into big-nosed, teenaged sluts?"

"No." I said immediately, and then thought about what I was saying. "Well, yes, but I think with the proper shading, she could de-emphasize her nose and bring out her better features, so guys wouldn't even notice her nose."

Suddenly, Jennifer's arms were around me. "Oh, Vinny. I always wanted an older sister." She hugged me tight.

Mom stood up and started stacking plates. "Well, I think everyone's done eating."

Reacting quickly, Dad clamped his hands down on either side of his plate, holding it to the table. He had been picking at his green beans and potato, saving the steak for last. "Sweetie, I'm not done."

She strained, pulling the plate away with all her strength, and inch-by-inch, it slipped out of my father's grasp. "Oh... Yes... You... Have..." With a final tug, she pulled the steak from his grasp.

My father looked pleadingly at us, his face full of torment. He winced at the sound of the garbage disposal. "Thanks a lot, kids. Your mother is currently throwing away eight ounces of perfectly cooked and seasoned top sirloin."

"Sorry, Dad," we said in unison.

Mom came back and dropped a cake, still in the rectangular cake pan, with the words "Congratulations Vinny" written on it. "We got this to celebrate your first night working alone." She set plates in front of Dad, Jennifer, and I. "I'm going to go take a bath."

"Honey," Dad said, "don't you want a piece of this beautiful cake you've baked for Vinny?"

"I said I'm taking a fucking bath. Now eat your cake."

"I'm not so hungry anymore," I said. Mom was obviously having some kind of breakdown, and I just wanted to get out of there.

"Me neither," Jennifer said.

"I made you this cake, Vinny." Mom plunged her bare hand into the heart of the pan, smashed together a fistful of cake and frosting, and slammed it down on the plate in front of me. "Now, eat your goddamn dessert."

I picked up a fork and ate a little piece of the mess in front of me. "Yummy."

My mother relaxed just a bit, but it was still obvious she was out of sorts. "Now, I'm going to go have a bath. Have a good night at work, Vinny." She staggered up the stairs, leaving a trail of frosting all the way up the railing.

The victimized cake lay between us. There were long fingernail tracks in it. My father laid a napkin over its wound. For a moment, no one said anything.

Jennifer stood up first. "I have a lot of homework to do."

"It's Friday night," Dad said.

"Early bird gets the worm," Jennifer said. She climbed the stairs slowly, as if she didn't want to chance running into Mom on the way to her bath.

I picked up my plate of pulverized gunk. I could still see Mom's finger marks in the compressed ball of dessert. "This cake is so good that I'm going to take it downstairs and save it for later."

My dad just sat, looking at the napkin-covered cake, shaking his head.

I made myself scarce, returning to my room until it was time to leave. Finally, when I could not wait any longer, I fixed my face and headed upstairs. Dad was waiting for me. He looked a lot better. He held out his car keys. "I think you needed these?"

"Thanks, Dad. I don't think I could make it halfway across town with my sample cases." I leaned over to give him a kiss on the cheek, like Jennifer did before she left on a date, but he intercepted me and gave me a firm hand-shake instead.

My family sure was acting weird lately. I gave my ny-lons a firm tug and walked out the front door.

Leaving after the sun went down meant rushing to my destination—the party wouldn't start for an hour, but it was better to be set up before guests arrived. As I zipped around corners in my dad's Ford 500, I was glad the hostess lived in a new neighborhood without the blind corners made by large trees or shrubbery. I tried to keep the car on the road as I read a map printed from my father's inkjet printer, which was, for some reason, only printing bright magenta. I nearly missed a turn and squealed the tires as I turned down a street of freshly built starter mansions. A victim of a housing crash, a paint-flaked sign at the end of the street announced affordable homes between 9,000 and 15,000 square feet. Most of the neighborhood's houses lacked grass, and prairie flowers overran the front yards. A few of the ginormous houses didn't even have driveways, only weeds pushing through the gravel beds still waiting for concrete.

The house at 1313 Ravenscroft Lane stood in contrast to its unfinished neighbors. It had a lawn and a good deal of landscaping in place. The various plants and shrubs glowed in puddles of warm light from unobtrusive spotlights hidden in the yard, and the owners had gone to the expense of having mature trees transplanted into the lot, offsetting the visual affront of the oversized box of the main house.

I glided up to the front door, already an expert in my high-heeled pumps, and knocked, giving the door a dainty rap. After a moment, I gave it a pound with my fist. As the door opened, I put on my brightest smile. "Hi, I'm Sally with Lyle B. Loni couldn't be here tonight..." My voice froze in my throat.

I can't tell you what force brought me to that house on that night. Karma. Kismet. Vampire magic. Deus ex machina. But I try not to think too hard about things like that.

Standing in front of me was Vicky, the girl from the bar with the gift for projectile vomiting. She looked at me oddly, and I tried to avert my gaze as she stared into my eyes. I could see what was going to happen already. She would recognize me and call the police. They would find me via Loni and haul me off to jail, leaving me in a small cell with a window and no escape.

Vicky grabbed my shoulder and spun me around. She gazed into my eyes, and a jolt of electricity shot through my body. "Vernon," she said, grabbing me and pulling me close. "You came back to me. Oh, Vernon. Oh, Vernon."

"Vinny."

"Oh, Vinny. Oh, Vinny. I never thought I'd see you again." She kissed me full on the lips, and reached under my skirt, grabbing me. "Give it to me, ladyboy."

We did it right there in the foyer, our clothes thrown about in wild abandon. We tried to start slow, but soon I was pounding her mercilessly into the hardwood floor. She started saying, "Oh, Vinny," again. "Oh, Vinny. Oh, Vinny. Oh, Vinny. Oh, Vinny. Oooh! Vinny!"

I struck at her neck, and she screamed in what I hoped was ecstasy. Her sweet blood squirted deep into my mouth and down my throat. I fed with abandon, letting go of the idea that if I took too much I could kill this woman, who had just done some very nice things for me. When it was almost too late, I pulled away and rolled onto my back.

"That was great," Vicky said. "Do we have time to do it again before the party?" She was looking decidedly pale.

"Maybe we better hold off for a while. I don't want you to die or anything."

She shrugged. "I'm willing to take that chance."

"Maybe we should get dressed and find you some juice or something. Juice and a cookie, isn't that what you're supposed to have after donating blood?"

We got dressed, and I led her off in search of the kitchen. It was much easier guiding her empty of blood than it had been guiding her full of liquor. Mainly this was due to her blood coursing through my veins, making me strong. I found the kitchen—a very clean room, it didn't even have furniture, just a countertop covered in party food. I looked for a place to sit her down. She was small, so I laid her down on the counter amongst the appetizers while I checked the fridge. "You don't have any furniture."

"Yeah, my husband stole it. I'm waiting for most of the new stuff, but I have enough that we can still have the party."

"You have a husband?"

"Relax, I'm divorced. That's why I was getting all drunk and slutty the other night. I'm usually not that easy. Hey, as long as we're getting all close and personal, why're you wearing a dress?"

"Um, well, my Lyle B manager kind of insisted on it if I was going to sell. I guess women aren't really comfortable with buying cosmetics from men. Actually, I kind of like it." I pulled a bottle of apple juice from the fridge and passed it to her. "Here, drink some of this while I get ready for the party."

After fixing my face and retrieving my silicone boobs from Vicky's umbrella stand, I got to work setting out my products, catalogs, and order forms in Vicky's living room, which was, thankfully, furnished. With that done, I went back and checked on her. She was woozy, but still conscious, so I propped her up in a chair in the corner of the room, and went about getting her hors d'oeuvres, and greeting people as they arrived. I apologized for Vicky, telling her friends she had a cold, and in an effort to be the perfect hostess, she had taken too much cold medicine.

I made over two thousand dollars on the party that night. Vicky's friends had some money, and they really freaked out over my before and after pictures. When the last order form was filled out, I took Vicky to bed and we had sex again, including the biting, but without quite so much drinking. After I finished, I fell back, panting. "So, do you know what you want for your hostess gifts?”

"How about you?”

"What do you mean by that? You just had me.”

"I mean, how would you like to move in here, and be my boy toy?" She fell asleep with her face buried in my neck.

Some days it feels good to be a vampire.

Where Vinny leaves home

The next day, I was riding so high on Vicky's blood, I couldn't sleep. I cleaned my room. I watched Oprah. I put away and sorted all my clothes. I even had Jennifer bring over her classmate Rebecca and gave her a makeover, showing her how to hide her gigantic nose—she was so happy, she signed up to do a party later that month, assuming we could get her mother's permission.

I strode up to dinner that night wearing a vintage Atari t-shirt and faded blue jeans, hoping that seeing me in my regular clothes might make my mother a little happier after last night's fiasco. Dinner was informal, while still being in the meat-potato-vegetable context—fried chicken, American fries, and coleslaw. When Mom presented the steaming plate of chicken, she glanced over at me and relaxed considerably. The dead-chicken smell still bothered me a little though.

Dad said the blessing, and I felt no ill effects. Then, we ate quietly. I think we were all nervous after Mom's freak-out. Finally, my father, who considered a lack of dinnertime conversation near to sacrilege, felt compelled to speak. "So, Jennifer, I understand your last final was yesterday. How was your first day of freedom?"

"It's okay, but I really am going to miss everyone when I go away to school in the fall. Today Rebecca came over and Vinny gave her a makeover you wouldn't—"

Mom stabbed her chicken breast roughly, rattling the table.

"—so that was fun," Jennifer finished lamely.

There was a moment of silence, and then my tactless father turned to me. "So, Vinny, my boy, anything new with you?"

"Yes. I've decided I want to move out of the basement—"

"Well, my boy, that's a fine idea. Do you want your sister's room when she goes away for school?"

"No, I want to move out of the house."

There was a moment of silence while Dad mulled over the idea. "I don't think that's a good idea. You've only done one of those parties, which can't be that much money, and then there's first and last month's rent, security deposit—"

"Dad, would you let me explain?"

My father paused and nodded. "Very well, my boy, you have the floor."

I wasn't really looking forward to explaining this part. "Well, it's kind of like this. I really hit it off with Vicky, the hostess of last night's party, and she has a big house, and she's all alone."

Dad raised his eyebrows. "A woman? That means you and Kyle—"

"Dad, there was never anything between me and Kyle."

My mother's eyes brightened at this news and she nodded like one of those plastic bobble heads. "So, it's a big house. Are you going to pay her rent? Are you even going to have your own room?"

I shrugged. "Honestly, we didn't talk about the details. She offered, and I accepted."

My father shook his head. I could see the battle between his urge to protect me and his need to get me out of his house fight across his face. He opened his mouth to speak twice before any sound came out. "Well, just be careful."

Jennifer crossed her arms. "This sucks. I like having you around the house."

"Don't worry. I'll only be a phone call away, and until you leave for college, I'll just be across town."

"When are you leaving?" Mom asked. "How soon until you move to this Vicky woman's house?"

"Actually, I was kind of hoping I could leave tonight. I spent all day cleaning up my room and packing my stuff, and when I compared my schedule with Vicky's it just seemed like this was the best night for moving in. We are both going to be busy. Vicky works days, and I'm already booking shows—score!"

Mom didn't look happy. "All these years of living in the basement, and now, just when you finally have a job, even if you... You could at least have asked her to dinner."

"Sorry, with everything else going on, I just didn't think about it." Actually, I had thought of it, but every time I was going to bring it up to Vicky, the mental image of last night's eviscerated cake appeared in my head.

Before Mom could cross-examine me further, something thumped against the dining room window. Another thump came, and then turned to rhythmic knocking. We glanced around the table at each other. "I wonder what that is?" Dad said.

Dad stood up and walked over to the curtains. "Vinny, it is late afternoon, and the sun shouldn't be coming directly in, but maybe you should stand well back. We wouldn't want to trigger your nasty allergy." My father might be in denial, but at least he was practical about my condition. I nodded and crossed to the back corner of the room, into a spot mostly hidden by the china hutch. Dad drew open the curtains.

Outside, Kyle was pounding on the window glass with so much force, I was afraid it might crack. He was yelling something. The sound wasn't making it through the insulated, double-pane window, but it seemed to me he was just yelling, "Vinny!" over and over again. I stayed crouched behind the china hutch.

Dad closed the curtains. He took a deep breath, and pondered the situation for a moment. Finally, he said, "I wonder why he doesn't just go around and knock on the door? I'll go outside and see if he's alright."

"Maybe you shouldn't do that," I said, returning to the table. "I mean, something seems wrong with him."

"Kyle's your friend and my co-worker. If something's wrong with him, we need to figure it out and see if we can help him." He headed for the foyer.

Without my father there to keep the conversation going, the room had gone silent. "So, nice weather we've been having," I said. A thud-like sound came from outside.

A few minutes later, my father returned. "I tried to talk to him, but he just kept running away from me, hiding in the bushes. If he keeps lurking out here, I think we may have to call the police."

I glanced at my watch. "May I be excused? Vicky will be here soon to pick me up, and I need to get my stuff upstairs."

"Of course you can, my boy."

I spent the next half hour rounding up all my worldly possessions. It wasn't much to show for over a quarter century of living: ratty t-shirts and worn blue jeans, an assortment of holey underwear, a guitar with a hole in it, a suitcase full of dirt, a PlayStation with thirty games, and the discarded 19" color television from my dad's study, so old it still had the VHF and UHF dials. In addition, I now owned two pairs of low-heeled shoes, a collection of ladies' business casual outfits, with accompanying underwear, and a large collection of cosmetics. I piled the detritus by the front door.

The doorbell rang just after sunset. I hurried over and answered it. Vicky stood in the doorway, and something about her looked a little off. "Are you okay?" I asked.

"Yes, it's just that there's a strange looking man hiding in your bushes."

I leaned out and saw Kyle skulking in the shrubbery. "Oh, that's just Kyle. He's a friend." She looked at me expectantly. "Oh, please come in," I finally said.

Before she was in the door, my father joined us in the foyer. "Hello, I'm Vincent's father, Burt Lester. Welcome to our home. You must be the special lady who's taking our Vinny away from us."

"Yes, that's about right. My name is Vicky. Vicky Swanson."

"And how do you expect to support my son?"

"Dad, stop," I said.

My father held out his hand to silence me. "No, my boy. To me, you are still my little Vinny, and I need to know Vicky here can keep you safe and be a good provider for you."

"Well," Vicky said, "I work a phone job, calling people for a collections agency, but honestly, I don't really need to work. I am finalizing the divorce of my first husband, and the settlement will be substantial."

My father nodded. "It looks like you have a pretty solid plan for the future." Up the stairs, I saw my sister and mother watching the conversation.

"Don't worry, Dad. I'm not going too far. I'll be right across town, a phone call and a half hour drive away.

Maybe we can have you over for dinner in a week or two, once we're settled in."

My father grasped my shoulder. "I want to tell you something, and this is straight from the heart. I know it's been tough on you, and maybe your mother and I could have been more tolerant of your condition. I know in the past, I may have seemed a little disappointed in your accomplishments, but over these past few weeks, you've become more than just a son to me." He paused, choking on his emotion. "You've become the daughter we never had." He paused. "Except your sister, of course."

We all took a moment to let Dad's speech sink in.

The speech would have been a perfect sentiment to end the evening on, but we still had to load my stuff into Vicky's car. My mother and sister came downstairs to help. I loaded up everyone with my stuff and followed them outside holding the guitar with a hole in it.

I stepped out the door just in time to hear a loud whine coming from the bushes. Kyle emerged running straight at Vicky, who had a garbage bag of my t-shirts in one hand and my PlayStation in the other. "Master!" he screamed. "Dude, she has your PlayStation." He let out an inhuman yell and launched himself at her.

As Kyle closed in on her, Vicky dropped the bag of t-shirts, lifted the PlayStation over her head, and brought it down perfectly on his head. I'll never forget the horrible sound it made, the crunch of plastic, the sound of the eject door skittering across the concrete, but even worse than the physical damage to the chassis, was the knowledge the laser alignment would never have survived that sort of punishment. Kyle seemed fine, a little dazed, but otherwise unharmed. He swayed back and forth for a moment and then ran back into bushes.

The enormity of the situation took a moment to sink in. I looked over to my family, frozen in place with puzzled looks on their faces, and back to Vicky who still held the broken video game console. I felt like I should say something. "Crap! I've had that PlayStation for twelve years. It was modded for imports and everything."

Vicky walked over and laid a hand on my shoulder. "I'm sorry Vinny. I'll see if I can find another modded PlayStation, and until I find one I'll buy you a PlayStation III."

I couldn't believe what I was hearing. "Really?"

I stepped in and gave Vicky a quick hug. "Okay, let's get this stuff in your car. Can we go shopping on the way there?"

"Sure we can."

My father shook his head like he was trying to un-see Kyle's outburst. "I suppose I should have a word with Kyle at the office tomorrow."

I shook my head. "Don't worry about it, Dad. I'm sure he's just as embarrassed as we are. Just put it out of your mind and never think about it again."

Dad nodded. "I'm sure you're right, Vinny. Let's just forget about the whole thing." Since his preferred way of dealing with any issue was ignoring it, he had just needed a little push in the right direction.

After the car was loaded, my mother came over and gave Vicky some papers. "These are things you might need to know: emergency numbers, our family doctor, our dentist, and a list of foods Vinny can tolerate."

Vicky smiled. "Don't worry, I know exactly what he likes to eat."

After the awkward silence had passed, Dad walked up and shook Vicky's hand. "Well, I'm sure you want to get going. Lots of moving in to do. Once again, it was a pleasure to meet you and I want you to take good care of my little boy."

I walked over to Vicky's car and started to open the door, but my mother ran over and gave me a long hug. "I'm so sorry. I've been so hard on you the past few weeks." She held me at arm's length and looked me in the eye. "I think you look beautiful in your dress."

As we drove away, my family stood in an all American family pose: Jennifer in front, Mom and Dad in the back, Mom's head resting on Dad's shoulder, and their suburban two-story behind them, framing the shot. I tried to memorize them there like that, hoping as the centuries went by and this world around me turned to dust, I would be able to take this memory with me.

The only thing that slightly marred the moment was Kyle, running after Vicky's car, waving his arms, and screaming at us.

Vicky barely spoke as she drove, and I wondered if something was bothering her. Maybe Kyle had freaked her out? I tried to hum to pass the time, but after my second time through "Paradise City," I had to ask. "Is something bugging you?"

"No, why do you ask?"

"I was a little worried Kyle's behavior might be freaking you out. He's really a good guy. I just think he's going through a tough time."

"It's not Kyle. Actually I really feel for him. I can totally empathize with his situation. I wouldn't like you ignoring me."

"What do you mean by that?"

"Well, I just mean I've always felt there was something missing from my life, and no matter what I did, I still wasn't happy. I married a wealthy man, but that didn't help, so I had him build me a big house and buy me an expensive car, but that didn't help. Then, I got a job, and it was crappy and miserable, and I really don't like the people I work with. So then, one day, I'm arguing with my husband about having a baby, and I realized having a baby with him wasn't going to make me happy either, especially with the husband I didn't even like. So I got a divorce, and at least I didn't have to pretend to love the stranger I had married." She paused for a moment, collecting her thoughts. "Then one day, I woke up and as I walked around my empty house and I looked back on my life, I realized all I really wanted to do was get drunk and let some jerk take me home, just so I could have someone to hold me, even if just for a moment."

"So that would be when we met."

"Yes, I went out looking for a cheap lay and ended up with a vampire. At first, I was really pissed about that—"

"I noticed." Just thinking about it made my balls hurt.

"—But after a few days, I started to have these feelings for you, and I realized you were what I had been looking for all my life. You could fill the emptiness I felt, and all I wanted to do was to make you safe and feed you."

At this point, I was beginning to think Vicky was a little crazy, but she was also rich and she was going to buy me a PlayStation III.

"And that's why I can feel empathy for Kyle. He seemed a little freaky at first, but I get where he's coming from. I hate to think of what I might do if you were ignoring me."

"Why, what might you do?" I didn't want her hurting herself.

"We don't have to worry about that, because you and I will always be together."

"Yeah, sure."

Vicky turned her car down the long empty street on which she lived. "I hope you don't mind. I invited someone over to help you move in."

"Great. Less for us to carry."

"One other thing. Would you mind having your own room? I mean, you're welcome in my bed any time of course, but I just got this new bedroom set, and your things don't really fit the décor I'm going for. I have a nice room in the basement we can fix up. There are no windows."

I'd been living in a basement all my life, so I decided to stick with what I knew. "Sounds good. I'm all for a room without windows."

Vicky smiled. "I'm glad. All I want to do is make you happy, Vinny. In fact, I have a sort of present for you."

"Besides the PlayStation III you're going to buy me?" It just kept getting better and better.

"You know how I invited a friend over? Well, she's a girlfriend of mine. Her name is Margot, and I've spent an hour today telling her what a great lover you are. I told her if she came over here, I would... share you with her."

"Really?" That was almost as exciting as the PlayStation.

"I told her you were by far the best I'd ever had, and then she said she wished she could try you out, and I told her she should."

"And she took you up on the offer?"

"Oh yes. Of course, Margot is my only friend who I'd make that kind of offer to. She's very liberated. She sees men as feebleminded creatures put here for her amusement."

"You did this for me? You invited one of your best friends over to be my food?" My head was spinning with the possibilities.

"Well, I'm a little short on blood right now, and I thought you might enjoy a snack after moving."

Vicky pulled her car into the driveway and a woman opened the front door of the house. She was tall and blonde, older than Vicky and I, maybe in her early forties, but she was quite attractive. For a moment my libido actually competed with my unquenchable thirst, but then my thirst returned, made even more immediate by my desire.

We got out of the car and Margot gave me a wary look. "This is your new boyfriend? He looks a little young."

"He's older than he looks," Vicky said. "Come on and help me get his stuff inside."

When she was done turning up her nose at me, Margot turned up her nose at the collection of low-grade crap that made up my worldly possessions. "Vicky, can we talk alone for a minute?"

"Sure, Vinny, honey, here's the front door key. Just start putting everything inside and we'll sort it out later." She handed me a ring of keys with one separated from the bunch, and then pulled Margot aside to talk.

I collected an armload of stuff and walked to the front door, but thanks to my acute sense of hearing—augmented by drinking Vicky's blood the night before—I was able to hear their entire conversation.

"Are you kidding, Vicky? He's the best lover you've ever had? He's so scrawny."

"Well, we met a few weeks ago, when he attacked me in an alleyway, and I've been looking for him ever since. Then, through sheer luck, we ran into each other last night, and he rocked my world."

"He attacked you in an alley? Is this some sort of Stockholm Syndrome thing?"

"No, I only thought he was attacking me. We had a misunderstanding. Besides, I think you can only get Stockholm Syndrome if you're kidnapped."

"But didn't he stab you in the throat?"

"That was the misunderstanding. He was trying to bite me and I moved at the last minute."

"Wait, he's a biter?" Margot didn't sound too pleased at this revelation, but I wasn't worried. From selling makeup, I knew there were two types of people who agonized over decisions: those who were trying to justify something they'd already decided to do, and those trying to reason their way out of a decision they didn't want to make. Margot fell into the former category, either through desperation or curiosity, she'd decided to have sex with me, sight unseen. Now that she had come face to face with my lackluster appearance, she had to justify that decision. I wished Vicky had told me about her plan sooner. I would have put on some makeup.

"It's biting in a good way. Trust me. You'll see what I mean."

"All right, but it better not hurt, and he better not leave any marks."

I stopped listening and concentrated on carrying my stuff inside. There wasn't a whole bunch and by the time Vicky and Margot were done talking, I had most of it inside. I started taking it down the stairs. There was only one room downstairs with no windows. It had an ancient queen sized bed with a flowery comforter that smelled quite distantly of cat pee. Vicky came into the room, holding my guitar with the hole in it.

"Do you own a cat?"

"I used to, my husband stole it."

From atop of the bundle I'd brought inside, I lifted my broken PlayStation. Even with the promise of the new PlayStation III, I felt like I'd lost an old friend. I took a deep breath and sighed, thinking of all the wonderful moments I'd had with the little plastic box.

Margot walked in with a load of my stuff. She looked at Vicky, holding the guitar with the hole in it and me holding the shattered PlayStation. "My god, Vicky. He's an animal. Are you sure you want him in your house?"

Vicky turned to me and gave me a very serious look. "You should take her now. She is ready for you. Do you want me to prepare her?"

"Prepare her?" I asked.

"Do you want me to undress her?"

Margot took Vicky lightly by the shoulders. "Vicky, dear, I am more than capable of undressing myself. I've been doing it all my life. Now if you want me to sample your boyfriend, why don't you wait outside?"

Vicky looked to me for guidance. I gave her a nod, and she turned and left the room without another word.

Margot watched her leave and close the door and then turned back, giving me a scrutinizing look. "That is not the way Vicky acts."

"Really? You find her behavior odd?"

She nodded. "Oh yes. I don't know what you did to her, but I have to admit I'm kind of curious." She started unbuttoning her blouse. "I want you to know I'm not usually the type of person who does this sort of thing, but Vicky was very insistent, and honestly, younger men have their advantages." She gave me a look that might have been called "smoldering."

I glanced down at the floor. "So... Um—" I was kind of at a loss for what to do. I mean, I knew what to do, but this was such a weird situation, like something out of a Penthouse letter.

"Aren't you going to get undressed? I mean you're not doing much to put me in the mood here. Is foreplay not your thing?" I gaped for a moment, and she gave me an exasperated look, stepped forward, and peeled off my Atari shirt.

"Be careful with that, it's an antique."

"Maybe it would be better if you shut up." She pulled off her bra, leaving us both naked from the waist up, and kissed me. After a minute, she grabbed my right hand and shoved it to her left breast. I squeezed, and her kiss became less forceful, more yielding. I was just thinking I could stand to kiss her for a long time, when she pushed me back onto the bed. After finishing undressing, she undid my belt, and started yanking off my pants.

In many ways, making love to Margot reminded me of making love to Veronica all those years ago. All the elements were there: a domineering, older woman had undressed me and taken the initiative. Me, lying on my back, consumed with the pleasure of the moment. The big difference was I was the one planning to take the blood.

When my pants were off, she impaled herself on me with surprising athletic talent, and started thrusting downward. Her pendulous breasts hung down in front of my face, and I tried to lift myself up so I might bite one, but I found it impossible with the ferocity of her undulations. I tried to push myself up to get my fangs close to some part of her body, but she put a hand on my chest and drove me back into the bed. "No biting."

I took hold of that hand. I caressed and sucked her fingers. I continued to kiss and massage her hand until she let down her guard, losing herself in the moment. I grabbed her arm, turned her wrist over, and bit deep into her artery. Or at least I tried to. The human wrist isn't really a great place to bite. It has a lot of different bones and cartilage and things to get in the way. I barely broke her skin, and she pulled away from me almost immediately.

"You fucker! You really bit me." Even as she continued to ride my dick, she started punching me in the face, and she could hit really hard. I think she came then, because she stopped hitting me, leaned back and screamed. Then it was like she took all the power of that orgasm, snapped forward, and hit me in the nose. I heard bone crunch. "You little shit. Vicky told me you were a biter." By the time my eyes stopped watering, Margot had already run from the room, slamming the door behind her.

I bit my lip, reached up, and snapped my nose back into place before it healed crooked. The sound was sickening. Tears streamed out of my eyes as I tried to fight back the pain. I lay there for a moment, wishing Margot had let me finish. "Vicky? Are you still out there?"

Fifteen minutes later, Margot snuck into the room to retrieve her clothes, as Vicky and I were busy finishing what she had started. In retrospect, I should have done or said something to her, knowing what my bite had done to Kyle and Vicky, but I was preoccupied.

Where Kyle and Margot return

For the next week, Vicky and I were like a regular couple. Every day, Vicky went to work, and I played games on my new PlayStation III. Every night we had crazy-good sex. I really felt like Vicky understood my needs. Still, no longer having to deal with harassment from my parents gave me more time to think. I found myself asking questions. Why did I seem to have this hold over Vicky? Was it some kind of vampire power? Had Kyle flipped out for the same reasons? And what about the woman who bit me all those years ago? Did she know of my existence? Did she care? Could I find a modded PlayStation One on the Internet, so I could play my old, import games?

On Thursday, I had my second party. Vicky's friend, Barbara—an autumn, petite, oval face, medium-dry skin, worry lines around the eyes—was officially hosting. Vicky had let Barbara use her house. Barbara's husband was one of those jerks who wouldn't let his wife have her friends over. In a way, Vicky's thieving husband made her house perfect for hosting Lyle B. All her furniture was uncluttered with memorabilia, as all her things were stolen—a situation Vicky was not wholly displeased with as she had gotten enough money in the settlement to "make new memories." I was an hour into the show, just into my speech about the benefits of being a hostess, when I heard a noise from outside. All eyes turned to the large picture window in the front of the living room.

Kyle stood at the edge of the lawn, bathed in the light of a streetlamp. He was wearing his salesmen clothes, sans jacket, and had a bit of a wild look about him, like he had slept in those clothes. Above his head, he held a boom box, which was playing Aerosmith's "I Don't Want To Miss a Thing." Tears ran down his face. Vicky and I looked at each other and then back to Kyle.

"Who's he here for?" asked Barbara. "Vicky? Do you have a secret love?" I turned to see the other women in the room looking expectantly at Vicky.

"He's here for me," I said, saving Vicky from the explanation. "We used to be friends, but he wanted to take it further. I should go talk to him." Kyle and me had been friends too long to throw it all away.

I walked outdoors and started across the lawn, trying to stop my sharp heels from sinking into the soft turf. As I approached, Kyle turned off the boom box. "I didn't think you'd come outside."

"I had to. I have customers inside. They think we're acting out some scene from a romance novel." I looked back at the house. All the women were at the window, watching us intently.

Kyle took my hand. "Look, I... Why are you wearing a

skirt?"

"I'll explain later."

"Okay. Look, I know I treated you badly, and I scared your family. I'm really sorry about that. I lost myself for a while, but I'm feeling much better, now. I'd like to be your friend again if you'd let me."

I nodded. "You can be my friend again."

"Can I come and live with you in your big house?" Okay, that was going a little too far.

"You'll have to ask Vicky," I said, afraid that saying no would make him flip out again. "It's her house."

"Can I have a hug?"

"Sure." I wasn't a really touchy person, but there was nothing wrong with a hug. Kyle wrapped his arms around me and pulled me close. I glanced over at the picture window and saw the women inside applauding and cheering—if they only had a clue of what was really going on. Kyle squeezed my ass.

"Kyle, stop that."

"I'm sorry. Just, in that outfit, you're smoking hot. Do you think maybe later we could have some drinks and maybe fool around a little?"

"Kyle, you do know I'm still a man under the clothes and makeup?"

"Of course you are. I'm not stupid. But, ever since we were together in the elevator, I realized I had a Vinny-shaped hole in my life. All I want is for you to fill that hole, dude."

"The answer is still no," I said firmly. "But if you want to, you can come inside and wait until the party's over and then we can talk some more." I wasn't thrilled by the revelations Kyle was making, but like it or not, he was part of my life. He had stayed with me after my attack. No matter what weird vampire mojo I had inadvertently laid on him, he would always be my friend.

"Okay. I'll behave."

We went inside and I pointed him to the basement stairs. "Go down there. You can play PlayStation until the party's over."

Kyle gazed at the floor. "I thought your PlayStation was broken. You know the night I... outside your house."

"Oh, Vicky got me a PlayStation III."

"Score!"

"My sentiments exactly."

When I returned to the party, Barbara was filling everyone in on Margot. "It's awful. All the doctors got out of her was that some wild animal had bitten her on the wrist. They treated the wound, but they wanted to keep her overnight for observation, just in case she'd caught something. Then, they were running some blood samples and they found something odd, and wanted to keep her for another couple of days because there have been some rabies cases lately. When she found out they were going to keep her, she freaked out."

"Did she have rabies?" one of the women asked.

Barbara shook her head. "No, she just threw a fit, so they strapped her down and sedated her. I went to visit her and they had her totally stoned out of her mind. The nurse told me every time the drugs wear off she starts screaming." Vicky gave me a conspiratorial glance. I knew what she was thinking. Whatever hold I had over her and Kyle must have affected Margot as well. If this was going to happen every time I bit someone, I might have to think about going back to starving.

The party was wrapping up. I wrote up the last order, gave a few last beauty tips to the women who stayed back to talk, and finally, Vicky and I were alone. Then came the hard part. I walked down to my room, where Kyle was sitting on the bed, playing PlayStation. I sat down next to him, and Vicky sat beside me. "Kyle, can we talk?"

"Yeah, of course." Kyle pushed buttons for a few more seconds and then paused his game.

"You know you're my best friend, and I'm really flattered by your attention, but I don't think we should take our relationship to any new places. I mean, I don't really see myself as being intimate with you."

Kyle nodded thoughtfully. "I can respect that, but I think you're wrong. I really want to be a bigger part of your life, and I'll do anything to make that happen."

"But Kyle, you're straight."

"Yes. I am, but that doesn't mean I can't be in love with you." He put his hand on my knee.

Vicky reached over and put her hand on my other knee. "I love you too," she said, just in case I'd forgotten.

I sighed. "But that doesn't make any sense. You like girls, Kyle." Why was this so hard for him to understand?

Kyle's voice took on a dreamy quality. "Love doesn't have to make any sense, dude."

"But you weren't in love with me three weeks ago."

"Three weeks ago, I was a different person. I thought selling more plumbing fixtures than anyone else would make me happy. I didn't realize you were the only thing that could make me happy. Then you came on to me in the freight elevator."

Vicky straightened. "You came on to him?"

Suddenly, I was on the defensive. "I told you it was a long story. We had been drinking, and Kyle cut his forehead, and there was a lot of blood, and one thing just sort of led to another. All I did was bite him, no fooling around or anything."

"You totally had a boner."

"I was excited about the blood." I held up my hands. "Okay. Let's just take this back a notch. Kyle, you want to live here so I can take your blood whenever I need it, correct?"

"There's no need about it. I gladly give my body over to whatever makes you happy."

I held up my hand, in the universal "stop" signal. "I really don't think that will be necessary."

"I'm just saying, dude, don't be shy. The offer is open. If you have any needs or desires I can satisfy—"

"For now, let's just stick to the blood."

"And after the blood we can have sex?" He gave me his best salesman smile.

"No, Kyle, not going to happen."

He gave me a look like a small child who'd just lost his ice cream.

I shook my head. "Okay, talk's over. I want a beer."

"If you're thirsty," said Kyle, "drink me."

"Me! Me!" said Vicky.

I stood up. "I'm going to go to the kitchen and get a beer. Does anyone else want one?"

They both raised their hands and then looked at me expectantly as if waiting for further direction. "Just relax for a minute. I'll be right back. Talk amongst yourselves."

I returned a few minutes later with the beers. I handed one to Kyle and then twisted the top off Vicky's and passed it over. "So, what did you two talk about?"

"Vicky says we are in some kind of supernatural thrall," said Kyle, "which makes sense, as she's kind of out of your league, and I'm way out of your league."

I nodded. I didn't think I was that far out of their leagues, but if it helped Kyle figure it out, so be it. I had to admit Vicky had a point. There must be something supernatural going on, something related to the biting. I have found I'm more open minded to supernatural stuff since I died and then got better. "Good."

"And that," said Kyle, "is why we have to go to the hospital and rescue Margot."

"That's— What?" I was pretty sure there were more links in their chain of logic, they just hadn't given them to me.

"Yeah, dude, if we're in thrall of you because you bit us, and you bit her and she's freaking out in the hospital, she must be freaking out because of your bite. As our lord and master, you are responsible for her now."

"What are you saying?"

Vicky put her hand on my shoulder. "You have to break Margot out of the hospital."

Kyle put his hand on my other shoulder. "Don't worry dude, we're going to help."

Flanked by Vicky and Kyle, I suddenly felt claustrophobic. "Wow, that's great, Kyle, really, but it's getting kind of late. Why don't you go home?"

Kyle opened his arms and announced, "I am home, dude. I live here now."

Vicky nodded. "We discussed it while you were getting the beer."

"I wasn't gone five minutes, and you invited Kyle to live with us?"

Vicky nodded. "Why not? There's plenty of room. Besides, I feel bad when I think of Kyle having to go home to a lonely apartment, so far away from you."

"And," said Kyle, "it will be more convenient when we start sleeping together."

"No!" That definitely was never going to happen.

Vicky rolled her eyes. "He's going to keep asking, and knowing you, you'll give in sooner or later, so you might as well surrender to the inevitable."

"I'm not surrendering to anything."

Kyle squeezed my shoulder. "It's okay, dude. I understand. We'll take it slow. Maybe I could start out by just watching you with Vicky, and then after you become comfortable with that, I could—"

"No!"

The next few days were a little like "Mission Impossible" at *Maison d'Vicky*. Vicky went to the hospital, doing reconnaissance on the pretense of visiting Margot. She determined Margot was strapped down and sedated, but she was not in a locked ward. Kyle used the Internet and his phone skills to track down hospital uniforms for us under the guise of a hospital administrator. He ordered "sample" nurse uniforms for Vicky and I, and he ordered an EMT uniform for himself. I was a little disappointed to learn modern nurses just wear scrubs and tennis shoes. I was looking forward to the white skirt and high heels. I would later find out Kyle had ordered one of those outfits as well, but that's another story.

The plan was simple. Vicky would put on a gray wig, cover herself up with a blanket, and I would dress up as a female nurse and wheel her to Margot's room, pretending she was an elderly relative staying on another floor of the hospital. Through his knowledge of plumbing, Kyle would create a distraction so the hospital employees forgot about us. Then while we were alone in Margot's room, we would put Margot in the chair, put the wig on her, and wheel her away, now watched over by two nurses instead of one.

I did not personally witness all of the following events. Some of the things happening in the hospital were related to me later by Kyle.

While Vicky and I were entering through a door close to Margot's room, Kyle entered the Emergency Room area dressed as an EMT. We planned to rendezvous near Margot's room, deep in the bowels of the hospital. However, as soon as Kyle tried to walk through ER, an overworked doctor waived at him. He was hunched over a patient performing chest compressions. "You! I have a code blue, cardiac. Crash cart's on the way. I need you to ventilate."

Kyle stood frozen for a moment, shock in his eyes.

The doctor looked at him expectantly. "Well. Come on!"

"Uh..." Kyle said.

"Either help me or go find the crash cart," the doctor yelled.

Kyle's flight or fight instincts kicked in. He turned and sprinted, only getting four steps before running headlong into a crash cart and the two nurses pushing it. Kyle went down, taking the cart with him, and true to its name, it did make a horrendous crashing noise as it hit the ground. Kyle scrambled out from under the equipment that had fallen on him, pulled himself to his feet, and ran away, assuming someone was going to make him pay for anything that was broken.

In retrospect, Kyle really hadn't even needed a uniform. He was in charge of the diversion, and we'd gone in during regular visiting hours, along with dozens of others off the street. We just got really excited about getting uniforms.

Vicky and I sat in Margot's room, waiting for Kyle's distraction, but nothing happened. Someone had turned the television to a home repair show. I picked up the remote and flipped through a few channels. They only had basic cable—as if the hospital wasn't depressing enough already. It disgusted me that people would die in this place without the basic human comfort of HBO. After a while, I poked my head outside and glanced down at the nurse's station. The nurses seemed absorbed in their work, but I doubted they were so busy we could leave the room unobserved.

Just then, Kyle ran out of a side corridor. Going full tilt, he didn't even see me as he disappeared around a corner. My hopes of a distraction dropped dramatically.

I ducked back into the room. "I think we're on our own," I said to Vicky.

"Okay, what do we do now?"

I realized there was only one thing we could do. "I'll be the distraction. Start loading Margot into the wheelchair and be ready." While I wasn't crazy about being the distraction, I also didn't care for the idea of detaching Margot from the I.V. and catheter tubing.

I strolled down to the nurse's station, trying to look casual. A very bitter looking woman stood behind the desk, watching me carefully. The photo ID clipped to her scrubs read, "Betty Brown, MSN." I didn't even know Microsoft was into nursing.

I smiled, "Hi there..."

She looked me up and down. "Are you new here, young lady? Where's your ID badge?"

"Just started. They were having trouble with the camera, so they couldn't give me a badge."

"They should have given you a temporary then."

"They didn't say anything about a temporary badge. They just gave me some scrubs and told me to take Mr. Karparti to the imaging room." On our way to Margot's ward, I had seen several signs pointing towards the imaging room.

She rolled her eyes. "That's just typical."

I glanced left and right and whispered conspiratorially, "You look like you know your way around. I wonder if you could help me with something."

"Of course, dear," she said in a brisk tone. "What do you need?"

"You see, I was bringing back Mr. Karparti from imaging and he had just had his um..." I made a south-of-the-border sign with my hands.

"Pubic region?"

"Um, yeah, pubic region shaved, and he's... Well, he's a little old, and he kept pulling up his hospital gown. He claimed he liked the feel of the breeze on it as I wheeled him around. Well, finally, he fell asleep with his... genitals hanging out, so I wheeled him into the stairwell."

"Why on earth did you do that?"

"He was asleep. I needed a smoke. Anyway, I think he made a run for it. Because when I came back, he was nowhere to be found. I think he's probably going around and showing people his shaved junk."

"So you left a half-naked, elderly patient in a stairwell while you went and had a smoke, and now you think he's going around the hospital showing everyone his shaved genitals?"

"Of course it sounds bad when you say it that way, but it's not like he wasn't wearing his gown, he just wasn't adjusting it properly."

"Well, I certainly haven't seen him. I think I would have noticed." She shook her head and sighed. "Well, what do you want me to do about your problem?"

"Could you help me search for him?" I squinted my eyes trying to make tears come out, but none did, so I decided to whine. "It's just that it's my first day in this hospital, and I don't know where anything is, and if they find out I lost a patient, they're going to fire me. It was a simple mix-up. It could have happened to anyone. I just got my degree, and if I get fired now, I'll never work in a hospital again."

"I still don't see how this is my problem. I'm off shift in a half hour. Just report it and take your lumps."

"I don't want to get fired. Haven't you ever done anything wrong? Hasn't anyone ever helped you out?" I buried my face in my hands and waited... and waited. Finally, a hand squeezed my shoulder.

"You're right. I screwed up when I was a rookie. I probably shouldn't do this, but since it's your first day, I'll see what I can do."

"Thank you. Thank you." I said, trying to sound as pathetic as I could.

She started walking down the hall towards Margot's room.

"No! Stop. He was this way." I pointed in the opposite direction.

"I'll help you just as soon as I give Ms. Cooper her sedative."

Ms. Cooper? Sedative? She was talking about Margot. "Just give it to me. I'll do it."

She kept walking, closer and closer to Margot's door. "Don't be ridiculous. This is my ward and my job. I'll only be a minute." She turned the corner into Margot's room and stopped.

I hurried after her, imagining the worst. In my mind, I saw Vicky standing in front of Nurse Brown, in the middle of moving her to the wheelchair. As I took the last few steps, Nurse Brown didn't even move, no doubt in shock from the sight of a strange nurse stealing one of her patients. I rounded the corner and saw Margot's bed empty. Vicky had done it. She had gotten Margot out of her room.

"She's gone," Nurse Brown said.

I ran over to the empty hospital bed and lifted the sheet as if a woman could hide under it. "Holy shit! It's an epidemic."

"In twenty years, I've never lost a patient."

"I told you it could happen to anybody." I took her by her shoulders. "Give me a description. We can split up, help each other."

She nodded. "Okay. Um, she's blonde, in her forties, and heavily sedated."

"All right. We'll split up and meet back here in an hour."

I walked out of the room and looked left and right. The corridor was clear. "Shit! There he goes." I took off at a run, leaving Nurse Brown behind, whipped around a corner, and took a cross corridor to the nearest stairwell, where I sprinted down to the ground floor, assuming I would find an exit there.

Following the signs, I headed at a little more than a brisk walk towards the parking garage where Vicky had parked. Suddenly, I smelled something odd, something that didn't fit with the smells of the hospital. Something I recognized. I skidded to a halt and followed my nose to the cafeteria, where they were selling mini-pizzas. Now that I was regularly getting blood from Vicky and Kyle, my appetite for human food was coming back, and I suddenly realized I had not had pizza for ten years. I walked up to the lunch counter and ordered ten mini-pizzas. I'd scarf one here and then take home a bunch to the gang.

As I was finishing up my mini-pizza, Nurse Brown ran by. When she saw me, she did a double take and walked over. "Did you find them?"

"No, but running around this place is exhausting. I decided to take a break."

"You're eating?"

"I know my rights. I'm entitled to a lunch break. You want a little pizza? I'm buying."

"No, I'm going to continue searching, and I recommend you do the same if you want to keep your job."

"You go ahead. I'll be right after you. And good luck." Nurse Brown rolled her eyes at me and then hurried out of the cafeteria, trying to look like she wasn't running.

I rejoined Vicky and Margot in the parking lot. Vicky sat patiently in the driver's seat, while Margot was still pretty out of it. She lay across the back seat lightly snoring. Vicky had put a sombrero across her face so she didn't look suspicious.

I sat down in the front passenger seat. "Where's Kyle?"

"I'm not sure. He hasn't been around here."

"Okay. He's a big boy. He can find his way back." He would later tell me he ran in circles for three miles through hospital hallways, and finding an outside door, stole a bicycle to ride back to Vicky's house. "Let's get Margot out of here before we get charged with kidnapping or something." I held up a paper bag. "I got some mini pizzas for later."

"Yea! How thoughtful."

As we pulled out of the parking garage, I had a thought. "So, now that we've broken Margot out, what are we going to do with her?"

"She can move in with us."

"Well, of course it's your house, but do you really want another roommate?"

"Sure. I don't mind living with people who I share interests with."

"You share interests with Kyle?"

"Sure I do, only the cutest little vampire in the whole world."

I nodded. "Great."

"Besides, Kyle has known you forever, so he can tell me all kinds of stories about your childhood."

"You really want to hear stories about Kyle and I staying up all night playing with our joysticks?"

"Oh, yes."

I sighed. "Not like that."

Where church goes to Vinny

We returned from the hospital raid around midnight. After we carried Margot into the house, Vicky went to bed
and I turned on the living room TV. A Star Wars marathon
had just started. About halfway into Episode I, Kyle returned.

"Where were you?"

"Dude, I kind of freaked out. Ended up stealing a bike
and riding it home."

"You stole someone's bike?"

"Yeah. It wasn't my best moment. I think I may have
been indirectly responsible for someone dying of a heart
attack, too."

"For stealing their bike?"

"No, they were separate incidents."

"Bummer. Want a beer?"

Kyle perked up like a dog scenting a fresh steak. "You want me to get you a beer, master?"

"Relax. I got it. I picked up some mini-pizzas too." I went to the kitchen to grab a couple beers and the last of the mini-pizzas, but by the time I returned, Kyle was stretched out in the recliner, snoring. I finished the beers and pizza, grabbed my guitar, recently repaired with the judicious application of duct tape, and tried to strum the "Imperial March." A few hours later, The Empire Strikes Back was on, and I had the song down pretty well. Maybe if I practiced for a few hundred years, I might actually get good. I made a mental note to talk to one of the minions about buying me a better guitar.

Margot woke up first. Apparently, her meds had finally worn off. She walked into the living room, freshly showered and wearing a pair of Vicky's silk pajamas, which were super tight on Margot and emphasized her curves. She sat down next to me and sniffed. "You smell good." She tried to snuggle up against me, but I was still strumming the guitar.

I angled my head down and sniffed in the general direction of my armpit. Ick, the body odor of the walking dead is not a pleasant thing. "No, I don't." I returned to strumming.

Soon, Vicky joined us, sitting on the other side of me, and trying to slide under the neck of my guitar. I blocked her with my elbow, but she kept squirming. "You play beautifully."

"No, I don't." I had realized a long time ago that I was to the guitar what Eric Clapton was to astrophysics. Usually, I didn't even bother to tune; it didn't really make that much difference.

Vicky looked across me. "Hey Margot, how about a man sandwich for breakfast?" She grabbed my crotch.

"Cut it out," I said. "They're about to freeze Han Solo. Besides, don't you have to go to work?"

"I quit. Work was taking me away from you too often. Besides, I have enough money to get by on for a few decades."

"What about you, Margot?" I realized I knew very little about the woman sharing my life, well, the other woman sharing my life. "What do you do?"

"Independently wealthy—life insurance," she answered. "I've been widowed twice—skiing accident and drunk driver."

"Ouch, that's harsh," I said, shaking my head.

"Well, yeah. I was really torn up about it for a while, but that's just life. People die, and you get over it eventually."

When Margot realized I wasn't going to stop watching Empire, she stood up and wandered over to the curtains. "I wonder what the weather's like today," she said, as she lifted a corner of the curtain, careful not to let any morning sunlight leak into the room. "That's interesting. A group of people has gathered on the front lawn carrying placards."

"They're probably realtors," Vicky answered. "Since the housing boom, they haven't been able to sell shit in this neighborhood. It's too far from the beltway, and the houses are expensive and lack character, kind of like my ex-husband."

"Actually, they look like protestors. Their signs say stuff about evil living in our house, and they came in a Jesus bus, one of those broken down school buses covered in leftover house paint."

I sighed. I had a feeling that a Jesus bus had nothing good to offer me. At this rate, I was never going to make it to the end of Jedi.

"What do we do?" I asked.

"Why don't we invite them in?" Margot said. "At least it will get them off the lawn."

"What, a bunch of Jesus freaks? They'll probably try to stake me."

Margot peaked out the curtain again. "Maybe. If they do, we can always kill them and drain their blood." I had to admit, she had a point.

———————————

I woke up Kyle and sent him outside with instructions to invite the protestors into the house. We made them keep their signs outside—I didn't like the look of the wooden handles. I waited for them in the dining room, so there would be an expanse of table between me and our "guests." Honestly, I was pretty freaked they might pull out wooden stakes or throw holy water on me or something. Not that I knew holy water would do anything, but at the same time, why risk it? I sat with my back to the wall and Vicky and Margot sat to either side of me.

A distinguished man with a black shirt and white priests' collar led the delegation. As soon as they walked into the room, the man threw himself on the floor. His followers followed suit, as followers are apt to do. Now the only one standing in the room, Kyle backed up against the wall.

I had to stand up to see the man over the edge of the table. "Um... Excuse me, sir. What are you doing on the floor?"

"We prostrate ourselves before the mighty Vampire."

I tried to think of a response to that. I had none.

Margot was a little quicker on the uptake. "What makes you think there's a vampire in this house? Seriously, what kind of priest are you? Vampires aren't real."

He cleared his throat, but stayed facedown. "I am..."

"Get up off the floor," she snapped.

The man stood. His followers didn't follow. "I am Reverend Billy Bisgrove, of the He is Risen Church of Immortal Life. Although I personally abhor the term, I suppose it would be simplest to describe ourselves as a vampire cult. I have been long watching for signs and portents.”

“There were signs and portents which led you to my house?” Vicky asked.

The man nodded. “Yes, they are clear if you know what to look for.”

“And what are the signs?” asked Margot.

“They are... very technical, but rest assured, they do work. After all, there is a vampire in this house. Am I correct?”

He seemed sure of himself, and I didn’t see any reason to be coy, so I raised my hand. “Here.”

The man dropped to the ground again. “We prostrate ourselves before you, my lord.”

“Vinny, call me Vinny.”

“Lord Vinny.”

“So,” I said, “what do I have to do to get you all to sit at the table like normal people? I mean, you’re awfully hard to see down there.”

The reverend stood immediately, and this time the entire group followed. “I am so sorry, Lord Vinny. We are but sheep, led to your divine slaughter.”

“Um, thanks.” I hoped that was metaphor or hyperbole or something. Even though Margot had suggested it, I didn’t want to slaughter all these people. Just think of the mess—someone would have to clean that up.

The reverend and those followers who could find seats sat down at Vicky’s big dining room table. The rest of the church members sat on the floor. Kyle stayed leaning against the wall. Everyone looked at me expectantly.

“This is just too fucking weird,” Margot murmured, just a touch too loud.

Reverend Billy stood, pointing a finger at Margot. “You dare to judge us? You who are under his thrall, you who live in the same house, breathing the same air as him, feeding him, caring for him, you who have everything mock us for wanting a silver... um, sliver of what you have?"

Margot held up her hands in a back-off motion. "Hey, don't go laying all that on me. I'm new here. All I've done is watch some old movie."

I shook my head. "Relax, Billy. And Margot, Empire is not just some old movie."

The Reverend took away his accusing finger and sat back down. "Of course, Lord Vinny, I forgot myself. I am supposed to be here to comfort you."

"Let's return to these signs and portents," said Vicky.

Kyle, who had been looking especially sheepish, made a face and stepped forward. "Yeah, I'm afraid that's on me. I did a site visit with one of our resellers. He was installing a new kitchen sink in their church and it was his first time using our new XJ-900 putty."

"Yes," said Reverend Billy. "And then Kyle told me that in plumbing supply all the exciting things are happening in the kitchen, and he told me of your embrace and the feelings he was having."

"You told him my secret?" I asked. Kyle was supposed to know better. We had discussed that if the government ever found out what I was, they would take me away to dissect me, like they did in the final episode of Alf.

"Do not punish Kyle, for it was fate that brought him to us," said Reverend Billy. "He needed help to understand his feelings, and he came to us who have searched for so long for a master, and who also needed a new sink."

"I'm sorry, I was having all these feelings, and with the way he dresses, I assumed he was a Catholic priest and he could do some mojo and hit me with the holy water and I wouldn't think about you naked anymore." Kyle kept his eyes on the floor as if he could not look me in the eye. "I'll go flagellate myself."

"I'm not going to punish anybody, Kyle. Don't worry about it." I didn't know what flagellation was, but it sounded bad, like something involving sharp objects and sensitive anatomy.

One of Billy's flock stood up, a tall woman with long, permed hair and black lipstick. "Reverend, it is just as you foretold. The Lord is merciful!"

I shook my head. "Call me Vinny."

The woman bowed. "Yes, Lord Vinny."

The room went silent for a minute as the reverend and his flock gazed upon me. I felt like it was my turn to say something. "So, Billy, how'd you come to start a vampire cult?"

Billy cleared his throat. "After many years serving as a priest in the Catholic Church, I was appointed assistant to the Archbishop of Nebraska. One night, I went into his office to retrieve a binder from his bookcase. It was stuck, so I gave it an especially hard tug, and a piece of trim came away from the shelf. When I tried to repair it, I found a cubbyhole containing an ancient, handwritten book. I knew I should put it back, but I was curious, and I knew enough Latin to begin to decipher the content."

I yawned. This story was taking forever. "Is there a point to this at all?"

"It was a journal of a woman named Eloise of d'Argenteuil, a twelfth century abbess. That in itself made the book priceless, but the tale it told shocked me to my very core. It told of a woman who was brought to her abbey after being attacked in the woods—"

"And she was attacked by a vampire?" I asked.

"Oh, you've read it then?"

"Well," I said, "you are here. So, to make a long story short, you found this book, and you've read a bit too much Anne Rice, and now you're ready to quit the church you spent decades serving so you can gain the favor of immortal life from me."

"Well, yes and no. I find Rice a little pedantic. I'm a much bigger fan of Charlaine Harris."

I nodded slowly. I didn't know if I believed the whole ancient tome, but either way, this guy was nucking futs. "So, what do you want from me?"

The woman who spoke before leaned across the table, grasping out to me. "Lord Vinny. Oh, Lord Vinny. All we want is to care for you and feed you. To worship you."

"What's your name?" I asked the woman.

"Tina."

"Tina, have I bitten you already?" She certainly sounded that way.

She looked confused. "No, my lord, however, if you wish." She pulled back the collar of her black blouse.

I shook my head. "Keep your shirt on, Tina."

"Forgive her, my lord," said Reverend Billy. "While she spoke out of turn, she did speak the truth. We will happily give you our servitude and life's blood, so we can be close to you, and hopefully, one day, you may even make us like you."

"Trust me, you don't want that."

The reverend's face clouded. "But master, we will devote ourselves to you for the rest of our lives if necessary. All we ask is your gift of immortality."

Vicky tugged at my sleeve, "Could we talk in the other room?"

"Sure." I stood up, and all the church members stood. I made a lowering gesture with my hands, and they sat back down. Under other circumstances, that might have been fun, but I resisted the urge to do it again. "Chill out. I'll be right back."

I walked into the living room, and Vicky, Kyle, and Margot followed.

"What's up?" I asked Vicky.

"I like the idea. I wouldn't mind having a few servants around here, and there's nothing wrong with finding a few new blood sources."

"Yes," said Margot, nodding. "You must expand your territory."

"I've already got the three of you bonded to me. Why would I need more people in my life? Especially freaky cult members."

"Dude, don't you see," said Kyle. "They'd be like your slaves. You could send them out for pizza and beer all times of the day. It wouldn't be that hard on them. They could take shifts."

Kyle had a point. I had really enjoyed those mini-pizzas, but they were gone now, and we were dangerously low on beer.

"And I wouldn't have to do your laundry anymore," said Vicky.

I looked at Margot.

She shrugged. "Don't look at me. I don't even do my own laundry."

I sighed. I might be able to back down from Vicky alone, but if all three of my minions thought this was necessary, I was inevitably doomed to lose this argument. "Okay, if you really want me to, I'll drink their blood, but just remember, I can't just take on a cult until I get tired of it. Once I bite them, we're stuck with them." I stared at my minions waiting for some sign that one of them might change their mind, but they seemed united in their front.

I stuck my head into the dining room. "Reverend Billy, if you and your flock are sure that you want to worship me, line up, and I'll bite you all."

"Oh, yes, my lord," Billy said, bounding out of his chair. "The line starts behind me," he announced to his unholy congregation, who lined up in an orderly fashion behind him, as if they had rehearsed it.

I took a deep breath and sunk my fangs into Billy's neck. I almost jumped back, expecting him to assault me in some way, but instead he just waited patiently as I took his blood. I found this to be a pleasant change. He had an odd aftertaste, a little like metal. Maybe he had a lot of iron in his diet. I bit another and another. The nectar ambrosia flavor of blood coursed through my mouth, but under that was the odd aftertaste that no matter how much I drank would not go away.

My head started to spin, and I felt heat in my cheeks. As I approached the end of the line, the room leaned sharply to the left. I grabbed at the couch, trying to catch myself and landed on the carpet. I heard the sound of a body hitting the ground far away. Then, I closed my eyes.

Waking up in a hospital bed is never fun, especially when you wake up dead. I glanced around the room, a typical hospital setup—industrial color scheme, lots of tubes and machines and adjustable beds with a television on the far wall, an amenity for those who aren't going anywhere for a while. Kyle had hooked up the Playstation III to the television, and he was playing Mecha Porko.

"Kyle, how are you playing Mecha Porko on the PlayStation III? It's a game that only worked on our modded PlayStation. What you're doing is impossible."

"Oh, it's cool. You're having a vision, dude." He hit another key combination instructing the mechanical pig to take out an enemy. "Just a second and I'll be at a save point. Then I can explain."

While it made no sense that the Kyle I was dreaming had to wait to save his game, I nevertheless waited for him to reach the save point. No reason to be rude. While he finished up, I examined the hospital room some more. I had been in this room before. Right after Veronica attacked and killed me, they put me in this hospital room and ran all sorts of tests. Just like ten years ago, I had two needles in my arm, one was an IV drip, giving me saline, and the other was an IV drip giving me human blood. I don't know if that blood guaranteed my transformation, but they gave it to me every day for two weeks before giving up. By the end of the first week, they had started shutting the curtains because I would scream and convulse every time sunlight touched me.

Right before they stopped giving me blood, a doctor told my father my blood pressure was 62 over 30 with a pulse of 10 beats per minute, my body temperature was barely above 80 degrees, and there was no medical reason why I was still alive. He said they were just going to make me as comfortable as possible. A week later, I was no more comfortable, so they released me.

Kyle saved his game and turned off the TV. "Okay, so where should I start? Like I said, you are having a vision. By your point of view, it's ten years ago, right after you got bit by that hot chick."

"Yeah, I figured that out. I was here, you know."

"And I brought you here to drive home the point that you are sick."

"You brought me here? Aren't you just a figment of my imagination? So really, I brought me here."

"More like a component of your psyche. Consider me your own ghost of Christmas past."

"What the hell are you talking about? Ghost? I hated that movie. You aren't dead, either." I thought about that for a moment. I'd been biting church member after church member, and I didn't think I'd bit Kyle, but then again... "Shit, you aren't dead, are you?"

"No, I'm not dead. It's a metaphor, you know, the ghost of Christmas past? From Dickens?"

"What does Dickens have to do with this?"

"Nothing. Okay, let's just say that I'm the Dr. Dre to your Eminem."

I shook my head. "I don't listen to rap music."

Kyle sighed. "Yes, you do. I'm pulling these references from your head."

"Why don't you forget the metaphors and just tell me what you have to say?"

"It's time to get off your ass, dude. These cultists are kind of freaky, and they know more about you than you do. If you want to keep yourself safe, you need to figure out exactly who and what you are."

"Really? That's all you've got? I've got to find myself?" I shook my head. "What a waste of a good hallucination. Where are the hot girls and the wild freaky sex?"

"Dude, you have hot girls and wild freaky sex in real life. You really need a kick in the butt. Your parents used to do it for you, at least struggling with them made you feel like you were doing something, but without that inter-action, you're going to get real bored real soon, and you don't want an eternity of boredom."

"Okay, maybe you have a point. Or maybe I have a point or whatever." That thought had been rattling around in the back of my head, but I had tried not to acknowledge it. "Maybe the old preacher could help me with that."

"Not the old preacher, dude. You need to find more of your own kind. You should find Veronica, the woman who bit you."

"Yeah, but Veronica was a decade ago. She's long gone. The trail is cold. How the hell am I supposed to find her?"

"Don't look at me, dude. I'm just a figment of your imag-ination."

"I thought you were Dr. Dre."

"Word to your mother."

I shook my head. "Dr. Dre didn't say that. Vanilla Ice said that."

"I thought you said you didn't know anything about rap music."

"You tricked me, you fucker."

He handed me a PlayStation controller. "You want to play some Mecha Porko before you wake up?"

"Cool."

Where Vinny tries to meet his maker

I sat bolt upright, jumped out of bed, and ran upstairs looking for my minions. I found Vicky and Margot having coffee in the kitchen. "Is this still Christmas day?"

Vicky raised her eyebrow. "It's August twelfth."

"So, you're talking crazy this morning," said Margot, taking a sip of her coffee.

I ran over what I had just said in my head. I was indeed talking crazy. "Nothing to worry about. I just had a weird dream. I'm still just a little fuzzy headed." I sat down at the table. "How about some coffee?"

After two oversized cups of black coffee, I felt like I was coming to my senses. I'm not sure if caffeine really affects me or if it's just a placebo effect, but either way, it works, so I'm not complaining. "Wait, it's currently August twelfth? I've been out for about three days?"

Vicky nodded. "Yeah, you were going through the church members, drinking their blood, and all of a sudden, you just passed out."

There was something I needed to remember about August twelfth. "Shit. I have a Lyle B show tonight."

Vicky nodded. "We were just discussing whether to cancel or to try to wake you again. Now that you're up, you have plenty of time to get your show ready."

Kyle walked into the kitchen with one of the cult members, Tina I think, on his heels. Like the other night, she dressed all in black and wore too much eyeliner. I really had to talk to her about that. If these people were going to be my followers, they were going to learn the proper cosmetics application.

"Dude, there you are. I went downstairs to check on you, and you were gone. I thought you might be sleepwalking."

I wondered how Kyle had jumped to that particular conclusion. "When have you known me to sleepwalk?"

"Well, never, but you're like becoming this badass vampire now, so I thought maybe it was a new ability or something, and dude, you'd be seriously fucked if you started sleepwalking and wandered outside during the day."

I wanted to argue whether or not sleepwalking could be considered an ability, but I was too enamored with the rest of his statement. "Yeah, I am becoming pretty badass, aren't I?"

Vicky rolled her eyes. "Oh please, you've been unconscious for three days. We had to ask Tina to watch Kyle so he wouldn't molest you."

"I didn't molest anyone," Kyle objected.

"Yes, we just found you naked, curled up in bed with him."

I gave Kyle my sternest look. "Kyle, bad."

"Sorry, dude." Kyle did his best to look pathetic, but I could tell he wasn't sorry.

"Okay, I need to spend some time getting my party ready, but when I'm done, I have something for us all to do."

"Finally, some action," Vicky said, unbuttoning her shirt.

I took hold of Vicky's hands. "Not that kind of action. We're going to track down the vampire who made me."

"The tramp with the Corvette?" asked Vicky.

I must have looked puzzled, because Margot said, "Kyle's been filling us in on your history."

I sighed. "Yes, as you say, the tramp with the Corvette. However, the Corvette was a rental, and I got the feeling it wasn't her style."

"I could check the car rental places. They probably don't keep records that far back, but we might get lucky," said Vicky.

Reverend Billy walked in drying his hair and wearing Vicky's pink robe and slippers. The robe barely covered the necessary areas. "Good morning, Lord Vinny. It is nice to see you up and around again."

I pointed my thumb at the reverend. "He's staying here too?"

"He was holding a vigil for you while you were unconscious," said Tina. "Now that you have recovered, I will be the only member of the church permanently in residence. However, you may call on us whenever you need extra personnel to... Satisfy your needs." She licked her lips.

He pulled back the collar of the robe. "Feel free to partake, my lord."

"I'll pass for now. But while you're here, what do you think happened to me? One moment, I was biting your church members, and then I was out cold."

"I do not know, my lord. Perhaps it is a side effect from too much blood, or possibly someone you ate didn't agree with you." So much for the resident vampire expert.

I looked around to the five minions in the kitchen. "Alright, listen up vassals, now that everybody's here." I paused, wondering if that was true. "Everybody is here, right? No church members lurking in the corners of the house or anything."

"No, Lord Vinny," said the reverend. "However, if you wish a larger retinue—"

"I think we have enough for now. What I need to do is find the vampire who made me into what I am."

"Your sire," Reverend Billy volunteered.

"However," said Margot, "would it be 'sire' if he had a female progenitor?"

Billy thought for a moment, "Perhaps not, but in relation to vampires, the masculine, sire, is the common term."

"Sire? Okay, we're going to find my sire. However, the trail is ten years old. Any suggestions?"

"I have a friend who's an artist," said Margot. "We could try doing a sketch."

"And I could put it online," said Reverend Billy. "I know all the vampire message boards, blogs, and news sites."

"Are there lots of vampire sites on the Internet?" I asked.

"Oh yes," said Reverend Billy, "but most of them are dedicated to homoerotic fan fiction." I glanced over at Kyle, who seemed to find this fact very amusing.

"All right, that gives us a plan. I'm going to go get ready for my Lyle B show. Tell me if you come up with any other ideas."

I left to work on my party, but Kyle followed me. "Dude, you didn't give me anything to do."

I was finding out the hardest part of being a vampire was making all your minions feel like they were different and special in your eyes. "Why Kyle, what do you mean? You have the most important task of all. You were the one who was there at the time. You have to search your memory for clues that will help us."

"Okay," he said, still not sounding too happy.

"And maybe tomorrow, if no one's come up with anything, we can go to Ernie's."

"Really?"

"Of course. That is where we met her. I need you to help with this. You are my oldest and best friend, you know."

"Awesome. Ernie's on Saturday night. I can't wait. Maybe we can even pick up a couple of chicks for you to bite." This, of course would be a bad idea, as the chicks that frequented Ernie's on a Saturday night were the hard drinking self-destructive type, not the angels of Karaoke Night.

"Maybe you can, but I'm not going to. When I pick them, they have a habit of staying picked, and I've collected enough people this week."

That night, I had a terrific Lyle B show, selling over a thousand dollars of merchandise. I had no great illusions that the money I earned from my shows would somehow help our little household in any way, but I liked the idea of making my own money. I came home to find the household asleep, so I went to bed myself. I woke up the next morning, ready to face the world, kick ass, and take names, but I ended up mostly playing PlayStation all morning with Kyle.

That afternoon, Margot's artist friend came over to do sketches. I half expected an artist to be some kind of tripped out hippie chick, but when I saw the woman standing in the kitchen, wearing a sensible business-casual outfit, black slacks and a jacket, I knew I had made a mistake. "Linda, this is my new life-partner, Vinny, and his friend, Kyle," announced Margot.

"Hi," I said, a little surprised at being introduced in such a way. Over the short time I had known Margot, one of us had been unconscious most of the time. Besides, Margot just seemed too cool for me. Sure, we'd had sex a couple of times, but one of those times had ended in assault.

Linda looked me up and down and raised an eyebrow to Margot. "Really, Margot, I didn't expect you to go the cougar route."

"For your information, I had no intention to 'go the cougar route.' I just met a young man with exceptional skills and one thing led to another."

"Really, what kind of exceptional skills are you taking about, Margot?" She kept eying me like I had two heads and it was only then that I realized I had not put on any makeup that day.

"Makeovers," I said. "I'm a genius with cosmetics."

"Well, Vinny, after we get done with these sketches, maybe you could do to me what you did for Margot." I seriously doubted that. Like I told Kyle, I'd collected enough people already.

Margot picked Linda's sketchpad up off the table and pushed it into her hands. "Maybe we should concentrate on one thing at a time."

"Of course. Now before we get started, I have to warn you I've never done this kind of work before, so we might not end up with anything useful, but we can at least try. So let's start with the hair..."

An hour later, we had gotten nowhere. Every time I would suggest something, Kyle would give contradictory information. Linda set down her sketchbook and shook her head. "The people who do this for a living must have some techniques to bring out details from a witness. I have to admit, I'm lost."

Margot, who had been watching the entire time, asked, "Would you mind trying one more thing?"

"All right, what should we do?"

"Have Kyle step outside, and let Vinny do the description by himself. Then, when he's done, bring Kyle in, and we'll see what he comes up with." She turned to me as if to ask if this sounded okay.

"Sounds good to me," I said.   "What do you think, Linda?"

"We can give it a shot." She didn't sound too enthusiastic.

Kyle left the room, and I went through the question and answer routine again. Without Kyle's help, it went more smoothly, and we had a reasonably accurate sketch in about a half hour. Then Kyle came in and I kept silent while he gave his description, or at least I tried to.

"Her eyes were blue, Kyle."

"I was sure they were hazel."

"Well, I spent more time with her."

"Yeah, you must be right, you're the boss."

Suddenly, I saw why Margot had asked us to do the descriptions separately. "No. Linda, this is Kyle's sketch, use his description. Make the eyes hazel."

Linda put down her pencil and glared at us. "Would you all shut up about the color of her eyes? This is just a pencil sketch. No pigmentation. No color. Got it?"

We all gave Linda our apologies, and she continued, finally ending up with two sketches, one from my description, and one from Kyle's. They were totally different.

"Well, fuck," I said.

The only solution, of course, was to go to Ernie's. Technically, Kyle and I were going there because Ernie was the only other person we knew who had seen the vampire, Veronica. Once we had Ernie's tie-winning vote, Reverend Billy had church members ready to canvas the community. Really, I just wanted to hang out with Kyle and Ernie and knock back a couple beers.

As I've mentioned before, Saturday at Ernie's was different from Karaoke Night. Most of the customers were regulars, those people who needed a fifth of vodka at lunch if they wanted to get through the day. If he'd had his druthers, Ernie would have choose a more sophisticated clientele, people less likely to vomit in the bathrooms before returning for more drinks. He liked to picture himself as an old-world innkeeper. Unfortunately, the people who carried the cash that kept him afloat were hard-core drunks. I think he would have kicked out the drunks and turned the place into a full-time karaoke bar a long time ago if he didn't also despise most of the karaoke singers.

Ernie gave me a hug as soon as I walked in the door. He smelled of cheap aftershave, stale beer, and fried chicken. He gave Kyle a playful punch on the shoulder. "Boys, where have you been keeping yourselves? I barely see you anymore. It's good to have you back and together again as well. The last time I saw this guy..." He gave Kyle another playful punch. "...he said you two weren't getting along so well."

I wondered just how much Kyle had told him. "Uh... We managed to come to an understanding. Can you talk for a minute?"

"Sure." He waved at Rita, who was working the bar. "Give me three pints of Coors."

I raised my eyebrow.

"I got a deal from the distributor," he said defensively. He grabbed the three beers off the counter. "Don't look a gift horse in the mouth. I'm giving you free beer." He led us over to an empty table, taking us away from the fresh alcohol-sweat stink of the regulars, and into the more permanent stink of stale beer with a hint of ancient vomit. "So, what's up?"

"Do you remember the first time I came here, the night I was attacked?"

He shook his head. "Oh, Vinny, of course I remember that horrible day. You were just a kid, and I should have been looking out for you. Instead, I was jealous you were leaving to get your rocks off with such a hot lady. If I had only known what would happen. You were a minor—"

I put my hand on his shoulder. "It's fine, really. I just want to know if you remember the woman who attacked me."

"Sure I do."

I set the two sketches in front of him. "Does she look like either of these two women?"

Ernie studied each of the photos for a minute. "Kind of. I mean she had this one's eyes, but the mouth and ears on this one look closer. She could be the sister of these women, but neither one is exactly right. She had a thicker nose, and her hair was shorter."

I leaned back in my chair and let my head drop back, staring at the ceiling. "Fuck."

"She's got to be long gone. Why do you want to know after all this time?"

I watched a fly eating something dark stuck to the air handler. "Tell me about it. I don't know, Ernie, maybe I'm being stupid, but I want to ask her why she did what she did. I want to see if she has this same blood condition that I have." While Ernie was close, I figured the vampirism and the "sire" stuff was strictly need-to-know.

"I don't really know that much. She had come in on and off for a couple weeks. She would order a beer and after that, she wouldn't talk. Guys would hit on her from time to time, but she always gave them the cold shoulder. I got the feeling like she was waiting for somebody, but nobody ever came for her. Then there was the night you guys came in, and as soon as she walked in the door, she cut a beeline to you. Honestly, I could barely believe it."

"And you never saw her after that?"

"Hell no. If I did, I would have called the cops."

I nodded. "Okay, thanks, Ernie."

"You talk to your dad lately?" he said, changing the subject.

"No, not really. Why?"

"After you were attacked, I offered to help with your hospital bills. I was deep in hock after buying the bar, but I wanted to do right by you. Your old man told me not to worry about it—a 'generous benefactor' handled what hadn't been covered by insurance."

"That's interesting." I certainly didn't remember anything like that. Then again, I hadn't even thought about hospital bills—my parents always handled those sorts of things.

"Even if you don't want to ask him about that, you should go see him anyway. I probably shouldn't tell you this, but he's been coming around from time to time, like he misses you or something. I think he's lonely."

"That's a good idea," I said, standing up.

Kyle gave me a pleading look. "Dude, aren't we going to hang out for a while?"

"I don't think so. I want to go ask my dad some questions."

"But, dude. You said we could hang out. Remember?"

"We have a lead to follow."

"Dude, can I at least finish my beer?"

I sat back down. "Okay."

I felt weird, knocking on the door of the house I grew up in. I suppose I could have just opened the door. I had a key and everything. Kyle and I waited about thirty seconds and then Jennifer opened the door. She was wearing sweatpants and a t-shirt, and she had added some highlights to her hair. She looked a little surprised to see me. "What? Did your sugar mama kick you out?"

"Can't I visit my family once in a while?"

"Well, yeah, but I didn't think you were too interested, too busy boning your milf."

"Jennifer, she's the same age as me."

My father, coming down the stairs, cut off her retort. "Vinny? Kyle? What are you boys doing here?"

"His sugar mama kicked him out," Jennifer said.

"No she didn't, and stop calling Vicky that."

Jennifer rolled her eyes at me. "Whatever."

"Hi, Dad," I said, talking over my sister. "We thought we'd come by and see what you were doing."

"Well, it's good to see you two. You don't stop over often enough, son. And Kyle, I hardly ever see you outside of work hours anymore. Can I get you anything to drink? Soda? Something stronger?"

"Beer would be great," Kyle said.

"Okay, you boys go wait in the den and I'll be in with some beer."

We waited in the den for my dad to return with the beers. "This is weird," I told Kyle. "He does the exact same thing with Jennifer's dates, but he kicks them out if they ask for anything alcoholic."

"Well, then I'm glad he didn't do that to us."

My dad came in with three beers and passed bottles to Kyle and me. "It's sure nice to see you boys. Do you want to turn the TV on? The Cubs are playing."

"No, Dad. I—"

He turned on the TV anyway. "Now isn't this nice—just the guys, sitting around with some brewskis, watching the game." As we watched, a Cubs batter hit a pop fly deep in left field, ending the sixth inning down by four.

Dad made a face and turned off the TV. "Then again, maybe we should just talk. What are you two up to? Going to sow those wild oats tonight?"

"Um, no, Dad. I was actually wondering if you know anything about the woman who attacked me."

He shook his head. "We never learned anything about her." This was the answer I had always been given.

I pressed on. "Ernie said there was some money. Someone handled the medical bills."

"Well, of course. The plumbing supply handled all of that. They have a great benefits package, don't they Kyle?" He looked to Kyle for confirmation.

"Dad, Ernie said someone handled the bit insurance didn't cover."

I saw indecision wash over my father's face. Then, he seemed to make up his mind. "I probably shouldn't have hidden this from you, but I... Your mother doesn't like me to talk about it. Still, I think you deserve to know. Shortly after you were attacked, someone rang our doorbell and left a duffel bag on our front steps. Inside the bag was twenty thousand dollars in cash. I don't know if it was a settlement from the person who... who did that thing to you or if it was just a donation from a wealthy Samaritan. There wasn't any record of the money. We kept quiet about it. We were afraid we might have to pay taxes on it."

"So there's no way to trace it at all?"

"No, I—"

Suddenly Kyle's head snapped up. He slapped my arm. "Dude! I mean, Mr. Lester. Do you still have the bag?"

"I don't know why we wouldn't. It would be in the basement somewhere. Let's go take a look. It's a leather bag, dyed red with the Cornhusker's logo."

We went down to the basement and started searching through layers of familial sediment—old camping gear, jigsaw puzzles with missing pieces, a bowling shirt from my dad's old team, the Plumber's Helpers. After a half hour of digging, I took a break and walked over to my old room. Other than the bed, it was empty. What I hadn't taken with me, my mother had thrown away. I sat down on my bed and looked up at the curtain that had been the bane of my existence.

Jennifer came in and sat on the bed next to me. We sat in silence for a few minutes. "I leave for Yale in a couple weeks. I was hoping you'd stop by a couple times before I leave."

"I'll see what I can do. I've been busy. Love the high-lights, by the way."

"Thanks. I don't know if I'll keep them, but I wanted to try something new. I kind of miss having you around the house, especially now that you have a makeup collection that puts mine to shame."

"Well, you can come by Vicky's any time..." I started thinking about my newest minions, the cult members. "Then again, maybe you better call ahead. Well, I should get back to the search. They're doing it for my benefit."

"What are you guys looking for anyway?"

"Oh, some old duffle bag with the Cornhusker logo on the side."

"Oh, that's upstairs in the laundry room. I was using it to take my gym clothes to school last year."

———

All four of us walked upstairs to the laundry room. Jennifer led the way in and pulled the bag from a corner. "I'd totally forgotten about this bag. It's been sitting here since April." Before I could stop her, she unzipped the bag. While the humans were simply repulsed by the smell, I was hit by a wall of stink so strong I left the room and watched from down the hall.

Jennifer rolled her eyes at me. "Oh, Vinny, it's not that bad." She looked inside the bag and made a face. "Okay, it is pretty bad." She turned the bag upside down, emptying the contents into the trash. "Here you go." She handed Kyle the empty bag.

"No!" Kyle yelled. "There might be a clue." He dropped to his knees and started searching through the moldy gym clothes and trash.

Jennifer took a step back. "Now that is gross."

"Kyle!" my dad yelled. "Get out of the trash. Stop fondling my daughter's dirty clothes."

Kyle stood up, shaking his head. "Sorry, Mr. Lester, but there may be vital clues—"

"Come on, Kyle," I called from the doorway. "Grab the bag and let's go."

For the drive home, we attached the bag to Kyle's luggage rack to abate the smell.

Where Vinny goes to the cleaners

We returned at twenty-three hundred and handed the bag over to our forensics department, which is how one of those cop shows would say we got home at eleven and asked Vicky and Margot to do something about the horrible smell. Vicky and Margot, not domestically inclined, tried smothering the bag with several types of cleaning products until they got sick of the smell and pitched it out the back door, hoping a day outside in the sunlight would kill some of the mold.

Vicky and Margot wanted to fool around a little, but I made an excuse not to. I had really been looking forward to the new Grand Theft Auto game—it had come out a year ago, but it was still new to me. Not that I'm more interested in computer games than sex, but with my current arrangements, I was worried about who might want to join in. If Kyle and Reverend Billy were out of the house, I would have tried it.

About an hour later, someone knocked on my door. "Come in." I was already tired of the Grand Theft Auto game. It was full of sex and violence, and reminded me way too much of my real life.

Reverend Billy came in. "I've been inquiring about your sire on the Internet, Lord Vinny. I am embarrassed to say the search has not gone well."

"Well, you did your best. I can't expect miracles." As far as I was concerned, doing anything useful on a computer constituted a miracle.

Billy shook his head. "No. You are a great vampire lord. I am a mere servant. You should punish me for my failure."

"I don't see a problem. I can't expect you to make things appear on the Internet just because I want them to exist. For all we know, she isn't even alive anymore."

"But you must punish me."

"Nope. You can't make me do it. I'm the boss."

"You humble me with your beneficence." Then, to my amazement, he bowed. "My flock has assembled upstairs, and we await the Great Feeding. I have arranged for fewer this time. Hopefully, this will be more agreeable to your constitution."

"Wait—"

He turned and left the room before I could protest. I followed upstairs, feeling a sense of dread. To think, just a couple months ago, I couldn't get anyone to give me their blood. Now I had so many they might be making me sick. When I arrived in the dining room, I barely even noticed the four church members. "When did you do all of this?"

The transformation of the room itself was startling. Heavy, black curtains covered the walls. Incense hung thick in the air, reminiscent of oriental perfumes or stinky hippies. Candelabras provided lighting. However, the general décor was nothing compared to the golden throne dominating an entire wall. Basically, it was one of Vicky's dining room chairs sitting on a platform two feet off the ground, but the whole thing was painted bright gold. I was already getting high off the leftover paint fumes.

"So, when did you have time to do all this?"

Reverend Billy stepped up, looking quite proud of himself. "I told them you would feed on them when your throne was done. They worked especially hard to make it. What do you think?"

I had never seen anything so ugly in my life. "It's great."

"Aren't you going to sit down?"

"Um, yeah. Sure."

I stepped up onto the platform and sat down in the "throne" made from Vicky's gold-painted dining room chair. The chair cushion made a squelchy sound, and I immediately knew they had not waited for it to dry.

They lined up in front of me for their reward and I bit them one after another, while I the gold paint soaked into the butt of my pants. When I was done, I didn't pass out like the last time, but I did feel woozy. I stood up, muttered my thanks for the blood and the redecorating. Then, I stepped off the edge of the platform like it wasn't there. Reverend Billy caught me as I fell.

"Whoa, there, Lord Vinny. Watch that first step. It's a doozy."

"Doozy, yeah." I made my way towards my basement room. My arms and legs felt like lead. I ran into something and looked up. Vicky was holding my arms.

"Are you alright?" She asked. "Oh my God! Your ass is bright gold."

"The church members have done something atrocious to your dining room." My voice sounded far away. "I'm going to bed now." I shook my head to stop the room from spinning and continued on to the basement.

I awoke to Kyle staring at me. "Um, hi, Kyle. What are you doing?"

"I was just watching you sleep. You're beautiful when you're sleeping, you know." Great. Now I'd never be able to sleep again.

"Why were you watching me sleep?"

"I'm waiting for you to wake up. We're going to look at that bag tonight. By now, it's probably about as aired out as it's going to get."

"Yeah, I suppose so." I pulled back my blankets to reveal the gold paint had dried, gluing me to my sheets.

"Dude," Kyle said, "Did you get freaky with a can of paint?"

"It's a long story, and no, I did not get freaky with a can of paint." After peeling myself off the sheets, I took off my paint-stained clothing and put on a pair of jeans and an ABBA t-shirt.

As we walked upstairs, I said, "I don't think we're going to find very much. I mean, it's an empty bag, and—"

"You're wearing my ABBA shirt," Vicky complained as I stepped into the kitchen.

"Sorry."

"Look, I don't mind everyone in my house, really I don't, as long as it makes you happy, but we need to set some serious boundaries. I don't want Reverend Billy wearing my bathrobe, and I don't want you wearing my ABBA shirt, and I really don't want people chopping up my dining room set and painting it gold and burning shitty incense!" Towards the end of her speech, she was getting a little hysterical. Knowing trouble when I saw it, I immediately slipped off the ABBA shirt and passed it to her.

Kyle grabbed me from behind, covering my chest with his hands. I pushed him back with my shoulder. "Kyle, W-T-F, seriously."

"Oh, dude, sorry. I um... I'll go get that bag." After a moment, he returned with the bag, which still smelled really bad.

Vicky pointed accusingly at the bag. "Take that thing out of my kitchen. Go to the garage."

I stood up. "Actually, that's a good idea." Kyle was giving Vicky a nasty look. "Kyle, come on. We're going to the garage."

As soon as we'd stepped into the garage and closed the connecting door behind us, Kyle turned to me. "Where does she get off?"

"What?"

"Vicky. How dare she give orders to you? She walks around like she owns the place."

"Well, technically, she does."

"She doesn't have to rub your nose in it."

"Kyle, you're complaining about a problem that doesn't exist. Vicky told me to take the stinky bag to the garage. Taking the bag out of the kitchen was a good suggestion. We use the kitchen too. Just because these church members go around calling me master doesn't mean I want blind obedience from my friends. Just let it drop."

We stared at the duffle bag for a few minutes. It was our only lead, and I had no idea what to do with it. I looked over at Kyle. He was staring at the bag intently as if, by will alone, he could make it reveal its secrets. "Any ideas?" I asked.

"Nope." His eyes lit up. "But on TV, don't they like look at the labels, and use them to track back to the retailer?"

"I'm pretty sure that just works on TV. Besides it's a generic, leather bag dyed with the Cornhusker logo. Do you realize how common those must be in Nebraska?"

"How about slitting open the lining?"

"It's not lined. It's leather."

Kyle stuck his hand in the bag and fished around. "There's no lining, but there is a hard bottom that's, like, bolted in." He stuck his other hand in the bag and pulled.

There was a loud ripping noise and a piece of heavy chipboard ripped out of the bottom, accompanied by a light piece of nylon cloth. Out of the bag fluttered a business card.

I picked the card off the floor. "Featherstone Dry Cleaning," I read to Kyle.

Kyle shrugged. "Great, they had the bag cleaned."

"Can you dry clean a leather bag?"

"Dude, you have a point. I don't think so."

We returned to the kitchen. Vicky and Margot were laughing about something and stopped when I came into the room. I ignored this and asked, "Would you take a leather duffle bag to the dry cleaners?"

"What, that old thing," Margot said. "It wouldn't be worth it."

"No, I mean could you theoretically have a leather duffle bag dry-cleaned?"

Margot shook her head. "Never take anything leather to the cleaners. It will end up worse than when it started."

I held up the card. "I think we have a lead."

Vicky didn't look so enthusiastic. "First, let me look in the phonebook and see if they're even still open. Then we can take a drive over there."

An hour later, Kyle was driving Vicky, Margot and I to Featherstone Dry Cleaning, which was still in business. Featherstone was in an old neighborhood, once the main street of a small town of its own, but now a victim of Omaha's suburban sprawl. Margot was navigating for Kyle and Vicky and I sat in the back seat. She was running her fingers through my hair. "You're never going to go bald," she said.

I made a face. "That seems like poor consolation for an eternity of teenage acne."

"You're just saying that because you have hair. My ex was going bald. He would soak his head in Rogaine every time he found a hair in the bath."

Kyle pulled into a parking space and stopped so quickly I almost slid out of my seat. "We're here."

The front of Featherstone Dry Cleaning was not very impressive, but when we went through the front doors, the inside was not very impressive either. It could have used some new paint, and carpet, and furniture. There was no evidence of clothes or cleaning, only a gold polyester curtain blocking my view from the rest of the store. A lone employee sat on a stool behind a sagging counter. He wore sweat pants and smelled as if he had not washed, or perhaps even moved, in several years. His hair looked oily enough to keep a family sedan running smoothly for 10,000 miles. He was watching a game show on TV. He didn't look up.

There was a bell on the counter, two feet from the elbow of the employee. I rang the bell, and he looked up, squinting at me for a moment as if willing his eyes to focus on something other than the TV. "Yes?"

"Did you, or do you know anyone who worked here ten years ago?"

"Toby has been here more than ten years."

"Well, can you tell me how to get ahold of this Toby?"

"Toby is right here," he said. He held his hand to his chest. "This one is Toby." Okay, Toby was a fruitcake.

I set the duffle bag up on the counter. "I need to ask some questions about this bag."

"It is leather. We can't do leather. We would have to send it out to a specialist."

I nodded. "Yes, I know it's leather. I was actually interested if you knew why it appeared on my parent's doorstep ten years ago with your business card in it." I handed him the card.

He looked over the business card. "This isn't our card. We got rid of these years ago."

"Could I maybe speak to someone else?"

"You could speak to the owner." He turned back to the TV.

"Is the owner here?"

"Yes," he said without removing his eyes from the screen.

"Well, could you get him for us?"

The man sighed dramatically, and picked up a telephone. "I have some people here to see you. They brought in a leather bag with the Cornhusker logo." He turned and looked me over. "Yes, I believe so." He set down the phone. "Please follow me. The owner would like to see you." He pushed himself up off the stool, and with great effort, staggered towards the curtain separating the lobby from the rest of the building. "My name is Toby," he said as an afterthought.

I nodded. "Vinny."

"This way, Vinny." He pushed back the curtain and stepped through.

I almost walked through the curtain without looking back, but I suddenly felt very alone and turned to see my entourage sitting in the lobby chairs. Vicky and Margot were talking amongst themselves. Kyle was playing a Gameboy. "Guys," I said, nodding at the curtain I was about to step through. They immediately hopped up and followed.

Behind the curtains was a room that took up the rest of the ground floor. Rows of clothing racks were packed into the room, leaving only narrow aisles, narrow enough that, as Toby led us through, the plastic wrappers over the clothing brushed against both my arms. The machines and chemicals I had expected were nowhere in sight.

Kyle asked the question I had been thinking. "Where do you clean the clothes?"

"We send them out to a larger facility which does the actual processing, allowing us to take in more clothing without investing in equipment."

The farther Toby led us into the building, the darker it became, until, even with my vampire vision, I was having trouble. I wondered how Toby could read the tags on the clothing. Finally, we reached the back wall, where ancient steps descended into darkness my eyes could not penetrate.

Toby pointed. "Go down there." I started to step forward, and Toby swept his pointing finger back to me. "But be warned!" he said. "Before you continue on, there is something you must know. Descend at your own risk, for the lower levels of this building are a hard hat zone, and having now been warned, you implicitly refuse the right of litigation against Featherstone Drycleaning in the event of an injury."

Stepping past Toby, I took a tentative step down. The stairs seemed stable enough, made from old stone, but they were wet and overgrown with slippery moss. I continued carefully.

Vicky, immediately behind me, put her hand on my shoulder and whispered in my ear, "Don't worry, a verbal notification like that would never hold up in court."

I took the steps one at a time, afraid my next step might find no stair at all and maybe dump me into some kind of bottomless pit. I tried to put this fear aside as being irrational, but I was not used to situations where I couldn't see in the dark. As I continued down, I eventually became aware of an extremely faint illumination somewhere below me. With something to focus on, I continued forward a little more confidently and eventually found myself on a landing. I still could barely see my hand in front of my face, but I could see a dim sliver, an edge of light squeezed around the outline of a door.

The darkness was so quiet I could hear Vicky breathing behind me. I reached out, tentatively, to gauge the distance to the door by touching it lightly. I over-reached a little and ended up pushing it open. It squeaked loudly, and I jumped back in fear, running into Vicky.

"Watch where you're going," she said, pushing me back.

I stumbled forward into the room. The musty smell was stronger. The room was black, and so large I couldn't see the far walls. In the center of the room, bathed in the light of a single candle, a man sat in a recliner, wearing an old-fashioned business suit, like last-century old. He was gangly, and his brown hair was unkempt. He didn't move a muscle, but I could tell he was watching me.

I took a few steps forward, careful of my footing in the darkness. "Hello. My name is Vincent—"

"The prodigal son returns," the man said, and I couldn't quite tell if he was being sarcastic or not.

I walked forward again, so I could better see who I was talking to. "Do you know who I am?"

"I know much about you, Vinny. I am Brad, Vampire Master of Omaha." He held up his hands to indicate the room around him. "And this is my underground lair. Do you like it?"

Again, I was having trouble determining if he was being serious. "I'm sure it's quite nice, but honestly, I can't see it that well in the dark."

"Forgive me." He clapped twice and florescent lights flickered to life, bathing the room in electric light. The basement room seemed to take up the whole underside of the building. Black curtains completely covered the wall. The ceiling was concrete and covered in conduits and pipes. "You see, I have all the modern conveniences." Apparently, "modern conveniences" meant the electric light. Brad sat in the middle of the huge, empty space, like he was adrift in a concrete sea.

"Do you have all these lights hooked up to a 'Clapper'?" I asked.

"No. I was just instructing Toby to turn them on," he said, pointing to a corner of the room. I turned around and jumped, surprised to find Toby there. He must have followed us down.

Brad continued. "Speaking of which, I see you have brought your ghouls."

"Ghouls?"

"You know, your human servants, people who we have bitten and made our property."

"Oh, yeah. I did wonder about the whole thing with the biting."

Brad gave me a concerned look and then continued. "It is good that after all this time, you have come to learn about your heritage."

"Um, yeah, about that, I was really hoping to meet up with the woman who originally bit me."

"Oh, Veronica Adamo. Yes, so sad."

"Sad?"

"Well, she bit you when you were underage by human society. When minors are sexualized, bitten, or disappeared, people, their parents or schoolmates, take notice. This exposes us to the outside world. Exposure is the greatest offense against our kind, and there is only one punishment—death."

"You killed her for turning me?"

"Not me personally, but the Master of New York, L'Isle Belmonte, who acts as the leader of North America. He is a cruel man. Pray you are never judged by him."

"So there are more of our kind?"

"Many, many more, Vinny. Some fit into the society, and some don't. If you lived in a different city, you might run into one from time to time, but Omaha is just a little too backwater for most."

"That's fascinating. You see, that's exactly the sort of thing I've come here to learn. I want to know all about vampires."

"Very well. However, there is much, and I am afraid I lack the comfortable amenities necessary for entertaining. Perhaps we could travel to your lair?"

That sounded like a great idea. "Of course."

Brad stood and walked through my minions as if they did not exist. We followed in his wake. When he reached the door, Toby grabbed his arm. "Master, I will prepare your vehicle."

Brad jerked his arm back. "Unnecessary, today, I will ride with Lord Vinny."

"But master, who will protect you?"

Brad backhanded him, knocking him to the floor. "You fool. I will be in the home of Lord Vinny. Do you think two vampires, one of them the Master of the City, cannot defend themselves?" And then he spat on Toby, which put me in the position of having to feel empathetic towards the disgusting, little man. "You must remain here to take in dirty clothes and answer the phone. Furthermore, you will have Chinese food delivered to Lord Vinny's house." He turned to me. "You do like Chinese?"

I nodded. "Sure."

He turned back to Toby. "Then, you will bring the car around to Lord Vinny's before sunrise so I may return to my lair. Do you understand, or do you want further explanation from the back of my hand?"

Toby put up his arm in defense. "No, master. Do not hurt Toby again. I live only to serve."

"Very good, Toby." He turned to me again. "Would you please give your address to my ghoul?"

I handed Toby one of my business cards, a gift from Vicky, which read, "Sally Waldon, Lyle B consultant" along with Vicky's address and home phone. He did a half bow and backed away from me.

"So, Brad," I asked, "You're the Master of the City. What does that mean?"

"Just a bit of paperwork every couple of weeks. Meet and greets with other vampires who go through our area, which in the case of Omaha, isn't many. It takes only a small amount of time, allowing me to manage my personal business."

"And what does that entail?"

"I have an interest in the Stor-All Storage Garages, this dry cleaning location, and I have a small ranch outside of town."

"What do you keep on your ranch?"

"Ghouls."

"You keep humans on a ranch?"

"Oh yes, they really like it there. In their off time, they can ride horses, and once a week, Toby takes them to the mall."

"Their 'off' time?"

"Well, yes. A ghoul must serve his master more than blood. We run a doggie daycare, and the ghouls also do telemarketing and medical transcription. Do your ghouls work?"

"Kyle sells plumbing fixtures, and Vicky and Margot are independently wealthy."

Brad nodded and lowered his voice. "Be careful. Going after the rich ones seems like a good idea at first, but unless you are good at investments, a good workhorse is more valuable in the long run. The rich ones are often lazy, and don't want to work once you run through their riches."

"Hey!" said Vicky. "Don't call me lazy."

Brad gave her a half-wave. "Be silent, ghoul." He shook his head. "Has she always been this lippy?"

I shrugged. "Well, yeah, I guess."

Vicky glared at me. "I'm right here."

Brad rapped her on the back of the head. "Silence. I'm guessing she is the first you bit?"

"Yes, how did you know?"

"The first human you bite is your Prima, or Primo in the case of the male animal. You will always be linked to her. The Prima can exert a little more independence than a common ghoul. They age very slowly, and as you gain power, may stop aging at all."

"Do you have a Prima?"

"Toby is my Primo." He waved his hand indicating the wretched, potbellied man. "But let us not stand around like cretins. Let us travel to your home, Lord Vinny." He led us up the stairs with Toby following behind, and Brad accompanied us back to the house.

Where Vinny joins Brad's organization

I was so excited. After a decade of being all alone, there was a vampire in our living room. The mood was only slightly spoiled by the fact he was drinking a Diet Coke and smelled like a musty basement. We sat in silence for several minutes, while Brad sipped his Coke and said nothing.

Finally, Kyle could take it no longer. "Well?"

Brad sneered. "Silence that impudent wretch, or I will silence him for you."

Kyle dropped his gaze. "Sorry, dude. My bad."

Setting down his Coke, Brad said, "You and I are descendants of the European line. Not much is known about that line before the Black Death, which decimated the population of Europe. It is thought the sudden loss of population made it more difficult for our kind to hide, as people became more suspicious of outsiders, and most were probably killed. The old ones took to the Carpathian Mountains. No one knows how they survived—maybe they just let themselves wither. A hundred years later, the patriarch of our clan, Vlad Dracula, a prince of the province of Wallachia in Transylvania, found the surviving old ones. Dracula, the greatest warrior of his time, vowed to destroy them. This he did, but not before he was turned."

I couldn't believe what I was hearing. "Seriously? The legends about Dracula are real?"

"Some are true and some are not. Like all the details of our existence have become garbled with silly stories about how we can't be seen in mirrors, or the idea any holy symbol can hurt us, when there are only a few that will do us harm. The legends of Vlad Dracula are suspected to be a mixture of truth and hyperbole as well."

"Wait," I said, "You said 'most' holy items. Some religious items can cause us problems?"

"Yes, but only if they are very old and have been in the presence of a true believer long enough to absorb some of their essence. An atheist cannot make a cross out of popsicle sticks and expect to be protected."

"So that's it then. There is a God, and he hates our kind."

Brad shrugged. "Perhaps. Then again, maybe it's the power of belief in the individual and not divine intervention. Would a just God allow our kind to exist and prey on his children?"

"I guess I hadn't thought of it that way."

"The branch of the Dracula line which we belong to, the Belmonte branch, came to the New World during the American Revolution, where we established our treaty with the Mexican clan, which dates back to the Aztec empire."

"This is all interesting stuff," I said, even though I was finding it a little on the boring side, "but what can you tell me about my sire, Veronica? You say she's dead now? Killed by this Belmonte guy?"

"She made a bad decision." Calling the decision to turn me into a vampire a "bad" one was an understatement.

Just then, the doorbell rang.

"Excellent," said Brad, "that will be the Chinese food. I hope you like pot stickers." He pointed to Kyle. "Go pay for the food."

"Why do I have to go?" Kyle asked. "You're not the boss of me."

Brad sighed. "You should discipline your ghouls more harshly. Toby would never speak that way to another vampire, let alone one who is older and of a higher status. A few beatings should set him to rights."

I shook my head. "I'm not really into beating up Kyle."

"Well, think about it. It's a great stress reliever."

Kyle stood up. "Look, I'm nobody's stress ball."

Brad stood up. "Control your animal, or I will control him for you."

Wanting to defuse the situation, I said, "Kyle, go pay for the food and set it out in the dining..." I thought of the garish throne that the church members had built me. "No, better set it out in the kitchen."

Kyle bowed deeply. "Yes, master." I could hear the sarcasm in his voice.

Brad watched Kyle leave the room and then sat back down. "Now, before we eat, I want to make you an offer. I have been long without a prefect, and I wonder if you would be interested in the job."

"Maybe, but I don't know what a prefect is."

Brad smiled. "Of course you don't. A prefect is a special assistant to the vampire master, sort of a deputy, usually another vampire, but in some smaller towns, a highly regarded Primo can substitute."

"So why didn't you just use Toby?"

Brad chuckled and shook his head. "No, Toby is weak-willed and unimaginative. He could never make a good prefect. I barely trust him to take in dry cleaning. That is why I have waited, and that is why you would be perfect for the job."

"What would the job entail?"

Brad held up his hands and ticked off job duties on his fingers. "You will be my voice in business dealings. You will assist me in conducting my business, both private and vampire. You will help me with paperwork and filing. And you will do any other tasks I may assign you."

Being prefect sounded like a lot of work. "I don't know. I already have a job with Lyle B."

"Are you sure you want to turn this down? It is not much work, and it is a great honor. I feel it would be a shame to turn down the opportunity. You could just take the job for a little while to see if you like it. Do it as a favor to me."

"Well..." I glanced over at Vicky. Her head moved left and right in an almost imperceptible no. "I suppose I could give it a try." While he had been a real jerk to Kyle and Vicky, he actually seemed to be taking an interest in me. He was the only other vampire I knew and the master of the city.

"Excellent. You should come to the dry cleaners tomorrow night, and we will have your induction ceremony. And then afterwards, we'll go out to dinner, somewhere where they serve bloody steaks."

"There's a ceremony? Do I have to get dressed up? What do I have to do?"

"Business casual will do, but if you want, I can send over some fancier clothes. We have a good deal of unclaimed formal wear, a perk of the business. The ceremony is really simple, just a bunch of old gobbledygook."

"Sure. I guess."

"Terrific, be there at midnight. Now, let's go eat some dumplings."

We went to the kitchen and finished the night eating Chinese food. The whole time, Kyle, Vicky, and Margot glared at me.

I woke the next day in a warm bed surrounded by my minions. Hot breath tickled the back of my neck and warm flesh touched almost every inch of my body. I languished in the sensuality of it for a long while, and the feel of Margot's ample breasts, firm and yet so soft, pressed against my shoulder started to give me an erection. A hand circled around it, squeezing, and I emitted a low groan, almost a growl.

I looked down to see who was holding me. "Um, Kyle, could your move your hand?"

"Yes."

"Not like that, I mean take it away." I might have pushed him off, but Margot had my right shoulder pinned, and Vicky had my left arm pinned.

"Are you sure, you seem to be—"

"Kyle! Stop!"

Kyle sighed and let go of me. "I was just trying to give you a hand."

"I know what you were trying to do. Just drop it."

"I already did."

"The topic, Kyle. Drop the topic."

"Okay, fine." Kyle put his head on Vicky's stomach and went back to sleep.

When Vicky suggested we all sleep together, I had been kind of into it. It sounded really sexy and fun. I hadn't really thought of the reality of it. Now that I was experiencing the downsides, I wasn't really excited about doing it again.

I looked to the left and right, hoping Vicky or Margot might be awake to finish what Kyle had started. No luck. I tried to nudge Margot awake with my shoulder and she rolled over and punched me in the balls. Needless to say, that hurts, even if you're dead.

I couldn't even reach the remote. With nothing else to do, I eventually went back to sleep.

The next time I awoke, I was alone. I crawled out of the bed, walked upstairs, and nodded to three women sitting around the table. "Good morning, Vicky, Margot, Tina." For once, Tina looked like a living human being. Her makeup was well done, and she wore earth tones, an improvement over all black. I imagined it was the influence of Margot and Vicky, who had not let their association with the undead alter their fashion sense. I felt a little bad for not inviting her to sleep with me last night, but I still didn't think of the church members as my ghouls. Once things were settled down with Brad, I needed to spend more time with them as a whole, maybe visit their church.

"You have a smile on your face today," Vicky said, stirring some low-calorie sweetener into her coffee.

"Yeah, I guess so. For once, I think I have a place in the world. I'm not alone anymore."

"You were never alone, silly. You always had me."

"I know. You're right. If it weren't for your drunkenness at Ernie's that night, I would never be where I am today."

"I aim to please." She took a sip of her coffee.

"Kyle already at work?" I asked, knowing he was usually gone by the time I woke up.

"Yes," Tina said. "Do you need him for something? I can contact him, ask him to come back."

"Nothing all that critical. I just have to talk to him again about inappropriate touching."

Vicky set down her coffee. "Oh, because of what happened in bed this morning?"

I gave her an assessing look, and she returned an innocent expression. I didn't buy it for a minute. "I thought you were asleep."

"I was drowsy. I didn't want to interrupt. I was hoping you two would have an intimate moment."

I stood stunned, not knowing what to say.

Then Margot blurted out, "Well, I think you should sleep with him."

"What?! But he's a man. If you haven't noticed, I'm not into man-on-man action."

"Yes," Margot said. "He's a man, and you're a vampire. Your hold over him is supernatural. And he loves you as much as anyone in this room. Sooner or later you're going to have to acknowledge that, and the longer you wait, the more damage it will do your relationship."

The doorbell rang, and Tina popped up from the table as if she were wired to it. "I'll get it." She returned in a few moments with Toby. Between the two of them, they wheeled a six-foot-long clothing rack into the room. It was loaded with tuxedos and formal dresses. I resisted the impulse to ask Toby why he wore an undersized t-shirt with "Baby on Board" written on it. Pulled over his potbelly, I found the shirt rather disturbing.

Toby bowed low. "Lord Vinny. Your clothing for this evening."

"Wow," said Vicky, "these are all unclaimed from the dry cleaners?"

"Most of them. I don't even buy clothing. I just wait for unclaimed garments." This explained Toby's shirt. "Some of them are things which have not yet been picked up. If you become attached to any garment, please inform me, and I will compensate the owner of the garment with store credit."

"Is that ethical?" asked Vicky.

"Considering we occasionally lure clients to the basement so Brad can bite them, I consider dry cleaning ethics to be relatively unimportant." This was the most intelligent thing I had ever heard come from Toby's mouth.

I nodded. "That's good enough for me."

"Also, Lord Vinny, I must ask you if these are all of your ghouls."

I was about to answer yes, but then I looked at Tina, and thought of the church members. "Um, not really. I sort of have a cult." I was still a little embarrassed by the church members and I wished I had more time to help them with their makeup and fashion sense before I had to introduce them to Brad. We'd barely gotten Tina dressing like a normal person.

"Excellent, you should have them come early to the dry cleaners. Brad wants them to help with the ceremony."

"Actually, I think I might leave them out of this one."

He gave me a look like there was something wrong with my brain. "You must bring them. The master commands it."

"Um, yeah. Of course I will, I guess."

Toby bowed and started to back out of the room. "It was a pleasure to see you again, Lord Vinny, but I must return to Featherstone Dry Cleaning."

"You sure you don't want to stay?" I asked, not because I wanted Toby's company, but because I hoped he could tell me some things about Brad. "Would you like a cup of coffee? Or we could play PlayStation III?"

He shook his head as if horrified. "Toby can not do such things. Toby's only enjoyment comes from his master, not from distractions such as fun and games. Toby must leave now."

I held up my finger in a one-more-minute gesture. "Say Toby, you've been with Brad for a long time. Do you know if a vampire can get sick from drinking too much blood, like from a hangover?"

Toby's eyes went wide. "Toby would not dream of speaking to the health of a superior being. Lord Vinny would have to ask Master Brad. Please let Toby go. Do not make Toby answer such a question."

I sighed. "Okay, Toby. You can go."

Toby backed out of the room, bowing, but still managed to hurry. He misjudged the distance, backed into the door-frame, let out a little yelp, and was gone.

After he had left, we spent some time looking through the clothing Toby had delivered. The only things that came close to fitting me were a dark suit, which was two sizes too small, and a ruffled, powder-blue tuxedo, straight out of a 1970s nightmare. I was afraid of offend-ing Brad by breaking the dress code, so after struggling with the nice suit, I gave up. I was going to have to wear the tux.

Kyle, Vicky, Margot, and I arrived at the cleaners a few minutes early. I was wearing the powder-blue tuxedo. Kyle, Vicky, and Margot all had their own dress clothes, and looked considerably better than I did.

I looked around for Reverend Billy's church bus, but I didn't see it. I hoped Brad wouldn't be pissed off if they didn't show. We waited around for a couple minutes to see if they showed up, but then we decided to go in rather than be late.

The shabby lobby was empty, so I rang the bell. After a few minutes, Toby arrived from behind the curtains. He was wearing a powder-blue tuxedo identical to my own. "Oh dear," he said, "this is embarrassing."

I looked down at my own attire and then back to him. "Um, Toby, why are we wearing the same clothes?"

"There were from a matched set, a wedding party that never returned for their clothing. I hadn't realized I had put any of them on the rack I gave you, but if Lord Vinny would like, I can disrobe."

"No!" Vicky and I shouted at the same time.

"Very well, Lord Vinny. Wait here. The ceremony will start shortly."

I sat down in one of the dirty chairs and waited. My ghouls joined me and chatted amongst themselves, but I was too nervous to join in. After a few minutes, Reverend Billy walked through the curtain. He wore a hooded cloak that, despite his size, barely covered his large frame. In his hand he carried a wooden staff, six feet tall and capped with a fanged bat's head. He banged it on the floor three times. "I understand a Seeker is amongst you."

I stood up. "Um, hi, Billy. I wondered if you guys were going to show up. How's it going?"

"Are you the Applicant who wishes position with the Nosferatu?"

"Well, that's why we're all here, right?"

Reverend Billy didn't move a muscle. He just waited patiently.

"Seriously, what the hell?"

Billy leaned over and whispered, "Sorry, I don't know how much I am supposed to say. I got here early, and Master Brad asked me to participate in the ceremony. He said it was a great honor. The rest of the flock is downstairs with Brad's people, but he said to keep the rest of your ghouls with you. Now, just go along with the ceremony and tell me you're the Applicant."

We straightened up, and Billy asked in a loud voice, "Are you the Applicant?"

"Yes. I am the Applicant."

"Then follow me to the Master."

He turned and walked towards the curtain, not looking to see if I followed. I hurried behind him, and nearly ran into him. He had stopped just short of the curtain. He banged the staff on the floor three times.

Toby's voice came from the other side of the curtain. "Who wishes an audience with the ancient master?"

"I bring with me an Applicant, who wishes position amongst the Nosferatu."

"What is the Applicant's name?"

Billy looked at me expectantly.

"Vinny," I answered.

From the other side of the curtains, Toby let out a sigh. "What is the Applicant's full name?"

"Vincent..." I made a face. "Price Lester."

Behind me, I heard Kyle snort.

"Vincent Price Lester," Toby said, pulling open the curtain. "You may come into our home and request audience with the Master. By stepping beyond this door... curtain, you agree to waive your rights as an Outcast." I honestly didn't know what my "rights as an Outcast" could be, so I stepped through the curtain.

Reverend Billy led us back through the racks of plastic-wrapped clothing, back to the slippery steps that seemed to descend into nowhere. When we reached the bottom, he took out a little flashlight and pointed it at the floor, so the reflected light provided a minimum of illumination. He wrapped on the door with his staff, three times.

"My Master," The Reverend shouted through the door, "I bring with me a Seeker, who has given up his rights as an outcast to seek position amongst the Nosferatu. Do you wish to see him?"

"Tell him to go away," Brad's voice said through the door. "I have had a long day, and I am very sleepy."

I tried to push past Reverend Billy. "I don't get it—"

Billy took hold of my shoulders and guided me away from the door. "You will be given another chance," he whispered into my ear. Then, he said in a regular voice, "The Master cannot see you. I am sorry. Please follow me." He led us up the stairs and out to the lobby. "Wait here." He bowed to me, turned, and left.

I looked at Vicky, Kyle, and Margot. "Well, that was bizarre."

"Yeah, dude."

Vicky sat down, popped off her heels, and started rubbing her feet. "I think it's some sort of ritual."

"I agree," said Margot. "My first husband was a Mason, and they did stuff like this all the time. Of course, they aren't supposed to talk about it, but the less interested I acted, the more he would tell me."

After leaving us for fifteen minutes to cool our heels, Reverend Billy pushed aside the curtain and stood before us. "Does the Seeker wish to petition the Master again?"

I stood up. "Yes."

"Then follow me, Seeker." I followed, and my ghouls followed with me.

Again we stood before the door at the bottom of the slippery steps. Reverend Billy knocked again. "Master, the Seeker returns, seeking your boon. Will you see him?"

Brad's voice came through the door. "Today is the day I wash my ghouls, and I have no time for the petition of a Seeker. However, if the Seeker wishes to leave his ghouls with me, I will clean them."

"Do you wish to leave your ghouls?" Billy asked.

"Um. I think they're clean enough."

"Do you trust the Master with your ghouls?"

I didn't know what to answer. Brad didn't seem to care about the well being of his ghouls, but supposedly, all the church members were already inside. Was I a hypocrite to hesitate before sending Kyle, Vicky, and Margot? Then again, maybe I was worrying unduly.

"Don't do it," Vicky whispered.

This was probably just another part of the ceremony. I was probably showing I could trust Brad with my people. "Yes. Brad may... wash my ghouls."

The door opened, and Toby appeared, motioning to them to come inside. As each passed, I touched them, squeezing a hand or an arm. Then the door closed, and my three best friends were gone. Billy started moving up the steps. "Please, we must go now." I took a deep breath and followed him.

I sat in the lobby for a whole hour, alone with my thoughts, wondering what Brad was doing with Kyle,

Vicky, and Margot. I wondered if I had just let them down. Was there some nuance or hint I had missed? On a hunch, I had placed the welfare of my friends in Brad's hands. Would a smarter, more powerful vampire put up with this kind of treatment? Maybe I had already failed. Maybe they were just waiting for me to go home. Screw that, I wasn't going home without my people.

I stood up, took a deep breath, and marched through the curtain. Reverend Billy stood behind it. "Seeker, how dare you upset the domicile of the Master."

"Drop the bullshit, Billy. We're going to go see Brad right now."

"But the ceremony—"

"Fuck the ceremony. We're going to make sure our people are safe."

I pushed past Reverend Billy and hurried to the back of the racks of clothing. I dashed down the slippery stairs a bit too quickly and ended up falling down the last three. For a human, it would have been devastating landing on the rough stone floor, but I didn't even notice the pain. I raised my hand to grasp the doorknob, but someone seized my hand from behind. "No, Lord Vinny. Let me."

Reverend Billy knocked the staff against the door three times.

"What is it?"

"Great Master, I must report the most serious lapse of protocol. The Seeker has stormed into your home and demanded to be seen."

There was a pause on the other side of the door. Finally, Brad said, "Show him in." The door opened slowly, and Brad stood not two feet away from me. I took two cautious steps into the room, and suddenly Brad leapt forward. He slapped my chest with the flat of his hand, and I felt a sharp pain.

A startled gasp caught in my throat, and I clawed at the ruffles of my tuxedo. I fell to the floor, flopping around like a dead fish. Something was beating on my breastbone. No, I realized, something was pounding on the inside of my breastbone. I stopped fighting the sensation as my eyes widened in wonder. Brad had started my heart.

Brad held up his hand for quiet from the already silenced, black-robed people gathered behind him. "The Seeker is foolish. He surrendered his ghouls to me, even his Prima. He has come into the house of a powerful Master, with no guarantee of sanctuary. Not only does he fail to deserve my boon, but I cannot rest knowing one so inept as he dares call himself Nosferatu. Thus I have cursed him with life. Henceforth, this Seeker shall live and die an ordinary life. Henceforth, the Seeker shall be known as the Human." Brad whipped his cape around and walked away from me, a wall of dark-robed ghouls closing between us.

I lay on the floor gasping for breath, and all the time, a voice in my head repeated, "I'm alive. I'm alive. I'm alive."

Where Vinny does a bad thing

Toby leaned down to look in my eyes. He shook his head in disgust, dislodging his comb-over. "This man came to us as a Seeker," he said, as long strands of hair unraveled from his head. "He was once a mighty vampire, but now he is inferior, a mere human. What shall we do with him, master?"

With his back turned, Brad ordered, "Strip him of his finery." Two of Brad's ghouls stepped forward with long knives. They pulled me to my feet, and someone held me from behind as my legs tried to buckle. The ghouls started cutting away my tuxedo, only leaving me with my under-pants, a tiny pair of bikini briefs which Margot had bought me, with "Got Wood?" written on the front. Toby scowled at the briefs. "I would feed him to the master, but he is not worthy of such an honor. Eject him from our home."

Reverend Billy helped me, half-carried me, up the stairs. I tried to help him by putting one foot in front of the other, lifting them on to the stairs, but I wasn't having much success, and I was grateful for his strength.

"I'm alive," I gasped into his robe.

"I'm sorry," he answered, reminding me that he and his followers foolishly sought the condition from which Brad had freed me.

When we reached the lobby, Billy sat me down in a chair. "Wait here," he said, and hurried back through the curtain. As I waited, I felt the life returning to my legs, and after a moment, I tentatively stood.

As I waited, I contemplated my situation. I would be able to live a normal life now. I could go to college— maybe my grades hadn't been that good. Maybe I could go to work with my dad. He always had wanted to bring me into the plumbing supply business. I could have a normal relationship, without the blood and servitude. Then again, I wondered, would Vicky still be interested in me? What about Margot? After what he had gone through, would Kyle still want to be my friend?

A well-dressed businesswoman walked in. She glanced at me, shivering in my bikini briefs, and moved to the maximum distance the lobby allowed as she made her way to ring the bell. She was obviously uneasy, so I covered up the "Got Wood?" with my hands.

When the woman saw Toby come out in his powder-blue tuxedo, her eyebrows raised. "I'm not interrupting anything, am I?"

"Of course not, Mrs. Overton. What can Toby do to please you?"

"I was wondering if you had my blue suit done," she said, handing him a receipt. As Toby looked at the receipt, she glanced over at me.

Toby waved dismissively. "Do not mind him. He awaits the return of his clothes."

The woman started to nod, but then a puzzled look crossed her face. "I didn't know you had cleaning machines here."

"We don't," Toby said, looking at her like he couldn't imagine why she would think such a thing.

I suppressed the impulse to laugh at the absurd situation, made all the worse by Toby's bewilderment. I ended up snorting a little, and they both turned to look at me in my skimpy underpants. My snort turned into a laugh, and I fell back into the lobby chair.

Mrs. Overton snatched the receipt back from Toby. "On the other hand, I think I'll come back tomorrow."

"Toby will only be a moment—" Toby started to say, only to be cut off by the door closing. He turned to me, and I thought he was going to give me crap about scaring the customers, but instead, he said, "What are you still doing here, Human?"

"Reverend Billy told me to wait, and Kyle drove me, so, I kinda—"

"Your presence is no longer wanted. You gave your ghouls to the Master. You have no business here, Human." He spat the last word.

I stood up and pointed my finger at Toby. "Just one damn minute, those are my ghouls... I mean, those are my friends, and I'm not going to leave here without them."

Toby shrugged. "What should Toby do about that?"

The night had been a little emotional for me, and I was feeling kind of crazy. I ran at Toby, grabbed his powder-blue lapels, and dragged him over the counter. "You go downstairs and tell your Master that unless he gives my people back, he shall rue the day he ever messed with Vincent Lester." For emphasis, and because he was getting a little heavy, I dropped Toby to the floor.

"Very well, Human, Toby will talk to the Master, but if Toby were you, Toby would pray he is in a good mood."

Toby retreated through the curtain.

I stood in the lobby shaking my head. I could not believe what I'd just done. I actually used the words "rue the day."

Reverend Billy returned, the staff in his hand, and he pounded it on the floor. "Human, you have come threatening the Master, and for that offense, he could kill you. However, he is benevolent and invites you to plead your case. Do you accept this invitation?"

"I do." I wasn't thrilled to be returning to the basement to beg for Brad's mercy, but Vicky, Kyle, and Margot were down in there, and I had a feeling this was the only way I would ever get them back. And, okay, I supposed I was going back for the church members too.

For the third time, we went all the way back to the basement door. Reverend Billy knocked three times. "This Human craves your presence."

The door opened to reveal a room full of dark robed figures. They parted to reveal Brad, sitting in his throne. "Approach me, Human." He beckoned to me with a finger that would have been more impressive had it been long and spindly instead of short and stubby.

I walked up to Brad's throne, and stood defiant.

Brad spent almost a full minute contemplating me. "What can I do for you, Human?"

"I want my ghouls back."

Brad smiled and shook his head. "Only vampires have ghouls. You're not a vampire, thus you cannot have them. You have failed your test. All you can do now is go home. No one here will stop you. From this day forward you can age, go out in the sunlight, and have a normal human life." He waved his hand dismissively. "Go. I set you free."

I didn't move. "Look, Brad, there's got to be some way I can leave here with my friends."

He seemed to consider for a moment. "I don't see how. To own ghouls you must be a vampire, but you are a human, so..."

I finally realized what Brad wanted of me. It wasn't fair, but to save my friends, it was the only way. I got down on my knees. "Please Master, make me like you. Make me a vampire, so I can reclaim my ghouls from you."

Brad considered this for long moments. "Very well, but if you truly wish to be reborn as Nosferatu, you must walk the path—"

"Sure, whatever."

"...of pain."

"What?"

"It's a perfectly simple concept. You must walk the path of pain."

"Is it going to hurt?"

Brad rolled his eyes. "It's called the path of pain. What do you think?"

I sighed. "Well, crap. How do you walk this path?"

"You have made a wise choice," Brad said. He stood up and walked to me. He held out his arms, letting his robes fly back to reveal a black tux underneath. His musty smell wafted over me, like the dank of the basement but more concentrated, and I wondered how long he'd spent down here. Had he had started to mold?

Brad wrapped his arms around me, and I felt intense pain, like being kicked in the nuts, but a hundred times worse. I looked down to see a sword sticking out of my stomach. Brad had pushed the sword so far into my back that the point had emerged from my front and now hovered a fraction of an inch from his tuxedo, and the force of the cut had already splattered a little blood on him.

From our audience of ghouls, I heard Kyle cry out, "Dude!"

"Be silent!" Brad commanded.

He pulled on the handle, turning me around. When he stopped moving me, I was again facing a wall of ghouls. I wondered if they were all my church members, or if they were Brad's ghouls, but then Brad pulled the sword out of my guts, and I stopped thinking about such trivialities.

The ghouls again parted, and before me, there was a table covered by black cloth. Someone had covered the floor around the table with plastic sheeting, and there was a circle of duct tape on top of the plastic.

Brad walked to the table, and stood within the circle. "Circumambulate the table, Human," he commanded.

"Do what?" I asked.

Brad rolled his eyes. "Circumambulate, it means walk in a circle around the fucking table."

I walked around the table, following the duct-tape circle and trying not to fall on the slippery plastic. I stopped when I had made one full circle and stood for a moment wondering what Brad would do. Brad pulled back the black cloth to reveal an assortment of evil-looking tools.

"Oh shi—"

I stopped short as Brad picked up a large knife from the table and stabbed it through my guts. This time I actually heard the splatter of blood hit the plastic. I was afraid to look down at the wound, afraid at what I might see.

"Dude, no!" Through the fog of pain, I saw Kyle struggling with Brad's people.

Brad pointed at Kyle. "If the ghoul cannot control himself, bind and gag him." Kyle disappeared in a swarm of dark cloaks.

Though worried, I was sure Kyle would be all right. I had walked the circle of pain, and as the blood pumped out of my body, I knew it must be only moments before Brad would change me back to a vampire, I would heal, and I would get my people back.

Brad returned his focus to me. "Good, Human. Now continue on the path of pain, circumambulate the table again."

"Son of a—"

He slapped me. "Silence."

I moved forward, step by bloody step, over plastic made even more slippery by my own blood. I bit through my lip, trying to distract myself from the pain, pushing forward inch by inch. The path wasn't that far, and I was almost there. I rallied, stumbling the final steps.

"Very good, Human," said Brad. He picked up something that looked like a dagger with a hook on the end, and plunged it through me with one swift motion. When he pulled it out, a piece of me came out with it. I would have thrown up if I weren't already so far gone. I dropped to my knees, trying to hold my guts inside of me. "Now walk around the circle once again."

I barely remember walking the path that final time. The pain consumed me, making every step, every breath, an agony. My vision was a narrow tunnel I focused on the line of duct tape. I didn't even realize when I had finished. Someone had to grab me by the shoulders to orient me towards the table. I raised my head and looked upon Brad's face.

"Congratulations, Human, you have walked the path of pain." He raised something that looked like a samurai sword, and through the waves of pain surrounding my body, I felt another sharp pain. "You shall now be known as the Dead."

Without realizing it, I spoke. "You bastard. Did you just stab me in the junk? You mother—" But then, I couldn't say anything. I fell to the floor like my engine had just stalled.

Brad kneeled beside me and lifted my head, pressing something to my lips. "Drink from me and live forever." Even through the fog of death, I felt disgust as I realized he was quoting Anne Rice, and I considered refusing, but this was for my friends, for their well being. I drank, and Brad's blood burned as it went down, but I swallowed every drop.

Brad's blood was potent. Almost immediately, I started to heal, feeling odd discomfort as my lacerated guts stitched themselves back together. Brad helped me to my feet, and within moments, I was able to stand on my own.

Someone turned on the bright overhead lights, and

Brad said, "Congratulations. I knew you could pass the test."

Reverend Billy walked up to me and handed me a scroll. "Recite this."

I unrolled the scroll and read. "I, Vincent Price Lester, do swear to uphold the will of Lord Brad, Master of Omaha. I vow to obey him in all things, defend his territories and chattel. I will remain his prefect until he releases me from my duties." I rolled up the scroll and handed it back to Reverend Billy.

Brad walked over to the table of torture weapons, and just as I was starting to panic, he pushed them to the side, opened a drawer in the desk, and took out a stack of documents. He crooked his finger to beckon me over, and then tapped different places on the pages. "Sign here. Now here. Initial here." After I was done with them, Brad went through the pages, filling in some blanks of his own, and finally, Toby signed them as a witness. Brad looked over the papers again, and then handed them to Toby, who passed them off to another of Brad's ghouls.

Standing, Brad announced, "I present to you my prefect, Vincent Price Lester. When he speaks, he speaks for me. When he fills out monthly paperwork, he fills out monthly paperwork for me. When he kills, he kills in my name." A cheer rose up from the assembled ghouls. I was so surprised at how suddenly the ceremony had ended; it took me a moment to realize they were cheering for me. Amongst the ghouls, I saw familiar faces, Vicky, Margot, Reverend Billy, and Tina, as well as a few people I recognized as church members, but I was more surprised by how many I didn't recognize. For a guy who hung out in a basement with Toby, Brad had a huge organization.

Brad embraced me, engulfing me in his nasty smell. "My prefect." As if that wasn't bad enough, Toby joined in the hug.

I disengaged myself from them. "So," I asked, "what do we do now?"

"Now, we are going to O'Brannon's."

"The place with all the crap on the walls?"

"They have a nice back room which will seat all of our ghouls, and they let me have it for free," Brad said, as if he was inferring that O'Brannon's didn't let just anyone schedule the back room, which, of course, they did.

I hesitated for a moment. I still occasionally forgot that since I started drinking blood, I no longer had issues with human food. "Sounds great."

"I am very fond of their Wagon Wheel Burger," Brad informed me.

Toby touched Brad on the arm, in a conciliatory gesture. "I'm sorry, master. They no longer make the Wagon Wheel."

Brad smashed his fist into his palm. "But that's the best thing on the menu. Call Mr. O'Brannon and arrange a meeting."

"It's a corporate name, I don't think there is a Mr.—"

"Don't argue, just do it."

Someone must have cut Kyle's bonds, because he ran up to me, and embraced me. "I was so worried," he said. Then, before I had time to react, he kissed me on the lips. It was quick, but long enough to leave me momentarily dazed.

As I left the room, I noticed some of the ghouls were already starting to clean up. They had moved the table and rolled up the plastic and they were carefully squeezing my blood into a stainless steel bucket. I guess not everybody was going to get a burger.

We caravanned to O'Brannon's. Brad and I rode in Brad's Oldsmobile Delta 88 convertible with Toby at the wheel. We were followed by Kyle's Jeep, the church bus, and the minibus that usually transported Brad's ghouls to the shopping mall once per week.

In the backroom of O'Brannon's, Brad, Toby, Kyle, Margot, Vicky and I sat around one big table. I was surprised to see the church members and Brad's ghouls intermingling rather than keeping to themselves.

Part of me wanted to hate Brad for what he had done, but supposedly, any vampire who wanted to be a prefect had gone through this ceremony, and he was still my only link to that world. My desire to find out more about vampire society overrode my indignation at being stabbed in the junk. "So Brad, do you mind if I ask you some questions?"

"Shoot," he said without looking up from his menu, which he seemed to find most dissatisfying.

"What just happened to me? I mean I was alive, I could feel my heart beating like a racehorse's." Even though I had just promised myself to Brad, I still held out hope I could once again experience whatever it was he had done to me.

Brad shook his head, laying down his menu. "Not at all. I had a needle concealed in my hand, and when I hit you in the chest, I gave you a shot of chemicals directly to the heart, a refined psychotropic mixture of herbs and chemicals that simulate the feeling of being alive and slows healing ability. Basically, you experienced a state of altered reality brought on by hallucinogenic, drug-induced physiological reactions and suggestion. I'm glad you were surprised. Most people have already seen the prefect ceremony by the time they go through it, and in my opinion, that ruins the fun."

"So I thought I was experiencing a miracle and you really just got me high?"

"Essentially, yes."

"Did you really have to disembowel me?"

"Not really, but I think the traditional formula adds a sense of occasion to things. After all, if I'd just done the bare minimum and had you sign the paperwork, would you feel truly initiated?"

Yes, who would trade some paperwork for being stabbed in the junk? "Um... I guess not. And what would you have done if I had decided to stay 'alive,' knowing there was no way to really do that?"

"That rarely happens. After all, the Applicant wants to climb the vampire hierarchy, not be removed from it."

"But what do you do?"

"We remove them from the hierarchy." Well, that was evasive enough.

"And after you remove them from the hierarchy, they are free to live their lives?"

"Well, yes and no. They are free from us, but before they leave, we cut off their heads and run stakes through their hearts. I mean, it's not like they're going to magically become human."

So much for my fleeting hopes of mortality. Brad didn't have any magic, just a cocktail of drugs designed to convince me I was human. Later that night, at O'Brannon's, I indulged heavily in alcohol and blood, wanting to wash away my sorrows. Despite my indulgence, I dreamed that night of Brad cutting off my head, again and again, and the next morning I woke up feeling like crap.

Where Vinny runs errands for Brad

Finally, I was learning about the vampire world. Unfortunately, I was learning though doing paperwork, working through Brad's backlog. Being the Master of the City meant doing about three hours of paperwork a week, and from what I could tell, Brad had quit doing his in the 1970s. Paperwork must have gotten in the way of him skulking in the basement of the dry cleaners, which was the only thing I ever saw him do, other than the ceremony where he had cut me to ribbons.

The documents that shocked me the most were the census forms. Brad was expected to provide his superiors with a detailed account of all the vampires working under him. Names were required for all vampires over one hundred years old. Many of the census forms had been filled out but never sent, and I noticed that in the year I was made, the number went from one—Brad, who was listed in the over one hundred blanks—to two. Apparently, I was being counted in the census. From the amount of blank space on the form, I could tell Brad's one-vampire operation was tiny compared to other cities, and while Omaha might be relatively vampire free, there had to be cities in the U.S. with dozens of old vampires. I wondered why none of them had come to Omaha. Maybe they just didn't like Brad.

I didn't like Brad very much myself. He was arrogant and rude, and he disrespected my friends. Still, he was my only connection to a larger world, which I was desperate to join.

I was looking through the 2001 forms, and Kyle was massaging my neck and shoulders, sore from leaning over the paperwork, when Vicky walked into the kitchen with Toby trailing behind her. Toby was wearing a mint-green jogging suit with a decidedly effeminate cut. It accommodated his paunch well. I guessed it was a maternity outfit.

Toby nodded so deeply it could have been a bow. "Lord Vinny. Greetings from Master Brad."

"Hi Toby, how are you doing?"

"The master is doing well, so Toby is doing well. Toby lives for nothing but to serve."

"Tell me, Toby. How did you become Brad's Primo?"

"Brad and Toby were partners in the dry cleaning business. When Master Brad was bitten, he made Toby a partner in a much more significant way." I tried not to visualize what that might mean.

"Well, that's great." There was a long pause, and I felt like I should say something. I searched for common ground with Toby. "So, that was quite a ceremony the other night."

"Yes, Lord Vinny."

I tried to think of something else to ask. "Oh, something I was wondering about. After the ceremony, I noticed some of the ghouls were collecting my blood in a bucket. What's up with that?"

"Vampire blood is very highly prized in Chinese communities as an aphrodisiac. It can go for up to $600.00 an ounce. We should make a minimum of $40,000.00 off your blood, even with spillage."

"Do they drink it?

He shook his head. "No, I think they stick it up their—"

I held up my hand, "So, what brings you here today, Toby?"

"Brad needs you to visit a man tonight. His name is Kenneth Donahue. He has discovered the secrets of the Nosferatu, and he must be eliminated." Toby pulled an envelope from his jogging outfit and handed it to me. "This contains pictures and contact information for your target."

"What am I supposed to do? Go to his house? Scare him?"

"Toby believes Brad would prefer him dead. Your instructions are in the envelope."

"Seriously, Brad wants me to kill some guy?" I hadn't signed up for murder. I thought being a prefect was all about the paperwork.

Toby nodded. "A great vampire lord should have no problem. You have the immortality thing going for you. Think of it this way, either he will kill you, or you will kill him. Worrying about it does you no good either way."

"Thanks a whole bunch, Toby," I said, not trying to hide my sarcasm. Sure, I had the whole immortality thing, but there were some pretty serious caveats to immortality almost everyone knew. At least some of those stories were wrong. Crosses and garlic didn't affect me, and I did have a reflection. Still, I didn't want to kill anyone. I wanted to yell at Toby, to scream at him for bringing me such a horrible task, but it wasn't Toby's fault Brad was such a prick.

"It is Toby's pleasure to serve, Lord Vinny," Toby said, bowing and backing out of the kitchen and forcing Vicky to step out of his way.

Not that long ago, my biggest worry was Uncle Ted giving me a job. Now I was conspiring to commit murder for Brad, who had grossly misrepresented my job duties. I suppose all jobs had some hidden downers, but I didn't want to kill anyone.

Still, I was ready to do anything to make Brad happy. He had been cruel to me and lied to me, and maybe I should have taken that as a sign, but he was still the only vampire I knew, and I wanted to show him I was worthy. Maybe all vampires were coldblooded murderers. After all, we had to drink blood to survive.

I was also frightened of what Brad might do if I didn't kill for him. I mean, look what he did to me at the ceremony, and that was how he showed his approval. I went back and forth over these things in my mind, and I decided I had no choice. Even if I didn't kill this man, Brad would, or he would find someone else to do it for him.

The biggest problem I faced in planning my first assassination was my poor driving skills. I didn't drive that often, and I sometimes did stupid things when I got nervous. Contemplating what I was about to do, I had long since moved from nervousness into anxiety. In the end, we decided Vicky would drive. She had the fastest car, a BMW M5, and she had taken a defensive driving course to lower her insurance rates.

With Vicky driving, I think Kyle and Margot wanted to help too. Despite her dislike of Brad and my mission, Margot offered to top off my blood supply, and Kyle lent me his gun. I was a little surprised Kyle owned a handgun, but then again, he listened to rap music.

An hour after dark, we arrived at the address Toby had given me. Vicky put the car in neutral and pulled on her emergency brake. "Are you sure you don't want me to go with you?"

I shook my head emphatically. "No, Toby was right, I'm the immortal one. I should be able to handle anything they throw at me." Yeah right, I could barely use the dishwasher.

I walked up to the front door, brushing my skirt and blouse to remove any wrinkles. I rang the doorbell, and after a few moments, an attractive, older brunette answered the door. I had no idea what I should do. I hadn't realized anyone else would be in the house. Would I have to kill her too, or could I somehow get her to leave?

The woman gave me a speculatively civil look. "Yes, can I help you?"

"Hi, I'm Sally, Kenny's girlfriend. Is Kenny home?"

The woman froze, and her face lost its expression and color. "You're Kenny Donahue's girlfriend?"

"Yes. Look, if he's not here, when you do see him, just tell him I'm going to keep the baby."

The color drained from the woman's face. "Maybe I should introduce myself. I'm Kenny's wife, Susan." As she said the words, she raised her hand, made a fist, and swung at me.

I put up my arms and waited for the inevitable impact of her fist, but none came.

She took a deep breath and lowered her arm. "I should hit you. I should knock your block off, but it wasn't your fault, was it? I can't hit a pregnant woman."

"Honestly, I had no idea he was married. I'm sorry, I'll just go."

Susan shook her head, and stood back from the door. "No, please, come in. I believe you. I knew Kenny had a wandering eye, but I never thought... Come in. I'll make you some tea, and you can tell me all about that cheating bastard. Then, I'll decide what I'm going to do to him."

"All right, thanks." Maybe if I played my cards right, I wouldn't have to kill Kenny after all. Maybe the wife would do it for me.

Susan Donahue led me into the kitchen and poured water into a white coffee maker with "Tea" written on the front in black magic marker. "I actually expected Kenny home by now. He's having some trouble with his business partner, Brad."

"Brad? Brad Featherstone?" I had a sinking feeling.

"Yeah, do you know him?"

"I think I may have met him in passing."

"You'd remember him. He's a real dickhead."

"Yes, that would be Brad."

I decided to steer the conversation away from Brad. Dickhead or not, he was my master, and I had committed myself to him. "I'm surprised you aren't saying the same things about Kenny after what he said about you."

"What has he been saying?"

"He told me you were separated, and you were the one sleeping around. In fact, when you opened the door, I thought maybe he'd hired a housekeeper. We even ran into Brad once when we were out on a date, and he told Brad you were cheating on him."

Susan got up from the table, and she stood in front of the sink, staring out the window into the darkness. "Maybe I should leave, just go and never come back."

"Look, don't make any harsh decisions. Maybe you could just get away for a few days, stay with some friends or family. Go somewhere where he can't find you. Get your head clear." I walked up behind her and put my hand on her shoulder.

She turned to face me. "But what about you, Sally? What about you and your baby, his baby?"

"I'll get by somehow... I guess I'll get a job or something."

She shook her head. "A young, single mother, on your own. You'd never..." She closed her eyes and seemed lost in thought for a moment. I really wished she would leave before I had to kill her. "Maybe we could raise the baby together. You can get child support, and I will sue for alimony. We can get a place together, and I'll help you take care of the baby. What do you say?"

"I... I... I'll do it." Anything to get her to leave.

She grabbed me and pulled me tight.

"...but for now," I added, "you should get out of here. Seriously, go clear your head, just like we talked about. Give me your cell number, and I'll call you in a couple of weeks."

"Are you sure you will be okay?"

I nodded and patted my lower abdomen. "The baby's not going anywhere. It's not even showing yet. Take care of yourself right now. We have months to make plans.

"Alright, I'll go pack a bag."

"No!" I needed her out of here now. "Don't pack a bag. Buy yourself new clothes. Take the credit card. He'll end up with the debt."

"You're right." She gave me another hug. "What are you going to do when I'm gone?"

"Well, first, I'll have to tell him I'm going to have the baby."

"Are you sure you want to do that by yourself?"

"I'm sure. This needs to be about the child, not about infidelity."

"Okay, but you call me soon, all right?"

"I promise," I said, trying to make my lie sound genuine. Why could I casually consider killing this woman's husband, but lying to her was making me feel guilty?

"Are you sure—"

"Go. Now. Get out of here."

"Okay. I will. Call me."

She gave me one more look as she walked away. A moment later, I heard a car start in the attached garage. I took a moment to relax—I wouldn't have to kill the wife.

Then I turned off all the lights and headed upstairs. I had to forget about Susan and focus on killing her husband.

I looked through the Donahues' clothing, finally selecting a black lace bra and panty set and a see-through nighty. I turned off the light and lay down in the bed. Now, all I had to do was wait for Kenny to come home.

Over an hour later, I heard footsteps downstairs, along with the sounds of car keys being dropped on a table and boots dropping to the floor. Then came a creak on the stair. As he walked into the bedroom, I could follow his movement by the sound of his heart beating.

"You awake?" he asked.

"No," I mumbled, trying to make my voice sound like his wife's, but disguised by sleepiness.

"That bastard Brad, he wants me to let those garages go for nothing, after I've been maintaining them and repairing them out of my own pocket. He even threatened me. He said that if I sold now, he'd keep me on as an on-site manager with a salary, but if I refused I 'would not like what happened.' What does he mean by that?"

I assumed the question was rhetorical, and kept my mouth shut, as I listened to Kenny walk around the room, getting ready for bed. I heard a heavy belt buckle clunk as it hit the floor, followed by a pair of pants. A moment later, he slid into the bed and his arm reached around me, running his hands down my body, groping my fake breast. "Hey, you're wearing that sexy underwear I bought you for your birthday." Something poked me in the back— okay, time to stop acting.

I rolled over and bit into his neck before he had time to see my face. I drank just enough to weaken him, so he would be in my control. "Kenneth Donahue," I said, reciting the words Brad had sent me, "by the order of Brad Featherstone, Master of Omaha, you are sentenced to death."

He made a couple futile attempts at escaping, and then he looked me in the eyes. "Please," he said. "Please don't do this. What do you want? I'll sell the garages. I'll give them to Brad. For God's sake. Please let me go."

"I'm sorry," I said, and I realized I really meant it. I didn't want to kill this man so Brad could add a handful of storage garages to his empire. But, I had sworn fealty to Brad, and even if I hadn't, I had shown this man my true nature, drinking his blood. I couldn't tell him to run, he would just come back, begging to be my ghoul. "There's nothing I can do."

I struck, and drained Kenneth Donahue to the point of death. Fear and adrenaline tinged the sweet ambrosia of his blood. His heart started to slow, and then he closed his eyes, never to open them again. I had killed my first human.

I rolled off from him and lay on the bed, staring at the ceiling. What had I become? I was now truly a monster, a dead thing that murders innocent men in the night, and I had Brad to thank for my transformation. What a dick.

I checked Kenny's pulse after I finished dressing. There was none. I pulled out my cell and called Vicky. "It's done. I'll be out in a minute."

"Are you okay?" she asked, an edge of concern in her voice.

"Not really, but I don't want to talk about it. Right now, I just want to get out of this house." I hung up the phone without waiting for her response. I calmly walked out the front door, making sure it locked behind me and rejoined Vicky in her car.

"Home?" Vicky asked.

"No, I want to talk to Brad. Take me to the cleaners."

Vicky drove in silence, only occasionally glancing sideways at me. I ignored her. I was too busy trying to think about what I would say to Brad. I knew I had to say something, but I was also nervous about pissing him off.

Vicky had no trouble finding parking in front of Featherstone Dry Cleaning at one in the morning. They had only turned on minimal lighting in the lobby and when I looked through the front window of the store, I could see Toby's face illuminated in the light of his little television.

Vicky opened her door and I reached over to grab her arm. "I want you to stay in the car. If anything happens to me..." I thought about what Brad had told me regarding the link between a Prima and her vampire. "Well, you should know if something happens to me. Don't come in to save me. Just go home. This might get ugly and I don't want you to get hurt."

"Don't pull any macho crap on me. I'm your Prima, and I'm your girl, Vinny. Don't you dare order me to stay in the car, not for this."

"Sure." She wasn't going to take no for an answer, and this was not the time to start an argument. Besides, if what I'd been told was right, if Brad decided to kill me tonight, Vicky might not survive anyway. I might as well give her the chance to fight by my side.

We got out of the car and walked into the lobby of the dry cleaners. The closing door jingled a little bell. Toby looked up and gave us a smile of recognition. "You're just in time," he said, pointing to his television. "They spray paint the guy's bald spot. He looks ridiculous."

"Yes, he does look ridiculous," I agreed, politically avoiding mention of Toby's hemispherical combover, which to get any longer, would necessitate growing an epic beard. "Say, Toby, is the master in? Can I go back and see him?"

I expected Toby to maybe pick up the phone and call Brad for permission, but he seemed too entranced with the head spraying to bother. "Sure, knock yourself out," he said without taking his eyes from the screen.

I pushed through the curtain that separated the lobby from the racks of clothing with Vicky on my heels, and stopped. The room was even darker than the last time we were here. The dim bulbs of two overhead lights did more to cast odd shadows than reveal the path in front of us. "Put your hand on my shoulder," I whispered to Vicky. "My night vision is better than yours."

I crept forward, moving by memory and touch more than sight, the reflections bouncing off the garment bags trying to trigger my vestigial fight-or-flight response. I reminded myself I was the big, bad vampire, the toughest predator nature had ever produced. Well, maybe the killer whale and the Komodo dragon were tougher, but vampires had to be easily in the top ten. After what seemed like three times the distance we had travelled on our previous visits, I put my foot over the edge of an abyss and fell.

I didn't fall far, just a couple feet, and then I did a face-plant into the far wall. Vicky, still gripping my shoulder had landed on top of me. I had found the open stairwell. I barely managed to stop us from rolling down the stone steps. "That's got to be illegal. I'm sure they have to have a rail or something." I whispered to her.

"I can call OSHA tomorrow," she whispered back.

"Don't bother. Brad will just order me to kill OSHA."

Through a series of intricate maneuvers, made easier by the familiarity with each other's bodies, we managed to stand up without falling down the stairs. Down the stairway, I could see flickering light and hear voices, like Brad had a visitor. I considered giving up my mission then and there. It seemed rude to interrupt. I grabbed Vicky's hand and started heading up the stairs.

Vicky gripped my arm. "You're going the wrong way."

"I heard voices down there. I think Brad has company."

"Listen again."

I listened intently and heard music playing. "I recognize that tune."

"Brad's watching Baywatch re-runs. I'm sure it's okay to interrupt that."

"Yeah, I guess so."

I turned again and headed down the stairway. We had been immersed in darkness so long, I could clearly make out the steps and landing from what I now knew to be the flickering of the television.

We entered Brad's throne room, and I found Brad sitting in his throne with his back to the door. A far wall, which had been covered in black curtains during our previous visits had been drawn back to reveal a TV that must have had a seventy inch diagonal.

"Woah," I said, walking forward. "Is that the new Sony?" On the screen, a pair of spandex covered breasts bounced as big as truck tires. I turned to look at Brad and immediately regretted my decision. He was... enjoying himself. His pants were undone, and his hand had disappeared inside. Apparently, our appearance had not been enough to dissuade him from his planned evening activities.

"Do you have something to say to your master?" Brad asked.

"Yes, but first, would you mind zipping up your pants, I mean really. You must have a hundred ghouls begging for a chance to do that."

"True, but they are all at the ranch. Only Toby is here. If my self-pleasure bothers you so much, I could call for him."

I held up my hands in a dual stop gesture. "No!"

Brad sighed, removed his hand from his pants, and zipped up. "Very well, what do you want, prefect?"

I'd been put a little off my stride by the big TV, the Goodyear breasts, and the auto stimulation. Still, I needed to call out Brad on the shit he pulled tonight. I took a deep breath, and let him have it. "You set me up tonight. You made me kill a guy because you didn't like the deal he was giving you on some lousy storage garages."

Brad shook his head. "I'm offended by that accusation. They're not lousy at all. I have exterminators come by regularly to spray them against such an infestation."

"Look," I said, trying to steer back on topic, "you did something really nasty to me. I thought I was helping you protect our kind, not making you a quick buck."

Brad nodded. "Yes, I did set you up, and I did make you kill unnecessarily, although why you care about something so trivial as human life is beyond me, but I did it for a good reason. I needed to know if I could trust you with important things."

"So you're saying that murdering Kenny was all about some stupid test? Is that supposed to make me feel better? You can't just have people killed because you don't like them."

"Ah, but I can. I did. And you helped me. How you feel about it is unimportant. I am telling you the truth. Do you really think I became over a century old by being soft? By respecting the rights of the lowly humans? If you want to see your century mark, you will have to be ruthless. Now, unless you have further questions, be gone so I may finish stroking one out."

"Um, Vicky, let's go." Without looking back, I strode to the door, stopping before I climbed the stairs to take Vicky's hand. When I heard Brad's zipper, I practically pulled her out of the room behind me.

I arrived home that night feeling awful. All I wanted was to be left alone, but several members of Reverend Billy's flock were there, waiting to feed. I drank gallons of blood, and by the time I was done, I felt awful. I was a murderer, and I had a horrible tummy ache. I dropped to my bed and slept like the dead.

Where Vinny goes on another outing

When I woke up, I got the feeling I wasn't in my own bed. I opened my eyes and saw an unfamiliar ceiling fan. I sat up and looked around the room. The bed was sitting on a gigantic area rug reaching nearly to the pine-paneled walls. There was a stocked bookshelf, as well as a conversation nook with a table, two chairs, and a television in a discrete corner. A cedar chest was pushed against one wall. Other than a lack of windows, the room reminded me of a hotel room, only slightly homier.

Kyle snored lightly at the foot of the bed, also sleeping in his clothes. I kicked at the bedding until I had a free foot, and poked him with my toe.

Kyle yawned and rubbed his eyes. "Dude, you're up."

"What's going on? Where are we?"

"You're in the guest room at Brad's ranch. The cops came to the house last night. One of Kenny's neighbors called the cops because of 'suspicious activity,' and they described a blonde woman in a car the same model as Vicky's. So when they found Kenny's body, they went around to question everyone with that car and hair color. When we saw the cops coming up to the door, we freaked out, threw you in Vicky's cedar chest and took you out the back. We strapped you to the top of the jeep and called Toby for a place to lie low. He directed us here."

"Why didn't you wake me up? If the police have Vicky, we have to save her." I jumped out of the bed, got my foot tangled in the bedding, and went down hard on the—thankfully lush—area rug. It still hurt. "Ow."

"Dude, chill. Everything's cool. The cops just asked Vicky a couple questions. And as far as being able to wake you up, dude, you were dead to the world," Kyle explained as I picked myself up and sat down on the edge of the bed. "I think you might have some kind of vampire sleeping sickness, like Nosferlepsy."

I rolled my eyes. "How long have you been waiting to use that one?"

"I thought it up on the way over, so about four hours. Would you have preferred Vampersleepy?"

While Kyle's joke might have been lame, it did advance a troubling idea. Could vampires get vampire specific diseases? "I wonder if Brad knows a vampire doctor."

Someone knocked on the door.

"Come in," I answered.

The door opened, and Margot stepped through. I could tell by her clothes she had left the house in a hurry. Margot never went anywhere unless she was elegantly dressed, and her current outfit looked thrown together. "You're up. Thank God." She ran over and started kissing me. "I was so worried about you. You were totally out of it," she said between kisses. Through Margot's onslaught, I became aware of another woman standing in the doorway. "Um, hello," I said.

The woman entered the room and flashed me a plastic smile. "Good evening, Lord Vinny. Welcome to the ranch." Attired in a knee-length skirt suit, she wore her dark brown hair short. She strode forward as if she was going to offer me her hand, but when Margot refused to let go of me, she continued. "I am Abby, Master Brad's business manager. The sun has gone down, so would you like the standard tour while you're here?"

"Sure. That would be nice, since I'm responsible for protecting Brad's interests."

Abby raised an eyebrow. "Really? Is that what Master Brad told you?"

I nodded. "Yes..."

She pursed her lips. "Interesting. Well, let's start with the barn." She took a few steps backwards, motioning to us like a tour guide. "Please, follow me." She turned around when she reached the door and led us down a flight of stairs. "The main house was standing on the property when Brad bought it in 1938. Since that time, it has been renovated and expanded twice, to serve as Brad's headquarters and provide lodging for visiting dignitaries. The Master of the United States, L'Isle Belmonte, has stayed here twice."

At the bottom of the stairs, she opened a door and stepped outside, motioning for us to follow. "Because Lord Brad does not keep cattle," she said, leading us across a large, gravel driveway, "we have converted the main barn into a telemarketing center." As she approached the building, I saw that a glass and steel entryway had replaced the traditional barn doors. She led us through that entryway and into a modern looking room packed with tables and telephones. A few people were still working.

"This is the heart of Brad's fiscal operation. Every day, fifty ghouls come here to sell everything from auto insurance to long distance. Currently, we've been contracted to do overflow work from Calltelestar Peopleconnect in Des Moines."

"What are those people doing here so late? Overtime?"

"Every month, we have a contest to see who can make the most sales. The winner gets to feed Master Brad. These are the frontrunners, afraid to leave their posts lest their competition moves ahead. One of the changes I made since taking over management of the operation was implementing a mandatory four-hour break per day. We can't have our best salespeople working themselves to death."

After Abby gave us a rundown of modern telemarketing, snore, she took us to a stable with a bunch of horse stuff, which she called the "tack room." Margot seemed especially interested in all the equipment, examining this thingy and that thingy—I don't know what horse thingys are called.

"Does Brad enjoy riding?" I asked, running my hand over the worn leather of a saddle and wondering if this was a side of Brad I hadn't seen before, having never seen him outside the dry cleaners.

"Oh, no. The master keeps to himself. He never leaves his underground lair, and only sends to the farm for ghouls when he absolutely needs blood. I've only met him three times myself. I try to encourage him to be a little more hands-on, especially with the ghouls basically worshiping him and all, but he doesn't really care to, and ultimately, he's the boss, so it's his choice."

"If you don't mind my saying so, you don't sound much like the other ghouls I've spoken to."

Abby let out a short, sharp laugh. "I should hope not. I'm no ghoul. Brad recruited me away from a major consulting firm. I have a MBA from the University of Nebraska, Omaha."

"And you don't find this all a little..."

"Odd?" She shrugged. "I suppose, but you should try to work in corporate for a while. Compared to some of the people I used to work with, Brad is the ideal boss."

"So you have no trouble working for a vampire?" I wondered why Brad didn't just bite her so he wouldn't have to pay her as much. Maybe he just hadn't gotten around to it yet—too busy skulking in his basement.

"Of course not. I'm a professional. That would be discrimination." She motioned for us to follow, stepping through the tack room door into the main stable. "This is, of course, where we keep our horses." I passed through the door and was amazed to find several stalls empty.

"So, where are the horses?" asked Margot, pointing out the elephant in the room, which was not so much an elephant, but a lack of horses.

"They're probably out on patrol," Abby answered matter-of-factly. "Master Brad has several enemies in the human and vampire world, and he is very security conscious. We keep a rotation of mounted gunman circling the ranch. The evening crew is probably out relieving the afternoon shift."

We exited the building and stood in the gravel drive. "So," said Abby, "do you have any other questions?"

I nodded. "Yes." I pointed to a big steel building with a rounded top. "We haven't seen in there yet."

"Oh, there's nothing in there, just some old farming equipment and storage."

"Could I take a quick look?"

"It's really greasy and messy in there. You'd ruin your clothes."

Kyle gave me a look. "Dude, this is way boring. Do you think they have a PlayStation?"

I shook my head. "I'm pretty sure they don't."

"I'm sorry," Abby said. "Most of our guests are centuries-old vampires, not big video game players." As she talked, she led us over to Kyle's Jeep. "Well, I hope you found the tour interesting. I'm sure you'll be wanting to get home."

"Yeah, sure." I might not be the greatest person in the world at taking a hint, but I could tell Abby had dismissed us.

As Kyle drove us home that night, I contemplated Brad's operation. Seeing the ranch had only gone further to confirm Brad used up other people according to his whims and paranoia. I regretted putting myself in the position of prefect, and I feared for my ghouls.

As soon as I walked in the door, Vicky was in my arms. "I was worried about you," I said.

"I was worried about you too."

We held each other for a moment, but then I pushed her away to arm's length. "What did the police say, are you in trouble?"

"No, they were grasping at straws. A neighbor on neighborhood watch duty pegged our behavior as suspicious. When the police showed up and found one missing and one dead, they started to think she might be on to something. She didn't get my plates though, and I don't think they can do anything without more evidence."

"Cool." I kissed her on the lips. "Now, let's order some pizza."

We settled in front of the TV with some beers and waited for the pizza. Vicky snuggled up to my left side and Kyle snuggled up to my right. I was getting more used to Kyle being affectionate, but it still creeped me out a bit. Margot sat in a recliner across the room as if she didn't care about touching me, but occasionally, I caught her looking at me.

A woman I didn't know, one of Reverend Billy's crowd, was curled up at my feet. I felt like I should say something. "Hello there."

"Greetings, Lord Vinny. My name is Jody, and I gladly make my body a gift to you."

I nodded. "Sure. Sure. That's great. I've noticed Reverend Billy hasn't been coming around much lately." In fact, I hadn't seen him for a week, not since the ceremony.

"He's been under the weather. That's why I got to fill in. Cool, huh?"

"Yeah, great. He have a virus or something?"

"I guess. I'm not a doctor."

To fill the time, we chatted about the ranch and Vicky's run-in with the police. After a half hour, the phone rang. "We should probably get that," I said, "The pizza guy's probably lost."

Vicky got up off the couch to get the phone, and Margot sauntered across the room and dropped into her spot. Vicky gave her a nasty look as she picked up the phone. When she heard the voice on the other end of the phone, her smile faded. "Yes. He's here." She handed me the phone.

"Yeah?"

"I have another task for you, prefect," Brad said from the other side of the line. "Come to the cleaners tomorrow night and we will discuss your assignment." He hung up.

I sighed. There was no way I'd be able to enjoy the pizza now. The thought of the next atrocity Brad would ask me to commit had ruined my appetite.

The next night, Kyle and I went to the dry cleaners. Vicky had wanted to take me, but I insisted she stay home until the police had long forgotten about her possible involvement with a homicide. The night air was prematurely crisp, and it reminded me the fall would be here any day, and my sister would be going off to school. Her life was moving forward.

"I need to go visit Jenny a few times before she goes away to school," I said aloud.

"Yeah. She used to be just this little brat that would bother us while we were playing PlayStation," said Kyle, "and now she's turning into quite a hotty."

"Don't even go there. I don't want to think of my little sister as being attractive."

"Change is inevitable though. We don't have to like it, but the only other choice is death. I mean she's going away to school, and even if she hasn't been sexually active yet—"

"Kyle?"

"Yeah, dude."

"Never speak of my sister again."

"Yes, dude."

The rest of the trip was spent in awkward silence. I tried to think about Brad, and how he had made me kill a man, a much nicer topic than the possibility of my sister banging a frat boy.

We pulled up in front of the cleaners a mere half-hour after sunset, the earliest possible time I could arrive without wearing several layers of clothing. The dry cleaners was lit for business, but as we walked up to the front door, I didn't see Toby in his accustomed place. A sign on the counter read, "Back in 5 Minutes." I waited at the counter, wondering what nefarious deeds Brad and Toby were planning. Then, I heard a toilet flush.

Toby walked into the room, refusing to make eye contact. He returned to his regular chair and turned around as if just noticing us. "He's waiting for you. Go on back."

This time, all the lights were on in the back room, although it was still surprisingly dim. We made our way to the back staircase and descended into Brad's lair. As per usual, he sat on his gold-painted throne. Fortunately, his pants were done up. He examined us for a moment and then spoke. "Welcome prefect and ghoul. You have a lot to do tonight, so I will get straight to the point. There is an artifact in this city, a small carving of a bat. It is very valuable to the Nosferatu, rumored to have belonged to Vlad

Dracula. It has been taken by a powerful man, stolen from another of our kind, and we cannot allow it to stay in the hands of a human."

I could see where this was going. "As your prefect, am I going to have to do shit like this all the time?"

Brad didn't move for a moment, other than to blink. "This is not 'shit.' This is a very important task. This is the work of a prefect. Just like the paperwork, which must be taken care of, so must this item be returned to us." He held out a folder. "I engaged a private detective. He tells me the man who has the artifact is attending the opera tonight. He also managed to obtain the combination for the man's safe. Go to his house and steal back the artifact."

"I'm going to do this," I said, as I took the folder, "but after this, I want you to slow down with these missions."

I had expected many things from Brad but not a look of incomprehension. "I don't understand. Why? It is an honor to work for your master."

"I just need some time to think. This has all been moving really fast. I need you to back off."

Brad smiled. "And what will you do if I don't 'back off?' " he said, his voice filled with contempt. "You are a true twenty-first century vampire, a soft, weak-willed boy with no stomach for killing."

"Honestly, I don't know what I'll do. But when I figure it out, it will suck for you."

He laughed at me. He laughed so hard and long, I thought he might damage something. "Well, now I'm scared," he said in a sarcastic tone. Then he went back to laughing at me. He nearly fell out of his throne. "Now, get out of here, and do your job."

"Come on, Kyle. Let's get out of here."

Perhaps some people, people smarter than me, would have forgotten about Brad's mission and gone home. Even with Brad laughing in my face, I was worried about my obligation to him. I had sworn some kind of oath, and

I was kind of afraid some kind of vampire police would come and arrest me, kind of.

Kyle stopped the Jeep. "I think that's the house over there," he said, pointing at a house which wasn't as physically large as Vicky's wannabe mansion, but of a nice size. It had the kind of finishing touches that told you the person inside had style, sophistication, and a stack of cash to put those things to work. I particularly liked the heavy stones that covered the outside of the house. A picture in the folder told me I was looking at the right house. "Dude, I think Warren Buffet lives in this neighborhood."

"The guy who sings all the beach songs? He lives in Omaha?"

"Never mind, dude."

After studying the house's layout, I folded it up and slid it into my pocket. Under it was a page marked, "alarm code," which Brad had neglected to mention. "So, Kyle, pull around the block, so we don't get into a neighborhood watch situation again, and I'll go get that thingy Brad wants."

"No, dude, let me go."

I put my hand on his shoulder. "Don't worry about me. I'll be fine. Immortal, remember?"

"Okay, but take this." He reached into the back seat and pulled a black hoodie off the floor. It was filthy and smelled of mold.

"I'm not going to wear that." I had worn my vintage Atari shirt, and I didn't want it to get dirty from the hoodie. Wearing a favorite shirt to go housebreaking was probably a stupid thing to do, but hindsight's 20/20.

"There's bound to be lots of people with security in this neighborhood. Some of them might have cameras."

I sighed. "Fine."

Kyle pulled around the block and parked, and after I assured him everything would be fine, I pulled the filthy hoodie over my beloved Atari shirt. I ran through backyards until I found the home I was looking for. Then, I did something really cool and vampirey. I climbed the outside of the house, using the stone blocks as handholds. I didn't stick to the wall, like vampires do in the movies, but I managed not to hurt myself. On the second floor, I slid open a window and gracefully flung myself through. However, on the way through, I knocked over a little table, which held a vase. I landed on the vase, and it shattered under my weight. I felt ceramic shards dig in my butt.

I would have liked to have a moment to recover, but then I realized I could hear a very insistent beeping noise from somewhere in the house. I had forgotten about the alarm. I knew the general location of the security panel, based on my examination of the floor plan, so I limped off in that direction, down the stairs, through the dining room, and into the kitchen. I tripped over a bowl of dog food and planted face first into the hardwood floor.

I scrambled to my feet. The panel showed a countdown with ten seconds left on it. I carefully took out the alarm code and typed it. When I was done, I pressed enter, and just like in the movies, the countdown stopped at one second. I stood for a moment to mentally recollect myself and pull some of the ceramic shards from my ass. I shook my head and walked back upstairs to the safe, with my pant-leg covered in dog food and my ass full of vase shards. This was not going to be a high point in my vampire career.

The safe was in a well-appointed study, filled with overstuffed leather chairs and polished mahogany furniture. A faint cigar smell hung in the air. The wall safe was a tiny model maybe six inches high and a little over a foot wide. I put in the combination and opened it.

After pawing over the contents, the first thing that struck me was the item Brad had sent me to find wasn't in the safe. The second thing that struck me was a Rottweiler. The big dog jumped, sinking its teeth into my forearm. Here's an interesting fact I looked up later: if you read a story about a human being killed by a dog, there's a good chance that dog is going to be a Rottweiler. I know some people, animal lovers, may judge me for what happened next, but in my defense, it was more caused by vampiric reflexes than anything else.

Sinking my fangs into the dog, I sucked every drop of blood from his body. I don't suggest it. It was really gross.

I dropped the Rottweiler's body to the ground. I took two steps back, still in shock from both my actions and the damage done by the dog, and spit out a tuft of fur. After a moment, I looked around the office and found some facial tissues. I wrapped a tissue around my tongue and tried to scrape off the doggy taste. It did not help.

I walked over to the window I had entered through and dived through, putting out my hand to catch the sill and flip around on the way out. I missed and fell, face planting into a landscaping block. When I had straightened my squashed nose, I jogged back to Kyle's Jeep.

"Jesus, dude, what happened to you?" Kyle said as I was getting into the Jeep. "Your arm's bleeding."

I snapped my fingers. "Phone."

Without another word, Kyle took his phone from his pocket and put it in my hand. I dialed the number for Featherstone Dry Cleaning.

Toby answered the phone. "Featherstone—"

"Put Brad on the phone. Now!"

After a moment, the phone clicked. "Yes," Brad said in a bored voice.

"First, your information is fucked up. That guy had a big ass dog, which bit me. Second, there is nothing in that safe. And third, fuck you, Brad."

I heard Brad sigh. "Look, you had a bad night, and you're a little upset. I understand. Just grab everything out of the safe and bring it to me. Maybe there will be something useful."

"So, what? You just want me to rip this guy off?"

"No, I'm looking for an artifact. If it is not in the safe, perhaps something in the safe leads to it or will give me some leverage against him. I'm not 'ripping him off.' Understand?"

"Yeah, I guess." I still wasn't very convinced, but I wanted to give Brad the benefit of the doubt. After all, he was my master, and I wanted to believe he was really a good guy under it all. In all likelihood, I would have to put up with him for a long time.

"Now, collect what is in the safe and come to the shop. I will be waiting for you." He hung up.

I handed the phone back to Kyle. "I need a bag or something. He wants me to scoop up everything in the safe." Kyle had a large collection of fast food wrappers in his back seat. I looked through them and found a bag from a Chinese takeout. There were still a couple of fortune cookies in it, so I tossed them back into the pile with the rest of the garbage.

"Dude, I was going to eat those." Kyle reached into the back seat for his cookies.

"Um, enjoy. I'll be right back," I said as I left the Jeep. I ran through the backyards again and scaled the side of the wall. I had left the safe open, and I started scooping out the contents.

"What did you do to my dog?" said a voice behind me. I turned, and in the doorway of the office stood a portly man wearing a tuxedo. He had a gun in his hand. He wasn't really aiming it, but we weren't exactly that far apart.

"Would you believe he's sleeping?"

The man's finger tensed, and the pistol cracked. "I'm sorry. I forgot my opera glasses," he said in way of an explanation.

Being shot is an interesting experience. I actually prefer it to disemboweling, but that's about all I can say for it. At first I felt like I'd been hit with a hammer, and for a second, it didn't hurt at all, as if my body was trying to register what had happened. Then I felt a burning sensation, like someone had stuck a hot coal in the wound.

"Ow." I grabbed the last of the stuff from the safe and rushed him. He shot me again at close range before I could push past him. Kyle would later tell me the guy must have had a small-caliber pistol, or it would have knocked me on my ass.

I'd been shot in the hip and in my left arm—a long way from my heart, as my father would have said, but it still burned like acid every time I took a step. I jumped through the window, somehow managed to miss the stone retaining wall, and landed face-first in the soft dirt, which I actually found kind of refreshing. I waited there a moment in the thick lawn, until I heard a thud and a spray of dirt spewed up not far from my head. Vampire or not, I didn't want to find out if I could recover from a headshot. As I was running away from the house, one more round hit me in the butt.

I limped through the backyards, not able to move as fast as I would have liked, trying to put trees and sheds between me and the irate man with the gun. I heard a crack behind me, and an evergreen tree just off to my right shook with impact. I didn't even have time to panic. All I could do was focus on escape. Kyle's Jeep was just ahead of me, and I could see Kyle watching my chase with interest.

"Come back here, dog killer," the man yelled, taking another shot for emphasis. The driver's side rear window shattered.

I didn't bother to run around the Jeep. The back driver's side door was closer, so I yanked it open and jumped in.

"Dude, you're getting blood on my seats."

"Drive!"

Kyle started the Jeep and put his foot down, squealing all four tires as we pulled away.

After a few blocks of frantic driving, Kyle slowed to the speed limit. "Where are we going now?"

I checked to make sure I still had the take-out bag filled with the contents of the safe. It was still clutched in my hand. "We need to take this stuff to Brad."

"Oh great, I love visiting Brad. It always goes so well."

"Please, no sarcasm. I'm not feeling well. I've been shot a few times. And my Atari shirt is full of holes and covered in blood. I knew I should have worn another shirt."

"Sorry, dude. We can probably find another one on eBay."

"It just wouldn't be the same."

"Yeah, I know." Kyle drove in silence the rest of the way to the dry cleaners. I assume it was out of respect for my Atari shirt, but he might have just run out of things to say.

When I walked in, I didn't even talk to Toby. I just walked past him, into the warehouse. I descended the stairs in back and held up the bag filled with the safe's contents.

Brad looked down at me from his gold-painted throne. "What took you so long?"

"You're going to complain about my timing? I've been shot."

"I noticed. You're dripping on my floor."

"Well, excuse me. The guy with the dog came home, and in addition to the dog, he had a gun. That wasn't in the folder either."

Brad shrugged. "It shouldn't have been important. He was supposed to be away. Sorry about that."

"Just take your stuff so I can go home."

Brad reached down and took the take-out bag. He riffled through it for a few moments. "Why does it smell like old Chinese food?"

"That's what originally came in the bag."

Brad nodded and continued to look through the contents. After a moment, he looked up. "You may go. Return to your home and await further instructions."

I did an about face and left the cleaners as quickly as I could. When we were back in the Jeep, Kyle asked, "So, is that it for the night?"

I shook my head. "No. I'm going to get cleaned up, and after I get some blood in me, we're going to the ranch. I think that Abby girl was hiding something in that big, metal building. She was really nervous when I wanted to take a look at it. There must be something in there Brad doesn't want me to see."

Where Vinny's investigation of the ranch yields a surprising result

I gathered my available minions in the kitchen. All of our church members were out for some reason, so it was just Kyle, Vicky, and Margot. I wondered if Reverend Billy knew his flock representative was MIA. Then again, I hadn't seen Billy around much lately.

Margot made coffee, and Kyle put out a little plate of sandwich cookies, the generic kind with chocolate on one side and vanilla on the other. I drank from Vicky's neck, and as her blood healed my body, the lead slugs popped out. I lined them up in a little row on the table.

After eating a cookie, Kyle picked up one of the slugs and examined it. "Yeah, dude. This looks like a .22 to me. If the guy had been packing a .38 or a 9mm, you might have been in some trouble."

I took one last lick at Vicky's neck to seal the wound and shook my head. I didn't get the whole Kyle-as-a-gun-nut thing. "Well, I guess we can be glad he wasn't."

Margot brought the coffee cups to the table, two in each hand. "So, why did you call us together, boss?"

"Well, as we all know, taking the position of Brad's prefect is not turning out as advertised—"

"No crap, dude."

"Thank you, Kyle," I said. "So I think we should find out more about what goes on at his ranch."

Kyle volunteered immediately. "I'm totally in," he said, but even as he said it, I doubted he was the right one for the job. He was exhausted and coming down from the adrenaline boost caused by the night's gunfire. I noticed a slight slur to his words, and he could barely keep his eyes open.

I shook my head. "No, Kyle. You've been through a lot tonight. You need to get some rest, buddy."

"We can take my station wagon," Margot offered.

"Okay," I said, wishing Margot didn't drive a station wagon. Because I still look like a teenager, I couldn't help think that riding with Margot would make me look like a kid being driven around by his mom.

"I'll go get changed," Margot said. She looked over my bloody Atari shirt. "You might want to put on some different clothes as well."

"Yeah, you're probably right." I descended to my basement room, and peeled off my bloody clothes. As I used my ruined Atari shirt to wipe off the blood, I examined my body in the mirror. The bullet holes had mostly healed, leaving only bright, pink scars, which would probably clear up in a couple of days. I pulled on a t-shirt and a fresh pair of blue jeans before returning to the kitchen.

I expected to wait for Margot while she got ready, but she was waiting for me, wearing rugged outdoor clothing and heavy boots that looked like they had been well-used. "About time," she said. "Were you busy gazing at yourself in the mirror?"

"Wow, where'd you get those cool clothes?"

"Africa," she replied, as if it were no big deal.

"No, seriously."

"I am serious. I spent a year in Africa, tracking down rare birds for my doctorate. My thesis involved irregularities in sub-Saharan migratory patterns of songbirds."

"You're a doctor?"

"I have a PhD in ornithology. It was interesting, but poor preparation for a life as a vampire's minion."

I have to admit, I was a little awed. "You lived in Africa? Studying birds? Did you see lions and stuff?"

"Yes, but you know, Africa isn't as wild as most people think. I was more worried about warlords and slavers than I was about lions."

"So, compared to your experiences there, this trip to the ranch must seem a little tame."

"That's pretty much the size of it. Still, we are breaking into an armed compound of vampire fanatics, at night, no less. I'm thinking we'll get enough adrenaline in our systems." She actually seemed to be looking forward to the danger.

I was not so excited. "Um, yeah."

"All right. Let's go, boss."

"Sure."

Margot led me outside to a large SUV. "Here we go," she said, activating the keyless entry.

"I thought you owned a station wagon." I'm sure I had heard her mention it at least once.

"That's what we called Land Rovers in Africa. The affectation makes me nostalgic. These American models are a far cry from the junk heaps we used to drive there, but they're a lot more comfortable too."

I was beginning to have the creeping suspicion I had massively underestimated Margot. Vicky had told me she was a widow living off her husband's life insurance. No one had ever mentioned running from African warlords or having a PhD. I felt a little guilty I had been using this woman as my errand girl.

Still, that couldn't be helped now. I stepped up into the SUV and pulled myself into the leather seat. I tried to think about something to say to Margot to tell her I had found new appreciation of her experience and education. Finally, I said, "So, I guess you know a lot about birds."

"More than you could possibly imagine."

"Cool." I went back to not talking. I doubted I could say anything smart enough to impress Margot or even make her believe I felt sorry for making her run my errands.

After another ten minutes of uncomfortable silence, Margot said, "We're almost there." Before I could reply, she jerked the wheel, and we hit the curb hard enough for me to hit my head on the roof of the SUV. I looked out the window. We were driving through a cornfield.

"We're driving through a cornfield," I said.

"Well, we weren't going to pull into the driveway with all the lights on, were we?" I could hear the cornstalks scraping along the sides of the SUV, and the ripe ears banged on the side panels. The ride was bumpy enough my butt cheeks only occasionally made contact with the seat.

"Is this safe?" I asked.

"Probably not, but if we hit anything, this vehicle has an excellent safety rating. You probably want to buckle up," she said.

An especially big bump made me slide out of my seat, banging my chin on the dashboard. I pushed back and tried to buckle the seatbelt, but the locking mechanism kept jumping out of my hand. After groping around for it in the dark, I found the belt receptacle, and I pushed the buckle forward. Just before I got it to click, Margot slammed on the breaks, and I hit the dashboard again.

"We're here," she announced.

I pushed myself back into the seat. "We're where?" All I could see was trees and corn.

"We're in a wooded tree break I spotted from the road. It will be good camouflage for the station wagon. We need to walk the rest of the way in."

"Why?"

"Remember, the ranch has an equestrian patrol. They might take an interest in the largest vehicle in the county driving up their back acreage in the middle of the night."

"Yeah, I guess so." Actually, I didn't, but that's just because I had no idea what an equestrian was. Maybe they were one of those ancient people the Romans fought.

"So just stay low and follow my lead, got it, boss?"

I thought I heard a noise and I glanced away for a minute. "Um, yeah sure. I'm right behind you." I looked back, and Margot was already several yards ahead of me. I hurried to catch up.

Once we got past the trees, a large pasture separated us from our objective, the building to which Abby had denied us access. Fortunately, the area was overgrown with weeds and prairie grasses, so we had plenty of cover. There were thistles taller than me with spikes almost an inch long. Brad really should send some of his ghouls out here to dig them up. I mean, it wasn't like he was short on labor.

We'd crept about a hundred yards into the tall grasses when Margot disappeared from sight. "Down!" she hissed from somewhere on the ground.

"What?" I said.

Margot grabbed my ankle and pulled my feet from under me. I landed hard, and made an *oof* noise. Margot crawled on top of me and put her hand over my mouth. Something sharp dug into my junk, and I realized I had landed on one of the thistles.

A moment later, I heard the thump of hooves nearby, and the beam of a flashlight swept over us. As I lay there listening to my heart beating at almost human speeds, I thought we were busted for sure, but a moment later, the hoof beats receded into the distance. I rolled off the thistle.

Margot crawled up beside me. "I think they're gone now," she whispered in my ear. Then she kissed me full on the lips. "The adrenaline's pumping now, isn't it? I wish we had a little more time." She slid off of me and rose into a crouch. "We're clear, get up." She offered me her hand and pulled me to my feet.

We continued creeping towards the building, and I became aware of something happening inside the building. As we got closer, I started to see slivers of light showing around the door. Then I heard the slightly distorted edge of an amplified voice, like someone was speaking into a microphone. There also seemed to be music playing.

"There's something fucking weird going on in there," Margot said. "Are you sure you want to go through with this?"

"Yes. Brad's hiding something, and I want to find out what it is. I will not be his puppet." The tenacity of my words surprised me. I'd always been such an easygoing person.

We reached the end of the tall weeds, and stepped on to the gravel surrounding the outbuildings. A large outdoor floodlight provided light for the compound, and I felt very exposed. However, I continued to creep closer, and as we approached, the amplified voice became louder and clearer. Something about it sounded familiar. Was it Brad's voice? Toby's? I was sure I'd heard it before, but the music—organ music?—and slight distortion caused by the amplification was just enough to throw me off.

I cautiously approached a side door, and I could hear people singing along to the organ. I came to the sickening realization they were singing "Amazing Brad," to the melody of "Amazing Grace."

"T'was Brad that taught my heart to fear, and Brad my fear relieved," sang the people inside. I tried to tune out the song. Any more, and I was going to be sick.

"I think I'm going to be sick," whispered Margot.

"My thoughts exactly."

"Are you still going to go in?"

"How can I hear that and not look?"

I turned the handle of the side door and inched it open. In the center of the building stood row upon row of church pews, and they were full of people. I assumed they were Brad's ghouls. I leaned in and opened the door a little more and turned my head to where the ghouls were looking. I felt Margot's hand grab my shoulder and pull back, as if I were leaning too far into the room. Still, I had to see what was going on here. I pulled against her and peered around the door. What I saw in that building, I will never forget if I live a million years.

A large altar dominated the front of the building. Above the altar hung a portrait of Brad, five feet across and eight feet high. Below that portrait stood Reverend Billy, or at least I thought it must be Reverend Billy, though since I last saw him, his skin had turned bright blue. He presided over the gathering like a giant, evil Papa Smurf.

"Come, children of Brad," he said into his microphone. "Come and drink so that your master's enemies will be weakened." He gestured to a table off to the side. It was covered in red plastic party cups, and if Billy hadn't pointed it out, I would have dismissed it as a refreshments table. I recognized every single person that walked to the table. I might not know their names, but they had all come to our house. I had come to think of as my church members. They each drank from one of the cups.

Blue Reverend Billy raised his hands. "As you swallow the colloidal silver, it will mix with your blood, and any vampire who drinks from you will be weakened. You are

Brad's Holy Soldiers called to do battle. And remember, even though I have been afflicted, there is a very small chance the drink will turn you blue."

I couldn't believe what I was seeing. We had been totally taken in by these people. We had given them an open invitation to our house, and all the time they pretended to feed me, they were actually poisoning me. "You fuckers," I said, perhaps a little too loud.

From the pews in my near vicinity, a dozen faces whipped around to look at me. Oops. Other Brad worshipers noticed those ghouls' reaction and followed suit, causing a ripple effect across the congregation. The singing sputtered and died. The organ music stopped, and finally, Blue Reverend Billy turned to us.

Blue Reverend Billy lowered his arm to point at us. "Brad's enemies! Get them!"

Margot grabbed my collar and pulled me backwards through the door. "Run, dummy!" she yelled, and then she took off running through the pasture, not waiting to see if I was following. I followed.

I was a little worried running through the field at night. It was rough terrain, and I was worried Margot might fall and twist an ankle, but she had on sturdy boots, and we needed to keep moving. It was only matter of time before the armed guards figured what was going on.

"Down!" Margot yelled.

"What?" I said. I heard a series of booming noises, and a bullet tore through my back and exploded out of my chest in a spatter of gore. I looked back to see one of the men on horseback reloading his rifle. "That hurt, you bastard," I yelled at him.

Margot was already back on her feet. She pulled at my arm, and considering the amount of damage to my chest, I was kind of glad she didn't tear anything loose. "Come on."

We were about fifty feet from the SUV when the second barrage found us, knocking out two of Margot's driver's side windows. I shook my head. If we ever got out of this alive, some automotive glass place was going to make a killing. Maybe we could get a bulk discount.

I ran around to the passenger side and jumped in as fast as I could, knowing Margot was not going to wait for me to get situated. I slammed the seatbelt home just as she started the engine. She yanked the wheel and pressed the gas, and there was an uncomfortable moment when all four wheels spun in wet mud, then the big SUV leapt back into the cornfield, and this time, Margot didn't spare the suspension. If I still had fillings, I think they would have vibrated out of my head.

After five minutes of slamming back and forth in my seatbelt, we dropped into a shallow ditch. The big vehicle hit the far side and shot up onto the road. We were airborne for about three seconds, which felt like about an hour, and then the SUV landed awkwardly with the squealing of tires.

For a moment, I sat in stunned silence until the smell of burning rubber brought me back to the world. I looked over at Margot. She was standing on the brake pedal. She was white as a sheet, white as a vampire, and I wanted to say something to make her feel better. "I think we survived the landing," was all that came out of my mouth.

"You're bleeding on my seats."

"Yeah." It was true. I was bleeding quite a bit on her seats. The flow had subsided significantly, but I would need more blood if I wanted to recuperate entirely tonight. "It hasn't been a good night for getting shot."

"No shit," she said, putting the SUV into gear and driving away from our launch site. "And just think, I thought hanging out with you was going to be boring. I haven't had this much fun since I left Africa. Hey, want to go get a couple beers? We can go to that bar you and Kyle are always going to."

"I don't think that's a good idea," I said, putting two fingers in the gaping hole in my chest for emphasis.

"Oh, shit. I forgot about that. I can pull over and you can feed."

"I can wait until we get back to the house."

Margot grabbed my crotch. "You can wait, but I can't."

An hour later, I was fully healed and we were lying in the back of the SUV. I felt like I had experienced one of those classic teenager moments, which I didn't get because I had been such a geek and then I had been dead. I mentally imagined a little window popping up saying, "Achievement Unlocked: Sex in Car."

Margot's phone rang, and she looked at the screen. She passed it to me. "Vicky," she said. "Probably wants you."

"Hello," I said, taking the phone.

"You have to get home, right now," Vicky said.

"What's up?"

"The house is on fire."

For a moment, I didn't say anything. I was struggling to comprehend her words. "Can you say that again?"

"Our house is burning down. Someone covered the side of the house in gasoline and set it on fire." Her words were coming out fine, but there was an edge of hysteria to her voice. Through the phone, I could hear the approaching sirens. "I swear to God, if I find out who did this, I'll—"

"You'll have to stand in line. Vicky, we'll be there as soon as we can."

Before I could even look at Margot, she said, "What is it? You sound really spooked."

"Vicky says the house is on fire."

Margot and I started pulling on our clothes as fast as we could.

It was hard to see the smoke in the night air, but the smell hit me blocks away. It wasn't the clean smell of a fireplace, but more like it smelled when people burned garbage. We rounded the corner and the flash of emergency vehicle lights became visible along with the flicker of firelight. Then I caught sight of the house. Flames poured from the upper windows, even as firemen directed their hoses to them.

Margot pulled up at the edge of the zone marked off by the emergency vehicles. There weren't many onlookers, which made sense considering our semi-deserted neighborhood. Vicky and Kyle sat on the back bumper of an ambulance, watching the house burn. The EMTs had wrapped blankets around them, and they looked like disaster victims, which I guess they were, which I guess we all were now. I walked over and put my arms around Vicky. Margot followed behind me and put her hand on Kyle's shoulder.

Tears ran down Vicky's face. She whispered in my ear. "You need to stop this. You need to stop them."

"Who?" I asked, afraid I already knew the answer.

"After I called you, I saw Toby wandering around with a gas can. Kyle ran after him, but he ran off."

I took her hands. "Vicky, I want you to stay here. If you don't, they're going to be asking a lot of awkward questions later on, but I have to go take care of this Brad situation."

"What do you mean, 'take care of'?"

"I'm not sure," I admitted. "But I have to do something. This town's not big enough for the both of us." I really wished I hadn't said that, but it was the best I could come up with at the moment. It barely even worked as a metaphor—Omaha is quite big, and two people can live here a long time without running into each other. For instance, I've never met that Warren Buffet guy.

Vicky kissed me. "Oh my god, you're so sexy right now."

I put my hand on her shoulder and pushed back lightly. "I've got to go." I turned and slapped Kyle's arm. "You're with me, buddy. Bring your gun."

Kyle shrugged off the blanket and stood. "I'll be right back." He jogged over to his Jeep, which fortunately was parked on the street and not in the garage. He opened the passenger side door and slipped something out of the glove box.

Margot and I walked over to the Land Rover and I pulled myself into the front passenger seat. Margot slid into the driver's site beside me. "What did Vicky say?"

"It was Toby. He used gasoline." I didn't think I had to say anything more. Obviously, Reverend Billy must have called the dry cleaners to tell them about our discovery, so Brad sent Toby over to take care of us.

"That little fucker burned down our house?" she asked.

"I guess so."

"That little fucker burned down our house." This time, she said it like a pronouncement.

As I sat in the front seats of the Land Rover, waiting for Kyle to return with his gun, watching water and flame battle to consume our home, I felt a sense of powerlessness like never before. We had made so many memories in that house in such a short time. Somewhere in that house was PlayStation III with all my saved games. I wanted to be sick. I wanted to cry. But more than anything, a feeling was rising deep inside. I really wanted to kill Toby.

Kyle hopped into the back seat, waving his black pistol. "I'm ready to go."

I shot Kyle a glare. "Put that thing away, there are tons of people around."

Emergency vehicles had blocked the street, so Margot had to take the next street over to get back on the beltway. She backed up the SUV into the non-existent driveway of a neighbor, and drove around the block to the next street. The houses on this street hadn't even been framed, and poured basements gaped on either side of the street like a mouth full of sockets that had lost their teeth.

Then, I saw Toby. He stood on the sidewalk of the empty street. He held a gas can and was watching the fire from across one of the empty lots, completely mesmerized by the destruction he had started.

Apparently, Margot saw him too. "Little fucker burned down our house," said Margot. She pushed her foot to the floor and acceleration pushed me back in the seat.

"Margot—" I said.

"Little fucker burned down our house," She said, turning the Land Rover onto the sidewalk. Okay, Margot had gone to crazytown.

Enthralled by the fire, Toby didn't notice us until we were going 70 miles an hour and he was mere feet from our bumper. He had just a moment to register surprise before the Range Rover hit him. I had expected him to go under the wheels, making horrible *thump thump* noises and feeling like a sickening speed bump. He did.

Where Vinny goes to the hardware store with murderous intent

The all-night, big-box hardware store is a must for the un-prepared vampire executioner. We were halfway to the dry cleaner's when Kyle had pointed out his gun would be pretty much useless against Brad, being he was a century old vampire. So Margot had stopped at the Home Depot, so we could supply ourselves with garden tools and sharp sticks.

I marshaled my forces at the front of the store. "Kyle, you go to the garden section, think machete. Look for long, sharp stuff. Ideally, I'd like to make this a nice, clean de-capitation."

"Dude," he said, loping off to find weapons suitable for head chopping.

I nodded to Margot. "Okay, we're on wooden stake duty." I set off towards the lumber section of the store, and after walking up and down several aisles, I shook my head. "Unless we want to stab Brad with a twelve foot fence post, I think we're out of luck."

"Well, let's just look around some more. I mean most of what they sell is wood. You think they'd have some sharp sticks somewhere." We walked up and down aisles, and with every step, I felt despair creeping farther into my psyche. If I couldn't find a sharp stick in a hardware store you could land a 747 in, what good was I going to be against Brad?

"What about these?" Margot asked. She picked up a sign proclaiming, "Beware of the Dog." Attached to the sign was a three foot long piece of wood, meant to be pushed into the ground.

I nodded. "I think that will do just fine," I said, gathering up a handful of signs, while Margot texted Kyle to meet us at the front of the store.

We walked to the checkout line and put our signs down on the counter. Before the guy at the checkout had scanned our signs, Kyle showed up with the cart full of weapons he had acquired. He had a machete for each of us, and something else. "What's that?" I asked, pointing at it.

"It's a cordless pole saw, basically a mini chainsaw on a pole."

I shook my head. "Put it back."

"But this would be perfect. You can saw off Brad's head, and you don't even have to get close to him."

The guy running our cash register was starting to look nervous.

Margot shook her head. "And Brad's going to stand still while we position it?"

"Well, um..."

I gave Kyle a stern look. "I think we'll stick to the machetes." I grabbed a machete from the cart and after taking a couple practice swings, set it on the counter. I noticed our clerk had stopped scanning things.

"Something wrong?" I asked, taking another machete from the cart.

He quickly shook his head no, and said, "Would you like me to put that on your Home Depot card?"

After we had left the parking lot and gotten back on the beltway, I said, "In the future, I don't think we should talk about cutting off people's heads in public. I think we made our checkout clerk nervous."

"Chill out, dude. That dude's just a schmuck in an apron. What do you think he's going to do, report you to the hardware cops?"

"I guess so. But Kyle, 'schmuck in an apron?' Let's try to be a little more respectful. He's just a guy trying to do a job."

"Sorry, dude."

I started to wonder if I had to worry about a police investigation. I guess we would have to hide Brad's body. Would there be a body? I didn't know. I'd never seen a vampire die before, except on TV of course. Would he turn to dust or explode in a bloody mess? Would he just leave behind a corpse? Was I going to need a body bag, a Dust Buster, or an industrial grade wet/dry vac? I really wished I had thought about this stuff while we were still at the hardware store.

Margot pulled up in front of the dry cleaners. The street was quiet. All the other little shops near the cleaners were closed. As far as the cleaners itself, the lights were on in the front of the store, but the open 24 hours sign was turned off, and no one sat at the front desk. Of course,

Toby wouldn't be sitting there, because we had left him on a sidewalk, dead as roadkill.

"Do we just go inside?" Kyle asked.

Margot turned in her seat to look at him. "We're here to kill the proprietor. I think we're beyond worrying about operating hours."

Kyle nodded. "Okay. Let's go." He got out of the Land Rover and started walking to the cleaners before I could tell him I was the one who should get to say, "Let's go." He held his handgun in one hand and the machete in the other. I had to admit, he looked badass. I scrambled after him, and Margot followed. I had a machete and a sign that said, "Beware of the Dog." Margot had a machete and a sign that said, "For Sale by Owner."

Kyle tried the front door. It was unlocked, and he started pushing it forward. I grabbed his shoulder and pulled him back. "Kyle, maybe I should go first. I appreciate your support, but this is my fight. I should go first."

He shook his head. "No, dude, I'm here to protect you. You're just going have to accept that. Besides, I have the gun. I can't shoot at them if you're standing in front of me."

Margot put her hand on my shoulder. "Listen to him. You're the important one here. Let us take our chances."

"But..."

Her hand tightened on my shoulder. "Don't argue. You're not going to win, and the longer you complain, the longer we're all standing in the street looking like we're going to a gang war."

I nodded. She had a point. "Okay, Kyle. Lead the way." I decided I didn't sound macho enough, so I said, "You have point."

Kyle pushed open the door and walked inside. It was quiet, except for soft murmurs coming from Toby's television. Kyle walked slowly, stopping to listen every few steps. When he got to the curtain, he paused long enough to stuff his gun into the waistband of his pants. Then, he took a handful of curtain and pulled.

The curtain came down, along with the curtain rod, which hit Kyle in the forehead. He swung his machete wide and Margot and I hopped back awkwardly as Kyle fought the curtain. For a moment or two, I though the curtain might win, but Kyle eventually managed to defeat it. He tossed the curtain and rod aside and peered into the room beyond. A bit of light trickled in from the lobby, but after a few yards, the long room was completely dark.

"I don't suppose anyone remembers the light switch location?" I asked.

There was a long pause and then Kyle said, "There should be a switch just inside the doorway." He reached inside and ran his hands up and down either side of the wall. He shook his head. "Dude, there's no way this building's to code."

"I don't suppose anyone has a flashlight?"

"No, dude. But next time we're in a hardware store, I've thought of something else we can pick up."

"Helpful," I said.

Kyle took baby steps forward into the inky blackness, his gun out in front of him and his machete raised and ready to strike. Margot and I followed, our machetes raised as well, but after a few steps, it became so dark even I, with my supernatural night vision, was unable to see him just a few steps in front of me.

"Kyle," I whispered, "stop for a minute. If we're going to walk any further, I'm going to have to put my hand on your shoulder. Otherwise, I'm going to lose you."

He stopped, and Margot and I stepped closer, putting our hands on each other's shoulders so we would not get lost in the dark. Again, Kyle started forward, but having my hand on his shoulder made me feel no easier. He was plunging into the darkness, unable to see where he was stepping, and we were holding sharp instruments. Also, somewhere in front of us, the open stairwell waited.

No matter how dangerous it was, we had to go forward. Brad had an army of ghouls, and I was sure he wanted to destroy us. We were acting out of desperation, not choice.

Somewhere in the plastic-wrapped clothes, I heard rustling. Before I could even guess where the sound had come from, someone jumped on me. I flailed wildly with the machete for just a moment until I realized I didn't know where I was aiming. Margot and Kyle were standing too close to me. If I kept swinging, I was more likely to hit them than any of our enemies. I heard a grunt of someone getting the air knocked out of them right in front of me, and then Kyle started firing his gun. The third shot ripped through my shoulder. The force of it spun me around and I dropped to the floor. This was not my day. Someone tackled me and held me down. I felt my hands pulled up behind me and heard the zip sound of plastic handcuffs.

The lights came on a moment later, and I found myself surrounded by Brad's ghouls. They wore black robes and hoods. There were at least thirty of them in the small area filled with plastic wrapped dry-cleaning. I looked to either side of me and saw Kyle and Margot had also been caught. My heart sank. I resigned myself to my fate, Brad was going to torture and kill us all. I wished they could have been spared, but I knew no amount of pleading would save them from Brad's wrath, because deep down he wasn't a good guy who'd just been put in a bad situation. He was a real dick.

I mentally checked out for a little while. I know I should have been the hero. I should have been looking for every little opportunity, planning our escape, looking for weaknesses. Instead, I gave into my exhaustion, both physical and mental. I'm not proud of it, but that's the way it happened. I was vaguely aware of Brad's ghouls carrying me down the stairs, mostly because of the immense pain in my shoulder.

Brad slapped me awake. I was lying on my back, which was cutting off the circulation to my cuffed hands. My shoulder burned like fire. I tried to roll over a little bit to relieve the tension on my injured shoulder, but Brad had other ideas. He stuck his finger right in the bullet wound and pushed me back down to the ground.

To either side of me lay Kyle and Margot. They also had their hands tied behind their backs. Around us stood Brad's ghouls, not all of them, but a few dozen for sure. They were all wearing the black cloaks. I recognized some of them from the church. They had been in my house. I had done my best to treat them as one of my own. They had poisoned me. Now, they were going to kill me.

"Right about now," Brad said, "you must be thinking about what a big idiot you are, coming to my house and trying to kill me. Pathetic." Then he got a far away look in his eyes, and his voice quavered. "I'm going to make you suffer so horribly for what you did to my little Toby."

"Actually, I'm thinking about how much my shoulder hurts." To tell the truth, I was feeling pretty stupid. Like I expected Brad to be alone? After all, he had sent Toby to burn down our house. And Brad himself told me a vampire could feel when his primo is injured or killed. Of course he knew we were coming. How had I been so stupid to expect him to be sitting alone in his basement?

"I wonder how you'd feel if I hurt one of your friends." He nodded to one of his hooded followers. The hooded figure stepped forward, and I realized it was Blue Reverend Billy holding one of our machetes. I could still see the price tag stuck to the blade. He walked to stand behind Kyle and raised the blade over his head.

"No!" I yelled.

Blue Reverend Billy brought the machete down on Kyle's head, but he hit it with the flat side of the blade. The force of the blow was hard enough the blade rang like a bell. Kyle's eyes rolled up in the back of his head.

"How do you like being a vampire now?" Brad asked.

"It sucks," I said.

He laughed. "You have only yourself to blame for your current predicament. You are an awful vampire. To be successful, you have to be smart. You have to be observant. These are the skills to keep a vampire alive for a century. How many times have you come to the store? Have you walked down the stairs? You never thought I might spend my time down here for a reason. I saw it in your eyes the first time we met. I asked you if you liked my lair. If you had been smart, you would have recognized it for what it was. This basement is only accessible through a long, dark room and a narrow, slippery staircase." He held out his arms. "This is a fortress."

I looked at him in astonishment. I had thought Brad was idiot. I had considered him a pathetic loser lurking in the basement. Now, I saw Brad for what he really was, a paranoid genius who had played me like a fiddle, a megalomaniac so afraid of another vampire in his territory, he was willing to lie to him, isolate him, and even poison him.

"If you had the least bit of wits about you, you would have run into the arms of your precious sire."

My eyes opened in astonishment. "But you said she was dead."

"Oh, you actually believed me? Yes, she's still alive. She was punished for making you. They killed her primo, but she is very much alive."

So, I had been doubly the idiot for believing Brad. He'd lied to me about everything. Somewhere out there was my sire, a connection to the rest of the vampire world.

"It's sad really. If you had done like I'd asked and helped me run the city, I might've let you live, but you had to go poking around where you didn't belong. Now, if you'd like to stand up and join me over here, I have a little surprise for you." He beckoned for me to follow, and the ghouls spread before him revealing the little table he'd used in my induction ceremony.

"Let me guess," I said. "You're going to cut off my head." Hands lifted me and pushed me towards the table.

Brad took his position behind it, and picked up another one of our own machetes. "No, first we're going to reenact your induction ceremony. I had so much fun the last time. I couldn't imagine not giving it another go." Without further ado, he plunged the machete into my stomach, all the way to the hilt. "Of course, before you are too cut up, I'm going to torture your friends. I want them to really suffer. You know, for Toby."

I staggered under the immense pain. Yes, I had experienced stabbing quite a lot recently, but familiarity didn't prepare me for two feet of cold steel slicing through my body. I fell to my knees. Brad stood above me, casually selecting his next torture tool, a medieval-looking sword. As I was kneeling there, thinking about how much pain I was in, I realized I could feel the sharp end of the machete sticking through my own back.

Brad selected another long knife, not one of ours this time, and looked at it appraisingly. "I just wish your precious sire was here to see you."

From behind him, one of the cloaked figures dropped her hood and said, "Your wish is granted, asshole." I recognized her; it was my sire, Veronica. She drew a sword from under her cloak and came at Brad, who barely had time to turn around before she raised her sword and started swinging downward.

Blue Reverend Billy ran forward and threw himself into her sword. The blade impacted with enough force to cut him nearly in two. Brad raised his sword and turned to attack my sire.

I knew I needed to do something, and I instinctually tried to get to my feet. In doing so, I pulled up sharply with my wrists, which were still strapped together with the large plastic tie. It pulled against the blade of the machete still sticking through my body. I pulled harder against the machete, and with a small pop, my bonds were cut. I was free.

A calm certainty came over me. I knew exactly what I had to do. I grabbed the first weapon I found, the machete still sticking out of my own stomach. I pulled it out, ignoring the pain, grasped the hilt tightly, and swung it through Brad's neck. It felt good, and I smiled as I saw his head fall to the floor, followed by his body.

I stood above him, clutching the blood soaked machete watching the ever-growing red puddle spread out from his neck, well at least the bottom part of his neck, the half that had gone with the body instead of the head. Had I just done that?

The air seemed to go out of Brad's ghouls. In an instant, they went from surrounding me with malicious intent to standing around, looking very confused. Their will to fight seemed to have left them. Which meant there would be less bodies to clean up, which was nice.

I dropped the bloody machete on the floor, and selected a more sensibly proportioned knife from Brad's torture table. Pushing past Brad's ghouls, I helped Kyle and Margot to their feet, using the small knife to cut their bonds.

Kyle gave me a thumbs-up. "Dude, that was wicked." I couldn't agree more.

I took him and Margot in my arms and hugged them. "Thank you," I said. "Thank you for coming here with me."

I walked over to my sire. She was cleaning Dead Reverend Billy's very red blood off her sword. I looked expectantly at her, but I was afraid to say anything. This woman was not only my sire, and I didn't really know what that meant, but she was also gorgeous, a super sexy Hollywood vampire.

"So," she said, "looks like you had a bit of a tough time here."

"I guess you could say that," I answered. "Um. You're my sire, aren't you?" The moment I asked the question I realized how lame it was. I mean, we had both been there.

"Yes, I am. In fact, that is why I'm here. I've been keeping an eye on you for a few weeks now."

Right then, there should have been a montage sequence, revealing the subtle hints I should have picked up on, so I could realize she had been here all along. It didn't happen.

Veronica continued, "I was shocked to see you working for..." She nodded at Brad's decapitated body. "...numb nuts over there, so I decided to watch you for a few days, and see what you were up to."

"He said you were dead. I thought it was my only connection to finding more like us."

"Well, honey, I think you more than showed your distaste for..." Again, she glanced at Brad. "... that one. L'Isle will be pleased."

"Who's L'Isle?"

"My boss and sire, L'Isle Belmonte, Master of the United States and owner of Lyle B cosmetics. He's taken quite an interest in you."

"You mean the Master of the United States owns Lyle B?" This meant I'd been working for the Master of the United States after all. I just hadn't known it.

"Of course he does. Lyle B is the world's largest vampire business. You didn't think they accidentally formulated a base that could protect our kind from the sun, did you?"

My mouth dropped open. I didn't know what to say. I'd been walking around all this time wearing makeup that would have protected me from the sun? "I had no idea," I said. "Brad never told me. That dick."

In retrospect, I wish I could say we buried Brad next to Toby in a beautiful pasture on their ranch, but at the time I had to make the decision, I was not feeling so generous. We had just gone to pick up Toby's body, which thankfully hadn't been found, and I saw all these empty foundations, surrounded by ditches waiting to be backfilled. We dumped Brad and Toby into one and pushed some loose dirt over them. Hopefully, the contractors would fill in the rest before the elements uncovered them.

We spent the next week tying up the loose ends of Brad's estate. Brad's former business manager, Abby, and Veronica handled most of the details. Veronica had handled the transfer of Vampire lands within the context of US laws before, and Abby knew all of Brad's business. At first, I'd worried Abby wouldn't be happy with me as a boss, but she saw it no different from any other hostile takeover, and she was just happy to still have a job.

"Yes, Dad," I said into my cell phone. "I have plenty of clean underwear. Yes, I know where my ticket is." I patted my pockets. "Can you hold on a minute?" I muted the phone. "Hey, Vicky," I yelled, "do you have my ticket?"

The past couple of days had been a whirlwind, both of activity and information. I learned Lyle B cosmetics was the front company for the vampire Master of the United States. I learned the cosmetics I'd been selling all along had some kind of magic vampire juju that would stop me from burning up in the sun, as long as I applied it correctly. I learned that by killing Brad, I was now entitled to his territory. I was to be the new Master of Omaha. All I had to do was go to New York and claim it.

However, there were other things I hadn't learned. Veronica kept alluding to some dark secret, some prophesy, some foretelling of my transformation into a vampire. Whenever I pressed the subject, she would say it was not her place to tell me, and all would be revealed to me soon. Whatever.

Veronica held up two sheets of paper and waved at me. "The tickets are electronic. You just need to know your flight number and have your picture ID."

I patted my pockets again. I was still getting used to my new clothes, and they felt uncomfortable. Veronica had insisted I buy a whole new wardrobe, saying my existing jeans and T-shirt motif was inappropriate couture for a Master of the City and a supplicant to the Master of the United States. She had even replaced a lot of my dresses, and some of them had been really nice. "Hey, Vicky, do you have my driver's license?"

"Your wallet's on the table," she yelled back.

I took the phone off mute. "No problem, Dad," I said. "Okay, give my love to Mom." After a moment searching for the off button, I ended the call and slipped the phone into my pocket.

I looked out the window, directly in the morning sun, protected by makeup and polarized sunglasses. The morning shift of ghouls was arriving to telemarket. "Do you think Brad's ghouls are going to be okay?" I asked Veronica. Over the past week, I had been systematically biting all of Brad's ghouls, binding them to me, so they wouldn't do anything to hurt themselves now Brad was gone.

"Usually, I would say no, but you're hardly a typical vampire. From what I've seen, your bite is many times more powerful than it should be for someone your age. I think they will make the transition fine. Although I still disapprove of you saving the ones that were poisoned with silver. You put yourself at terrible risk for a few humans who were themselves trying to kill you."

"Yes, but it wasn't their fault. They were in thrall to Brad." I decided to change the subject. "So what's the itinerary for the next few days?"

"We will land in New York and be taken to Belmonte House, where you'll announce your ambition to be Master of Omaha. Then, we'll take you to the Lyle B headquarters and you'll fill out paperwork to become a regional manager for Lyle B cosmetics."

"None of this is going to involve getting stabbed in the junk, is it? Brad stabbed me in the junk. I didn't like it," I understated.

Veronica rolled her eyes. "Don't tell me Brad used that version of the ceremony. No. We do not participate in genital mutilation. As long as no one else challenges you for Omaha, you'll be fine."

"Well, things are looking up already. But what's this challenge thing?"

Veronica shrugged. "Don't worry about it. Everyone knows L'Isle wants you to have a job. I doubt anyone would go against his wishes."

Vicky came down the stairs followed by Kyle and Margot, carrying my bags. "This should be everything you need," Vicky said. She handed me my carry-on reluctantly. "It's going to be really hard without you here."

"Vicky, it's only for a couple of days. I'll be back by the end of the week." I kissed her. Then I kissed Margot. And yes, I even kissed Kyle, but no tongue or anything.

"Don't worry," I said. "I'll be back before you know it."

"We need to get going," Veronica said. "Just because you're now a dignitary in vampire circles doesn't mean they will hold the plane for us."

"All right. Let's go."

I stepped out the front door, barely flinching in deference to my years learning to see the sun as my enemy. I felt hot sunlight on my face. I had spent decades hiding in shadows, but finally I could come into the light. I was now a powerful vampire, soon to be the master of a major American city. Of course, it was probably only a matter of time before something went horribly wrong, but until then, I would put on a brave face and try to be optimistic for the sake of the ghouls.

About Shannon

Shannon Ryan writes books about loser vampires, Greek gods, and Satanic telemarketers. Living in Iowa with his wife Stephanie, Shannon enjoys lying on surveys and relocating sofas for no specific reason. He has studied paranormal investigation and conspiracy theory. Shannon is often found in the company of psychics and computer programmers. His work has been read by Art Bell on the *Coast To Coast* radio program.

He can be found at http://weirdauthor.com/.

Also by Shannon

David Graves is having a bad life. A bill collector is threatening grievous bodily harm. His girlfriend thinks he's an incompetent loser. His human resources manager, a creature of nightmare, is sexually harassing him. His Satanist bosses have tricked him into signing a contract that dooms him to an eternity of telemarketing. And, when he finally meets a girl he likes, she's more interested in rebuilding transmissions and random acts of violence.

Can David escape his evil bosses, win the heart of a wrench-wielding psychopath, and—just maybe—save his soul?

Even the best families can have dark secrets.

Some people would say that Nick Baker has it all: the trust fund, the family connections, and the country club membership. However, the Baker dynasty is in decline, and being a Baker comes with obligations as well as a family history of insanity.

Already prone to panic attacks, when Nick sees a supernatural creature dancing outside his office window, he wonders if he's just hallucinating or suffering a complete mental collapse. However, the creature is all too real, and it has come to collect on a promise made by one of Nick's ancestors, the secret of the Baker's success. Nick must choose between thwarting the ambitions of his family or facing the wrath of an ancient god.

9 781940 509099